IDAHO

OFFICIAL STATS

NAME: Brad Chillicott

VITALS:
Age: 32
Height: 6'0"
Eye Color: Brown
Hair: Brown

OCCUPATION: Game warden

OBJECTIVE: Uphold the law, see justice done.

ADDITIONAL INFO: Brad is a man of honor and integrity. The son of the town drunk, he has faced prejudice which has motivated him to rise above his past. He will do what's right to protect the woman he loves.

DANGEROUS TO LOVE

DANGEROUS TO LOVE
USA

MARILYN CUNNINGHAM
SOMEONE TO TURN TO

Silhouette Books

Published by Silhouette Books
America's Publisher of Contemporary Romance

To my daughter, Cherie,
in this,
as in everything,
my inspiration.

SILHOUETTE BOOKS

ISBN 0-373-82310-X

SOMEONE TO TURN TO

Copyright © 1990 by Marilyn Cunningham

Visit Silhouette at www.eHarlequin.com

Printed in U.S.A.

MARILYN CUNNINGHAM

Born and raised in Idaho, Marilyn Cunningham left several years ago to work for the government. She lived in various cities, including San Francisco and Baltimore. Then ten years ago Idaho lured her back, and she began writing novels. At first she lived in an isolated cabin, but later moved to her present home—ten acres on a paved road. The paved road makes all the difference when the snow starts to fall!

Marilyn travels extensively, both to follow her own interests and to visit her children, a daughter and twin sons whose work takes them to many foreign countries, including Venezuela, England, Scotland, Mexico and New Zealand. She has used some of these countries as settings for her novels.

When she is home she loves to garden, hike the mountains that surround her home and read just about anything but the labels on canned food. She doesn't cook; that is left to her husband, John, who is a fantastic chef.

Also residing with Marilyn and John are their two poodles, Andre and Denali.

Books by Marilyn Cunningham

Silhouette Intimate Moments

Someone To Turn To #334
Enchanted Circle #355
Long White Cloud #441
On the Edge #527

Harlequin Intrigue

Under the Midnight Sun #492

Dear Reader,

This story is set in the high country of Idaho in the foothills of the Rocky Mountains in a place of rugged and pristine beauty. I wanted to write about the clash of cultures here, as the old-time values give way to modern ways and ideas. I chose to use the story of a powerful rancher who knows no law not of his own making and of the hero, a game warden whose determination to uphold law and justice pits him against the family of the woman he loves. Both the rancher and the hero struggle for the love and allegiance of Ramsey who is torn between them.

This is the country where I was raised and it is very dear to me. I believe this high country, perhaps because of its remoteness, breeds strong, independent people—men like Brad, who will fight against all odds for a principle, and women like Ramsey, who will fight just as hard for the man she loves.

I hope you'll like their story.

Marilyn Cunningham

Please address questions and book requests to:
Silhouette Reader Service
U.S.: 3010 Walden Ave., P.O. Box 1325, Buffalo, NY 14269
Canadian: P.O. Box 609, Fort Erie, Ont. L2A 5X3

Chapter 1

For several minutes after he parked, Brad Chillicott sat in his loden-green pickup emblazoned with the logo of the Idaho Fish and Game Department and stared moodily around the ranch. He took in the massive log house encircled by a veranda, the corrals where several quarter horses stared curiously at his truck, the large barns bursting with hay, and frowned. He could think of a dozen places he would rather be.

Then, with a shrug of resignation, he switched off the ignition and swung his long legs out onto the ground. He knew he was in for another frustrating experience and he wasn't a man who accepted frustration easily. Someday the Carmichaels would realize they didn't own the entire county anymore.

His square jaw tightened and his gray eyes darkened to slate. At least they didn't own him.

It was only a few steps up the walk, bordered with old-fashioned cosmos and hollyhocks, to the broad veranda, then across to the massive front door, but during that time

Brad's mind flashed back to the many times he had walked that path. The place still looked as imposing to him as it had when he was an insecure kid, and the Carmichael ranch, the Floating Eagle, represented all the things he wanted and could never have.

He set his mouth in a firm line, wishing he didn't have the feeling that he was about to engage in a boxing match with smoke. The Carmichaels had to realize that things had changed. Old Jacob couldn't keep on operating like a robber baron. There were game laws now, rules, fishing and hunting rights for the public, and the old outlaw had better accept them before he got into real trouble.

He lifted his hand to knock, then let it fall to his side as the door opened. He might have known they would have seen him coming, he thought, a wry grin twisting his lean face. No one came unseen to the Carmichael spread. The opening door reminded him of nothing so much as a drawbridge being lowered at some hulking, medieval castle. He took a deep breath. At one time, years ago, he had come here as a friend. Now he knew they all thought of him as the enemy. His lips tightened. He was the enemy. And would be until they learned to respect the law.

"Come in, Brad." A rotund, middle-aged woman with thick gray curls and red cheeks held the door open and motioned Brad inside, then turned and led him down the hall to the living room. She rubbed her hands on her apron and gave him an uneasy smile.

"I'll see if I can find someone—they're all around here somewhere."

"Thanks, Martha." He wondered whether the housekeeper would have an easy time finding anyone. The Carmichaels had a way of scattering when the game warden came to visit. But he was in no hurry. This time he was going to impress upon them that you didn't shoot at fishermen, even if they were fishing in a stream that ran through your land, even if you did shoot over their heads.

He leaned against the mantel of the mammoth fieldstone

fireplace and looked idly around the room. It was still the most impressive he'd ever seen, with its high-beamed ceiling, wide expanse of windows and walls of polished logs that shone like burnished copper. It spoke of tradition, stability, power, he thought, and yes—money.

He heard a door open behind him and turned quickly, tensed for the anticipated confrontation. Then his jaw dropped and he merely stared at the woman who stood poised in the doorway. Seeing her so unexpectedly was like a punch in the solar plexus. When had Ramsey Carmichael come home?

He stared at her silently, momentarily at a loss for words. She hadn't changed since high school, he thought, not essentially. She was tall for a woman, and her silk shirt and snug jeans accentuated her slender form, which was curved in all the places it was supposed to be. She still had the same wheat-colored hair that seemed to glow in the shadows of the room, the same clear hazel eyes that could look right into your heart. And her mouth, wide and generous, soft as flower petals, looked just as it had when he used to conjure himself to sleep with the thought of those lips pressed against his.

With a jerk, he brought himself back to the present. Only in dreams had he possessed those lips. Oh, she'd smiled at him, said a few words if they happened to be in the same class, but he'd never asked her out. They both recognized the gulf between them. Class distinctions might have fallen in other places of the country, but in the small, ingrown community of Tyler, Idaho, the granddaughter of the county's most affluent rancher didn't fraternize with a boy from Milltown.

"Ramsey," he said heartily, taking a step forward. "I didn't know you were home. How long has it been, anyway?"

"Brad Chillicott," she said slowly, her eyes widening with recognition as she put out her hand. He clasped it and for a moment they just stared at each other, both seemingly unable to break away. He was uncomfortably aware of the light fragrance of roses that drifted over to him, and of the warm softness of her touch. The years fell away, and he was a tongue-tied, awkward boy. If he didn't watch out, he'd be scuffing his toe on the carpet and blushing.

She retrieved her hand, brushed back her shoulder-length hair with a somewhat flustered gesture and motioned him to the sofa. "Brad Chillicott," she repeated, a smile curving her lips and shining in her eyes as she sank gracefully into an armchair across from him. "Martha said the game warden was here; that can't be you! I never figured you'd end up as game warden."

"What did you think I'd end up as? A bank robber?"

She gave him a quick look, perhaps alerted by the edge in his voice. "Well, I remember you were always studying! And so much smarter than the rest of us. I guess I'd have thought you became a scientist—or a mathematician. I certainly never thought you'd stay in Jade County."

She hadn't meant it as a slight, he knew. He was too touchy. He brushed back a shock of thick dark hair and grinned. "I never could have got that far away from my ranching roots. I'll always be a country boy, I guess. Anyway, what's wrong with me being a game warden?"

A blush colored her clear, flawless skin a dull pink and he felt a little catch in his throat at the sight.

"I just have trouble seeing you arresting anyone..."

"There's more to it than arresting people," he said shortly. "There's protecting the environment, for one thing, seeing that the wild creatures have a fair shot—" He stopped abruptly. Why was he justifying himself to her? He'd better get back to the reason he had come. "Is your grandfather here?"

"Martha went to find him. Has the old pirate been up to something?"

"Someone from here has been up to something," he said grimly. "A couple of dudes came running into the office yesterday, scared to death. Said they'd been fishing in Pine Creek and someone shot at them.''

"Shot at them!''

"Well, over their heads,'' he admitted. "But he can't *do* that! I know Pine Creek runs through his land, but it's open to the public!'' He doubled up his fist and pounded his leg in frustration. "And this isn't the first time; it's just one of a string of incidents.''

Ramsey started to protest, then shrugged and gave him a sheepish grin. "I guess he's a little out of touch with the game laws. He never thinks they apply to him. He lives in the past. Thinks things are like they used to be, before it got so crowded and he could do as he wanted on his own land.''

Brad bit back a sharp comment. There was such affection in her voice that he knew he would only antagonize her by arguing about the morality of old Jacob Carmichael's attitudes. And his quarrel wasn't with Ramsey. She hadn't been back at the Floating Eagle for years. Not since she married, he thought, and was surprised at the sharpness of the pain that hit him. He'd thought he'd gotten over that.

"I heard you were married,'' he said carefully, keeping his face expressionless. "Ramsey Delacroix, isn't it? Is Mr. Delacroix with you?''

He caught the quick look of pain that flickered across her face, but she gave him a broad smile. "No, he isn't. Mr. Delacroix is in Rome, and no longer my husband. He's married to an Italian countess, who, from all reports, is extremely beautiful and extremely rich.''

Although her voice was completely without inflection, he caught the effort it took her to say the words, and he didn't try to keep the warmth from his own voice.

"She couldn't be as beautiful as you are. You haven't changed, Ramsey. You still have those beautiful wide eyes all the boys used to dream about.''

Her laugh was light, but pleased. "You don't know how

good that kind of talk is for my ego. Even if you do say it to all the women.''

''I deal in truth, lady. Only in the truth. If you remember me at all, you should remember that.''

''I do remember you as rather solemn,'' she said, a sparkle in her eyes. ''Is that the same thing? I used to wonder if you ever had any fun.''

''When your folks were as poor as mine, you didn't have much time for fun,'' he said, totally without embarrassment. ''I figured early on there was only one way out. Study. College. Besides,'' he said, a teasing note in his voice, ''I can't believe you ever noticed me enough to see what I was doing.''

''You'd be surprised.'' Her tone was nearly flirtatious. ''I didn't think you noticed me...''

''Not notice you!'' Her comment astounded him. How could she not have known? It seemed to him his entire senior year had been spent adoring her from afar, wishing he could talk to her, touch her, knowing he didn't have a chance. Nights of burying his face in a pillow and vowing that someday she and her entire family would see him as an equal.

''You really were a big influence on my life,'' he continued, still in the light, teasing tone.

Surprise widened her eyes. ''I find that hard to believe. You came here to the house a couple times with Cousin Jeff, but I can't remember you and I ever holding a conversation for more than five minutes at a time.''

''That's because I had such a giant crush on you. I tended to stammer and dig my toe in the ground every time I got near you.''

''But how did I influence you?''

''Let's just say you were my inspiration.'' He hoped his tone was light enough that she might think he was joking.

Suddenly he was much too aware of her. The slight sheen on her high cheekbones, the pulse that throbbed in the hollow at the base of her throat, the scent of roses combined with the warm female fragrance of her skin, all proclaimed she was no longer the girl he remembered, a girl to be worshipped from afar, but a woman. A warm, desirable woman that a man could just reach right out and touch.... He clenched his fist. It was time to change the conversation.

"Are you staying long, Ramsey?"

He noticed that she swallowed slightly, and guessed she had been as aware of him as he of her. But he might have been wrong, her voice was calm enough. "Just until the fall school term starts; I teach at Berkeley and my son has to go back to school this fall, too."

"You have a son?"

"Yes." There was undisguised pride in her voice. "Stevie. He's eight, and I guess I really came back to the ranch for him as much as for myself. I wanted to give him a taste of ranch life..."

"It's a good place for kids," he said noncommittally.

"I hope it will be good for Stevie. Since the divorce he hasn't really been himself. It's been well over a year, but he's still so morose, so difficult..." Her voice trailed off, then she continued softly. "I think he's having a hard time getting over the feeling of abandonment. Of betrayal. He's holding in a lot of anger. I thought he needed the love and stability of an extended family, some relatives around him so he'd know he's not alone..."

"Like you do?" Brad's voice was gentle. When she had spoken of betrayal there had been something so forlorn in her voice that he'd wanted to reach over and comfort her.

Before she could answer, the heavy rhythm of boots came down the hall and the door swung open. Jacob Carmichael glared across the room at Brad.

Brad rose slowly from his chair and faced the old patriarch. Jacob was in his seventies, but as stiff and spare as a gnarled, weather-beaten pine. He still had a shock of thick white hair, and his prominent nose and craggy features made Brad think that the Floating Eagle was an apt name for his ranch; the old boy looked like a fierce predator himself. His expression was stern and accusing as he stared across the room at Brad.

The old man's hostile expression kindled a matching anger in Brad and he stared back uncompromisingly. The fact that he was tall enough to stare right into those flashing pale blue eyes always made him feel a little more in control of the situation. Although so far, he thought, amusement tingled with bitterness, all their confrontations had ended up a draw.

"What do you want now, Chillicott?" Jacob's voice was a harsh bark. "Don't you have anything better to do than harass us?"

Brad didn't reply, waiting until the two men who were right behind Jacob had also stepped into the room. "Hello, Karl," he said tightly, nodding to a powerfully built man with coarse black hair and a bronzed complexion who took his place, arms crossed over a massive chest, beside Jacob. "And Jeff," Brad added, inclining his head toward a slim man with light hair and aristocratic features who was eyeing him with a slight smile on his face. "I'm glad I have you all together."

Jeff's smile widened but his pale blue eyes were cold. "Not all, Bud's not here. But don't worry. We'll tell him what you have to say so you won't have to repeat yourself."

Brad felt an angry flush darkening his face, but his words were clipped and as cold as Jeff's smile. "This really isn't anything to make light of. I've warned you all before. Yet you continue to fish without licenses, hunt deer—"

"A man's got a right to hunt and fish on his own land," Jacob Carmichael broke in. "Who furnishes the feed for those deer, I'd like to know? They ate up half my hay last year. And we've a right to keep all those city dudes from trampling all over everything! My grandfather took this land from the Indians—"

"And you took it from everybody else!" Brad cut in. "Besides," he said more calmly, "it's not all your land. The Carmichael land borders the national forest, and people have a perfect right to use forest land. I have reports you've been chasing them off there, too.''

He saw the concerned expression on Ramsey's face, and suddenly wished he didn't have to continue. Why couldn't her name have been Jones! He swung his eyes back to the three men. "And Pine Creek may go through your land, but it's open to the public for fishing, as long as they stay within the high-water mark.''

''Access doesn't mean public!'' Jacob snapped.

''You don't shoot at people because you disagree with the law!''

Breaking into the silence, Brad continued. ''I have a report of a shooting incident there last night.''

The silence lengthened as Jacob looked from Karl Powers, his ranch foreman, to Jeff Carmichael, his distant relation and right-hand man. "Shooting?'' he finally said.

''A couple of dudes came into the office, shaking in their shoes,'' Brad said firmly. ''They were fishing where they had every right to be and someone shot at them.''

''Ah, I didn't even come close,'' Karl said, a disgusted look on his bronzed face.

Jeff's grin broadened. ''Tacky, Karl, tacky. You know you're not supposed to scare the city slickers.''

''If these people were on my land,'' Jacob Carmichael said confidently, ''they shouldn't expect a welcome. Time was when a man could do as he pleased on his own land.''

''You've preached that before,'' Brad said through gritted teeth. ''I'm tired of hearing it. You can't take the law into your own hands anymore. I've half a mind to issue a warrant—''

He broke off at Jeff's laugh, knowing he had gone too far. Arrest one of the Carmichael clan in Jade County? When half the judges probably owed Jacob their job? Not unless he actually came upon one of them in the very act of poaching or shooting at someone. But their arrogance, their smug assurance that there was nothing he could do, set his blood seething.

Ramsey slid from her chair and placed her hand lightly on Jeff's arm. Her smile, Brad knew, was calculated to defuse the tension that was building between the men. "There must be some mistake," she said soothingly. "An accident—"

None of the men paid the slightest attention. Brad's eyes held Jacob's in an angry stare. "This time I'm just warning you. But if I get any more reports of—"

The loud blast of a horn interrupted him.

Ramsey's eyes followed his exasperated glance out the window at the parked pickup truck. "What was that?" she said as the horn blasted again.

"My phone." Brad shrugged and headed for the door. "I'll be back in a minute."

"Take your time," Jeff said to his back. "We aren't going anywhere."

In the sudden silence, Ramsey moved to the window and pushed aside the curtain to watch Brad reach into the pickup cab for the phone. She realized her other hand, poised lightly on the windowsill, was trembling slightly, and she shoved it into her jeans pocket. It had been a shock, seeing him again after all these years...even if there had never been anything between them.

He must be in his thirties now, just a couple of years older than she was, but she had recognized him immediately. When she had known him in high school his face had been much more vulnerable, of course, unformed, not the hard, granite-sculptured features of the mature man. And his eyes, then guileless and direct, now seemed to screen even the slightest emotion. He had filled out, of course. The boy's body was now a man's, long and lean and well muscled. He moved, she thought, with the power and grace of a panther. And he seemed just as elusive.

Her response to him had flustered and surprised her; it had been so strong and so immediate. She'd sensed a feeling of warmth and excitement emanating from him, an intense sexual awareness that had matched her own. It had happened on a purely physical level, a mere chemical reaction, but had she ever felt that way about her ex-husband, Paul? She remembered that their attraction had been more of an intellectual amalgamation, a coming together of people with similar interests. Although, she thought, a trace of bitterness turning down the corners of her mouth, she had been wrong about the similar interests.

She turned away from the window, then glanced at the men with bewildered eyes. "What was that all about? Is there a war going on? I thought Brad was a friend."

Her grandfather snorted. "Not since he got that job as a game warden. The old one, Arnie Parkins, is bad enough. He's always trying to get something on us, too. I've warned him to stay off my land, and he's halfway reasonable! But Brad Chillicott—hell, he seems to have a personal vendetta going. Just looking for something to hang on us."

He strode across the room and put his arm around Ramsey's shoulders, his craggy old face suddenly tender. "Sorry you ran into this little argument, Ramsey, on your first day home. I wanted everything to be just like it used to be when you were a little girl..."

There was such wistfulness in the old man's voice that Ramsey turned to him and pressed her cheek fiercely against his chest. For a minute she was six years old, he once again providing the only security and the only unconditional love she had ever known. The mixed feelings of affection and guilt she was experiencing nearly overwhelmed her. She had stayed away much too long. She should have come back more often but at least she was here now with the people who loved her. It was a place to heal.

She had been proud of the way she had mentioned her divorce to Brad. Her voice had been completely devoid of emotion, betraying nothing of the hurt and pain that Paul's desertion had caused. It had taken time and effort to achieve that. Now if she could just get her interior to conform to her exterior, she'd be all right. Her return to the Carmichael ranch, where she had lived such a happy, secure childhood would help her as much as she hoped it would help Stevie.

She was sorry it had taken a disturbing letter from her grandmother to get her to come home. Until then, she hadn't guessed how ill her grandmother was, or that something might be wrong at the ranch.

At the thought of the letter, she pulled back and gazed lovingly into her grandfather's face. He appeared the same to her, older, perhaps even more majestic, but she couldn't see any of the worry that her grandmother, Delia, had hinted at. She would talk to Delia tonight about her puzzling message, find out what she had meant when she said there was something very wrong at the Floating Eagle, something that Jacob wouldn't discuss with her.

From the circle of her grandfather's arms, she surveyed the others. Karl, except for a slight, sardonic glance from his opaque black eyes, didn't move, but Jeff flopped down in a chair and dangled one long leg over the arm. His expression was affectionate and teasing.

"Might as well jump right into it, cousin. You can see he's out to get us poor folk. Why, I think ole Brad would like nothing better than to look at us behind bars."

Ramsey grinned back. Jeff, although only distantly related, had been just like a big brother ever since she'd arrived at the Floating Eagle, a frightened, orphaned girl of six. He'd been part of the warm, enveloping love that had always made her feel so special.

"You could try obeying the law," she said, smiling. Her family's attitude toward game laws, although she didn't really approve, was no surprise to her. In a way she understood. It must be hard to see a way of life crumbling around you. The Carmichaels were fiercely independent and thought the ever-encroaching hordes of people known as *society* were a threat to their freedom. Why should people who made their living in the city assume they could ride roughshod over the land that provided livelihood for others? All in the name of recreation. They just didn't accept the rights of the *public* that Brad was sworn to uphold and protect.

Karl gave her a dark look. He was also one of Jacob's strays, a half-Indian boy who had come to the ranch when he was sixteen and stayed to become the trusted foreman. "He can't *prove* one of us fired those shots," he muttered.

Jeff laughed. "But, Karl, you just admitted it. By the way, you were out pretty late last night—where were you? I heard you ride up around midnight."

Karl gave him a hooded look. "Just about the time you got in, right?" he said shortly.

Jeff swung his leg idly and reached down to pick a straw from his pressed jeans, then rose and walked to the window. "A man can't find everything he needs here on the ranch. Guess Bud would agree with that, he didn't get home until after we did. Where is Bud now, anyway?"

Ramsey had wondered the same thing. She and Stevie had arrived home late yesterday evening and had gone straight to bed, not even stopping in to see her grandmother since Martha had assured her the elderly lady was asleep. She'd expected Uncle Bud at breakfast, but he wasn't there, either. No one had mentioned his absence, and she'd remembered that Bud's presence or absence had never made much of an impact on anyone. As her dead father's younger brother, he still seemed to be living in his shadow.

"Here comes Brad," Jeff said, turning from the window with a sardonic smile. "And he's walking like he's ready for the shoot-out at the O.K. Corral."

The door burst open and Brad stood for an instant in the doorway, his narrowed eyes taking them all in. Then he strode wordlessly to the middle of the room. Ramsey felt a quick tightening in her chest. Something was very wrong. Brad had looked upset and frustrated when he left to take the phone call, but he was different now. He exuded a cold, hard anger that communicated itself to everyone in the room. His lips were pressed so tightly together that there was a thin white line around his mouth and his eyes, eyes she remembered as a warm gray, were nearly black.

The group stirred uneasily as Brad remained silent, his eyes coldly assessing each face. Finally Jeff broke the lengthening silence.

"Well, what is it, Brad? Back to give one of us a poaching citation?"

Brad's eyes swung to Jeff's face. He didn't smile, and Ramsey saw a muscle twitch in his clenched jaw.

"No, no poaching citation," he said calmly. "I think this time someone may really have gone a little too far. This time it's murder."

The words fell like a rock into a bottomless well. The silence seemed to stretch interminably on, although it was probably only a few seconds. In those few seconds, everything changed, changed from the light family atmosphere into something unspeakable.

Ramsey managed to tear her eyes from Brad's face to glance at the others in the room. Expression had been expunged from every face as though by an eraser. Karl stood solidly planted in the middle of the room, his black eyes betraying nothing. Jeff stared at Brad with eyes narrowed to half slits. Only old Jacob seemed visibly shaken; he sank heavily into a chair before he spoke.

"Murder," he repeated, his voice rasping. "That's what you're accusing us of, murder? Going a bit far yourself, aren't you, boy?"

"I'm not accusing you of anything," Brad said, although the tone of his voice certainly belied his words. "But I can assure you I think of it as a possibility. A very real possibility."

"Well, now," Jeff drawled, walking over to stand beside Ramsey, "before we start trying to defend ourselves, maybe you should tell us what's happened."

"That call was from the sheriff. Arnie Parkins has been killed."

"So that's it," Jeff said thoughtfully. "A game warden

killed, and of course you think immediately of us. Any reason, other than the fact that you don't like us?''

Brad faced him angrily. "Save your snide remarks. My partner was killed. A man doing his duty. Apparently he came upon someone with a poached deer, and he was probably shot in an attempt to apprehend the poacher. Some self-styled mountain man, I expect. Someone who likes to take the law into his own hands.''

Jacob raised a protesting hand, his mouth set in a hard, uncompromising line. "Why us?''

Brad swung around to face him. "Like I said, I'm not accusing anyone. But Arnie was killed at Three Tree Spring, and that's in the national forest, just a few yards over the boundary of your land. And as I think you'll agree, poaching isn't unknown to any of you.''

Anger flared suddenly in Ramsey, replacing the initial shock. Her family was right; Brad *was* harassing them! He had jumped to an immediate conclusion that a Carmichael was guilty with, as far as she had heard, only the most circumstantial evidence. How dare he! She had a feeling there was something going on here that she didn't understand. There must be something behind his hatred of the Carmichaels, some bitterness that had little to do with poaching. She started to speak, but a cautioning look from her grandfather stopped her.

Jacob Carmichael rose slowly from his chair, and Ramsey thought he looked like an old-time prophet about to call down the wrath of God on a sinner. "You will have to do better than that, boy,'' he said sternly. "We are not killers. You'd do well to find evidence before you talk like that.''

Brad gazed around the circle again, this time being careful not to meet Ramsey's eyes. "I'll do that.'' Without another word he turned and stalked out the door.

Ramsey turned stricken eyes to her grandfather, then impulsively ran after Brad. He couldn't just leave like that. He had something to explain. He was going entirely too far. Accusing them of poaching was one thing. He might even be right! But accusing them of murder was something else entirely. Anger welled up inside her, more powerful because of the feeling of dawning rapport and sexual awareness it replaced.

She hurried up to him and grabbed his arm just as he opened the pickup door. "Just a minute, Brad."

When he turned to look at her she thought she surprised a look of pain on his face, but if so it was quickly replaced by cold anger. "What is it, Ramsey?"

"Brad, you can't be serious. You've known the Carmichaels for years."

"I've known Arnie quite a while, too."

"But you're jumping to conclusions! It could have been anyone," she protested. "Other people must poach, outsiders could have known about the spring. You have no proof at all!"

His look softened, and he sighed. "I guess I let my anger get a little out of control. It just seemed the last straw..." He raised one eyebrow and gave her a half smile. "You're right, I'm probably going off half-cocked. But the place where he was killed—only locals know that place. Somebody was skinning out a deer when Arnie found him. And the Carmichaels *have* made threats."

Suddenly he cupped her chin in his hand and raised her face until he was looking deeply into her eyes. Her heart skipped a beat, then raced madly under the intimacy of his touch. She couldn't look away from those compelling eyes that held her as firmly as an embrace.

He seemed about to say something, then shrugged and let his hand fall to his side. "The sheriff had a good look around the place," he said tonelessly. "He thinks Arnie was killed sometime late yesterday, probably after dark. He doesn't seem to have much to go on."

Her skin still remembered the exhilarating touch of his strong hand, but her voice was even enough. "It's not your concern, is it? The sheriff is handling the investigation."

"Technically I suppose it's not," he said, and she saw a

muscle twitch in his clenched jaw. "But Arnie was a game warden, doing his duty. He was pretty near retirement, too. And he was my friend."

He swung into the pickup, shut the door with a solid crunch, then looked out at her. For a moment she might have been looking into the eyes of the young boy she remembered. Then he sighed. "I have to do what I can. I'll probably ride over to Three Tree Spring tomorrow to see if I can find anything he missed."

Outrage tightened her lips and she felt her face flush as she guessed his motivation. "Find any evidence that ties the killer to the Carmichaels, you mean."

He didn't answer and she watched silently as he drove away. She couldn't begin to sort out her emotions. She had been happy to see him, inordinately so, and her skin still tingled with keen awareness of his masculine vitality. She had actually trembled beneath his touch. It had been so long since any man had aroused such a response. It couldn't all have been based on her remembrance of him; anyway, she wasn't at all sure she even knew him anymore.

He had certainly changed, she thought, turning slowly and walking toward the house. That guileless, honest boy had hardened into a suspicious, arrogant man, a man of swift anger and harsh judgments. A man out to get the Carmichaels at any cost. Nonconformists her family might be, they might even skirt a minor regulation, but to think that they would have anything to do with murder was ridiculous.

The thought struck quickly, and she tried to ignore it, to push it back into her subconscious, but it kept bubbling back up. Every one of the men—Uncle Bud, Cousin Jeff, even Karl Powers, had been away from the ranch last night.

Chapter 2

Ramsey opened the door to her grandmother's room and a dynamo of energy in the shape of a small blond boy jumped off the edge of the bed and hurtled toward her. She noticed with amusement that a pair of western boots had been added to his usual attire of jeans and T-shirt. Had someone found a pair of her old boots that now fit Stevie?

His blue eyes sparkled with excitement as he looked up at her, his wide grin showing two missing teeth.

"Hey, Mom! Guess what! Grandma says I can ride a horse!"

A wave of tenderness almost overpowered her as Ramsey opened her arms to the small boy, who dived in as swiftly as a homing trout, then as quickly pulled away. She ruffled his blond head and bent to pull him close, steeling herself for his immediate stiffening. Stevie hadn't been so open and obviously happy for a long time. She had often felt completely frustrated; he didn't seem to know what he wanted. He hated for her to be out of his sight, yet resisted her attempts at affection. He was probably still angry and confused, grappling with his love for her while fighting the fear that she would abandon him as his father had. She had been right to bring him home.

"That's great, Stevie," she said, reluctantly loosening her embrace. "I'll come with you as soon as I talk to Grandma, and we'll saddle some horses."

"Nah." He struggled out of her arms and strutted to the door, looking for all the world like a little bantam rooster. "Karl's going to teach me. He said a man's got to know how to ride in this country."

With an amused smile, Ramsey watched him close the door, then turned eagerly to her grandmother. Martha had brought the old woman breakfast in bed, and this was the first opportunity Ramsey had to see her.

At the sight of the frail old lady, her porcelain face almost as white as the pillow she was lying against, Ramsey was nearly overwhelmed with affection. She rushed to the bed and gathered Delia in her arms, aghast at how thin and light her grandmother felt against her breast. For a long moment, neither spoke. Ramsey didn't trust her voice. Then she swallowed and drew back to look at her grandmother's face, hoping she wasn't going to cry. This was the woman who had taken her in when her parents died, the woman who had been unstinting with her love, the woman who, along with Jacob, had made Ramsey's childhood happy and secure.

"Thank you for coming, Ramsey." Delia traced her granddaughter's cheekline with a slender, trembling finger, her old eyes suspiciously moist.

"You didn't expect me to stay away when you said you weren't feeling well, did you? I'm just sorry I didn't come sooner. When Martha said you were sleeping when I arrived yesterday, and then when you didn't come down for breakfast, I was really worried."

Delia lifted her hand, a hand so thin it was nearly transparent, to stop Ramsey's torrent of words, and smiled wanly. "I'm not that bad off, dear. Not well, but I didn't call you back for a deathbed scene. I didn't mean to scare you—I just wanted to be sure I saw you alone.'' She glanced at the closed door as though to be positive no one was within earshot.

Puzzled, Ramsey sat down on the edge of the bed, still holding the old woman's hand. Why would she care that they might be overheard? "See me alone? What's going on, Gram?"

A shadow of what might have been fear passed over the older woman's face. "I don't know—maybe nothing. Perhaps I shouldn't have called you here. But I've had this feeling, something I can't put my finger on. Something isn't right."

"Not right?" An uneasy feeling trickled down Ramsey's spine. "Is something wrong with Granddad? Isn't he well?"

"It's not that," Delia said quickly. "Jacob is strong as a horse. Couldn't knock him down with a crowbar. But he's been acting very strange. As though he's worried about something. And you know he always used to talk things over with me." The old woman took a deep, quavering breath. "Well, he doesn't anymore."

It was the last statement that perturbed Ramsey the most, and she pursed her lips thoughtfully. Jacob Carmichael was noted for his temper and his autocratic manner to everyone but Delia. He had always shown his wife his softer side. Perhaps it was because her delicate, flowerlike beauty and gentle manner were such a contrast to his bull-like determination and oaklike physique, but he had never excluded her.

"Maybe if I talk to him, pretend I'm just chatting..."

Delia laughed, then clutched her chest. "Oh, Ramsey, that would never work! You're too open and sunny! You haven't a duplicitous bone in your body! Never have had. Always so honest and direct, just like your father. Jacob would know immediately that you were quizzing him!" She took a shallow breath. "No, I don't expect you to do anything. Just having you here will help. And if something is

wrong—well—'' she gave Ramsey a tremulous smile
''—I'd like a younger shoulder to lean on.''

"I may not be sneaky," Ramsey acknowledged with a
grin, "but I can keep my eyes open. Can't you tell me
anything else?''

Her grandmother shook her head. "It's just a feeling.
Like something sinister is going on. Jacob is so secretive
and he's obviously worried. And I hear the men whispering
sometimes.'' Her frail body stiffened. "I—I don't know
why—it's ridiculous—but I'm afraid…'' She clutched Ramsey's arm and the young woman tightened her grip protectively around her shoulder.

"Well, I'm home now," Ramsey said firmly. "Don't
worry about anything. Everything will come out fine, I know
it will.''

Delia gave her a wry grin. "I sometimes think that your
always believing everything will come out fine actually
makes it come out fine!''

They were both silent a minute, obviously thinking of
something that had not come out fine. Ramsey had written
about the divorce, and although she'd tried to sound matter-of-fact, she knew that her grandmother had undoubtedly
read her hurt between the lines. Delia broke the silence.

"But what about you, Ramsey? You're looking a little
pale. Do you hear at all from Paul?''

Ramsey shrugged. "No. Neither does Stevie." Her lips
tightened. "That's what angers me—that he's forgotten
Stevie. Oh, Gram, I had no warning at all. He had business
in Rome, and I expected to join him in a month or so. Then
I received a telegram asking for a divorce—and immediately
afterward he married an Italian countess.'' She pressed her
face against Delia's thin shoulder, inhaling the faint perfume
of lilacs.

Her grandmother put her hand under Ramsey's chin and
shifted her face until she could look thoughtfully into her
eyes. "No warning at all, Ramsey?''

Ramsey's marriage flashed before her eyes. Nine quiet

years when she'd assumed everything was all right. Didn't
the initial excitement usually fade? It was true they rarely
talked to each other; Paul was often traveling in his job, and
she was immersed in her schoolwork. And all that talk about
intensity and excitement was probably just a fairy tale, anyway, certainly she and Paul had never experienced it, even
in the beginning. She'd thought they had a good enough
marriage, a sound marriage, and if she sometimes cried unexpectedly, it was probably because she was working too
hard....

She remembered the flash of awareness she'd felt when
Brad had entered the room. She didn't recall ever having
felt that unexpected voltage when she looked at Paul. Had
she been wrong about her marriage? Was there some intensity she had missed, some feeling she couldn't even put a
name to? Had Paul felt its absence?

But it was a ridiculous thought. How could she contrast
years of love with the fleeting shock of attraction that had
raced through her when she'd first entered the living room
and seen Brad lounging against the mantel of the fireplace?

Delia sighed. "Well, at least you're home."

Home. The very word made Ramsey feel better. "I feel
almost like I did when I first came here as a child," she
said shyly.

The worried expression left Delia's face and she smiled.
"You were such a little waif. I don't know what your parents were thinking of, jetting around all over the place and
leaving you alone so much. You wandered around like a
little ghost for days."

"But I soon got over it," Ramsey said. And she had,
although she sometimes thought the early years, when she
had felt abandoned and unloved, had left a residue of in-
security that surfaced at unexpected moments. "I never can
thank you enough. You and Granddad gave me love, security, a feeling of—family! No matter what happened, I
always knew I had someone to turn to."

"Of course," Delia said serenely. "That's what a family

does—takes care of its own. You know there's nothing we wouldn't do for you, Ramsey.''

"Or I for you," Ramsey whispered. "That's what I want for Stevie, a knowledge that whatever happens, he has people to depend on." She sat up straighter, focusing her tear-filled eyes on Delia, and smiled. "Enough sentimentality! I'd better go find Stevie."

"He'll be fine with Karl. Why don't you back off just a little, Ramsey? Give him room to think, sort things out. And it will do him good to have men to look up to."

Ramsey rose from the bed and kissed Delia lightly on the cheek. The old woman's skin was like parchment, dry under the touch of her lips, and she felt the usual rush of tenderness. "You have such wisdom, Gram. Maybe I'll just ride around by myself this afternoon. See if I still know how to ride a horse."

As she moved to the door, Delia's voice called her back. "Martha said Brad Chillicott was here this morning. Something about a murder? What was that all about? Martha sometimes gets things a little confused."

Ramsey half turned, a frown on her face. "Yes. There was a terrible tragedy. Arnie Parkins was killed. I'm afraid Brad thinks the Carmichaels had something to do with it."

Delia gave her a quizzical look and Ramsey realized her voice might have given away more than she wished. She could still feel the touch of his hand burning against her skin. "I—I talked to him awhile. About old times. Gram, is something going on between Brad and the family?"

"Oh, he's always been such an intense boy," Delia said. "Puts his heart into everything he does. Right now that's upholding the game laws. And you know your grandfather." She smiled fondly.

"It seems like it's more than that," Ramsey said. "It's almost as though he resents us..."

"Well, a lot of people do," Delia said briskly. "You don't run the largest ranch in the county without making a few enemies. Now why don't you get on with your riding,

Ramsey? I'll try to get down to dinner, but if I don't, you come right on up here, you hear?''

Ramsey blew her a kiss, then walked out the door. Talking to her grandmother had relieved some of her anxiety, made her feel young and buoyant. She could handle things; life certainly wasn't over. Skipping lightly down the stairs, she decided she'd forget about everything for the afternoon—Delia's disturbing statements, Stevie's ambivalence, the unsettling memory of Brad's hand on her cheek. It was a blazingly beautiful late-June day and it would be a crime to stay indoors. Her old horse, Kelly, wouldn't be here anymore, but there must be another she could ride.

Just as she started out the door a masculine voice called her name, and she turned, a warm smile on her face. "Uncle Bud!"

Her uncle ambled toward her, a stocky blond man in his late forties with a sweet, diffident smile on his face. He looked just as he always had, she thought, rushing into his embrace. Time didn't seem to touch the innate youthfulness of his personality.

"Sorry I wasn't here to meet you," he said. "Welcome home, Ramsey." He held her a little away, his eyes taking in her blond hair tied back with a royal-blue ribbon that matched her silk shirt, her snug-fitting designer jeans and high-heeled western boots. "You look good, kid."

"You, too." She smiled up into his broad, friendly face. "I expected you at breakfast, but—"

She broke off at the dull flush that crept up his neck and colored his fair skin. Had she said something wrong?

He dropped his eyes uneasily. "I—I guess I was out a little late last night. Overslept this morning."

Recovering, he gave her an affectionate grin and patted her shoulder. "But I see you're dressed for riding. You don't want to hang around talking to me on a beautiful day like this. See you later."

Ramsey, puzzled, watched him walk down the hall and turn into the kitchen, then, with a shrug, she opened the front door and stepped out on the veranda. The afternoon breeze played around her bare neck where she had pulled back her heavy hair; the sun fell across her face like a warm caress. From far away she heard the soft knicker of horses, and the screech of a high-sailing hawk. The sights, sounds, smells of the ranch enveloped her like a comforting cocoon, and she experienced such a sense of well-being that for a long moment she just stood there, drinking everything in.

She skipped down the steps and along the path, idly reaching to break a hollyhock from its stately stem, and held it against her face as she walked toward the barn. She was home.

She entered the barn and paused, lifting her head to sniff the pungent, heavy smell of hay and horses, and giving her eyes time to adjust to the gloom. Walking to the first stall, she saw that one of the quarter horses was already in. She smiled slightly. Karl had probably anticipated that she would want to ride and picked out a horse for her. Luck was with her. Amber, a gentle quarter-horse mare, turned her liquid eyes from the feed rack to watch her approach. Soothing the mare with frequent pats and gentle words, Ramsey soon had her saddled and bridled. There are some things you don't forget, she thought smugly as she pulled the cinch tight.

She led the horse from the barn, pleased at Karl's choice. Amber was golden brown, trim and spirited, and with a toss of her head that set her bridle jingling, was off as soon as Ramsey swung into the saddle.

She wasn't sure yet just where she wanted to go, but an idea was forming in the back of her mind. Perhaps it had been there all along. Brad's face, tight-lipped and angry as he looked at her from the window of his truck, flashed into her mind. What caused him to be so hostile to the Carmichaels? And what caused her heart to speed up just a little every time she thought about him? She wasn't an impressionable girl, thrilling over any attractive man's interest. Maybe it was merely that he was a part of a childhood that she remembered as warm and wonderful. Anyway, she re-called that he had mentioned Three Tree Spring.

The more she thought of it, the better the idea seemed. She needed a destination, and Three Tree Spring wasn't all that far away. Gently, she neck-reined Amber toward an open field and nudged her with her knees. The mare broke into a lope and Ramsey took a deep, exhilarated breath, filling her lungs with the warm fragrance of the summer day.

At a ranch-house window a curtain twitched briefly, then fell back in place. The eyes that had watched Ramsey until she was out of sight now stared thoughtfully at a wall, see-ing nothing but the woman riding away. The mouth tight-ened to a thin line. He didn't like the direction she was heading in.

He turned from the window, a mirthless smile curving his lips. He would follow. Accidents could happen to a woman riding alone.

Tying Amber to a low-hanging branch of spruce, Ramsey walked on shaky legs to the spring, guided by the crystal sound of water trickling over pebbles. It had been a long time since she had ridden, and her thighs felt numb. Now that she was here she wondered if riding out alone had been such a good idea after all. She had this uneasy feeling that she was being observed, although she'd kept a sharp lookout and had seen no one.

She realized that the impulse to come here had been in the back of her mind ever since Brad had said he planned to come out and search the area for anything the sheriff might have missed. It seemed like a good idea to beat him to it. Obviously there would be nothing here incriminating to the Carmichaels, but might Brad, in his single-minded effort to find them guilty of something—of anything—mis-read some evidence?

She had come to Three Tree Spring often as a child. The spot was named from the three huge pines that rose like sentinels beside the deep pool. It hadn't changed. Kneeling, she trailed her hand through the icy water of the pond that formed where water gushed from the side of the mountain, the smell of damp moss and spicy watercress taking her back in time.

In spite of the uneasy feeling that underlay her every action, she smiled inwardly. Jeff had once told her that a troll lived under the water and might grab her and pull her down if she knelt to drink, and for a while she had believed him.

A rush of anger made her hands tremble as she absorbed the peaceful atmosphere, smelled the astringent scent of pine and felt the dampness of the moss-covered ground seep through her jeans. This was an enchanted place; violent death had no business here.

Sighing, she rose and glanced quickly around the secluded glade where water from the spring encouraged a lush green growth that made a natural enclosure. She would have to be quick if she hoped to find anything. The ride here had taken longer than she expected, and the light would not last long. Already the sun was touching the western horizon and the hollow was deep in shadow. In a few minutes the sun would dip behind the high peaks and night would follow quickly.

She saw immediately that it wasn't going to be easy to find anything that the sheriff had missed. The spongy ground was a mass of boot tracks; it would be impossible to separate those of the killer from the murdered game warden, the sheriff or anyone else.

Catching sight of an indentation in the ground, she went a little closer, and sucked in her breath at the sight of blood on the grass. The deer's? Arnie's? She fought back a rush of nausea, but forced herself forward.

After a meticulous inspection, she leaned back against the rough bark of a pine, her shoulders slumped, and let disappointment wash over her. What had she expected? She should have known the sheriff hadn't overlooked anything. All she had found was trampled grasses, deep footprints, dried blood. She shuddered. How her world had changed in one day.

The sun dipped behind the mountain, shooting its last feeble rays into the glade. The dying light glinted on an object just a few yards away. She stiffened. All she saw was a quick flash of silver, but her pulse raced and she was instantly alert. Probably nothing, but...

She walked toward the shining object and bent down to examine it. It was lying several yards from where the bodies of Arnie Parkins and the deer had lain and was half-covered in a blanket of dried pine needles. She would never have seen it if she hadn't been standing in just the right spot at the exact time the sun had begun its descent.

Kneeling, she picked up the object in a suddenly shaky hand. Glowing in her palm was a silver conch, the kind Navajo Indians wore on a hatband. Could it have been lost by the murderer? Maybe not, but it had certainly been lost recently. The metal was highly polished with not a hint of tarnish. It couldn't have been here much longer than overnight. She tightened her lips. The person who lost it might not have killed the warden, but it certainly placed him at the spot at about the right time.

Suddenly she tensed, instantly alert to the crackle of pine needles under approaching footsteps. Her heart raced and she was frozen in position, but she retained enough presence of mind to hide the conch in a tightly clenched fist.

"Well, Ramsey, imagine meeting you here."

The deep voice was right behind her, and there was an angry edge to it that made her want to rise hastily from her compromising position. Almost afraid to move, she turned her head gingerly to find the toes of western boots planted firmly in front of her. Her eyes traveled upward over long masculine legs clad in faded jeans, over broad shoulders straining a red plaid cotton shirt, and rested finally on Brad's stern face.

She struggled clumsily to her feet, managing to shove the conch almost subconsciously into her jeans pocket. "Brad! What are you doing here?"

His voice was grim. "I think maybe you'd better tell me what *you're* doing here."

Hastily she thought over her options. Defiance? Humility? She was lost? Or maybe just the plain truth? There was something about Brad's uncompromising expression that made the latter seem the best bet. She dusted her hand on her jeans, and pushed back the strand of hair that had escaped the ribbon. "I thought I might find something the sheriff overlooked."

"And you wanted to find it before I got here," he said, making no attempt to hide his anger. "Why, Ramsey? Do you know something about that family of yours that I don't? Like where they were last night? Were you *expecting* to find something incriminating?"

"No!" In her haste to help, was she getting them in deeper? "I just thought you might have your mind already made up," she said more quietly. "Considering what you've said, you admit you might be prone to jump to conclusions! Anyway," she continued, "you said you didn't plan to come out here until morning!"

"And you believed me?" His lips curved in a tight grin. "You should have seen your face when I said I planned on checking out this place. Anyone could see you planned to beat me to it!"

They stood toe-to-toe as she glared up at him with angry defiance. She had as much right to be here as he did. The sheriff, not the game department, was conducting the investigation. She stared into relentless eyes that were deep wells of darkness, refusing to drop her gaze.

She was hardly aware when the defiance changed to something else. There was an intensity in his regard that pierced right through her defenses. She was nearly hypnotized; she no longer had the power to look away. He was standing so close to her that she felt the heat emanating from his powerful body and caught his musky, masculine scent.

Finally she managed to disengage herself from his compelling gaze, but it didn't help much. Glancing downward, she saw that his shirt, open a couple of buttons, revealed a sprinkling of dark hair, moist with the perspiration that also covered his strong, muscular neck with a faint sheen. She quelled an impulse to reach out and twirl a strand of the dark, springy hair around her finger. Her mouth felt suddenly dry and, fascinated, she stared at the pulse that beat rhythmically in the hollow at the base of his throat. She felt the same rhythm beating in her own temples.

She tore her gaze away and again looked upward, managing to get as far as his lips. A thrill went through her as she saw they had lost their severity and were curved slightly upward, firm and full. The shiver that raced all through her body culminated finally in a sweet, heavy feeling somewhere in her lower abdomen, and she again shifted her gaze. But there was no relief in looking into his eyes. Dark and demanding, they held hers with relentless, hungry power.

Gathering all her resolve, she managed an impatient shake of her head, then turned her face away, somehow breaking the intensity of the moment. What had they been talking about before this fierce current of sexual awareness had hit them with the force of a thunderbolt? Oh, yes. He was angry that she had beat him to the punch.

"Okay," she said, wishing her voice weren't quite so tremulous. "I know it smacks of suspicion. Perhaps I shouldn't have come. But you'll have to admit you do seem to have your mind already made up."

He didn't answer, apparently trying to get his ragged breathing under control as his eyes traveled over her averted face with a look as intimate as a caress. Then, very carefully, as though reaching for something infinitely fragile, he took her hand and pulled her along beside him.

"I think we need to talk." He led her to a fallen tree and seated her as gently as though she were delicate china, then positioned himself beside her. She knew that the moment of intense sexual awareness had affected him as strongly as it had her, and guessed that he was trying as hard as she was to ignore it. It wasn't easy. She was very much aware that his thigh was only inches from hers; the firm muscles showed tautly through his snug jeans. She could guess at how hard and solid he would feel beneath her hand. And if she relaxed slightly, her arm would brush against the hard curve of his shoulder.

She sat stiffly erect and placed both clenched hands on her knees.

As though it were the most natural thing in the world, Brad reached over and covered her fist with his strong bronzed hand and squeezed slightly. Little currents of warmth and excitement danced along her arm, and she stared at his hand as though she had never seen anything like it.

He fixed his gaze straight ahead. "I guess I know how you feel, Ramsey. And I can't blame you." Was there a hint of tenderness in his voice? "You've always been extremely loyal, and naturally you'd want to protect the people you love. And I probably made it sound as though the Carmichaels were the only suspects."

"And they're not?"

He hesitated. "I radioed Sheriff Thorenson before I came out here. He's checking out everyone known to have been in the area. It will take a while, but he's not overlooking any possibilities."

"Then there is really no concrete evidence against anyone."

His face was glum. "Absolutely none. The bullet could have come from any one of a hundred rifles. Everybody in the county has one. And the rifle that fired the fatal shot is probably buried, or tossed in a canyon—or even sitting in plain sight among somebody's gun collection. Unless we find it, we can't match the bullet."

"The killer had to get here. Any hoofprints?"

"Lots," he said thinly. "Nothing traceable. Also, we're only a few hundred yards from a forest service road. The killer might not have ridden a horse; he could have driven in, killed the deer and been dragging it to his car when Arnie found him. There's nothing."

Ramsey repressed a quick surge of guilt as she thought of the silver conch in her pocket. There *was* something. But until she was sure Brad wouldn't go off half-cocked, she wouldn't mention it to him. She might even investigate herself. If she could prove someone else guilty, Brad would have to leave the Carmichaels alone.

He seemed to be turning something over in his mind, then sighed. "I wish you weren't involved in this, Ramsey. When I saw you yesterday I thought—"

"Yes?" she encouraged when he broke off in midsentence.

"Oh, I dunno." He dug his toe into the ground, and Ramsey smiled inwardly, remembering what he'd said about having a crush on her. Was the fact that she had known Brad so long ago the reason she felt such an affinity for him now? Even though he had changed from an eager, vulnerable youngster to a hard, implacable man?

"I guess I hoped we might get to know each other," he continued. "Just Ramsey and Brad, and forget Chillicott and Carmichael."

She gazed down at her hands resting lightly on her thighs. "It still seems strange to think of you working as a game warden. What made you choose this profession?"

"Because I love these mountains so much, I guess," he said slowly. "And there are so many pressures on the land. Not just from people like your grandfather and some other old-time ranchers who think the land is theirs to do with as they please. They're anachronisms, really. It seems to me we have a new kind of society, a rootless, violent society. People who see nature only as something to tear up. They spew out from the concrete on weekends, and raise havoc in the name of recreation."

She was surprised at the bitterness in his voice. "But surely people have a right to be on public land," she protested.

"Oh, sure." He shrugged, as though to shake off the thought. "What about you, Ramsey? What are you really doing back here? From all reports, you loved the city."

"Reports? You've been keeping track of me?"

He grinned. "You can't have been away so long that you forgot how news travels around here. You'd be surprised at how much I know about you."

She smiled, warmed somehow by the thought that she had been in his mind. "I suppose Delia has been talking." She glanced around the little glade, wondering how to put her thoughts into words. "I was happy to get away from the city. But this murder has changed things. Brought horror where it should never be. I'm not sure I should have come back. I never expected to, not for any length of time. I'd had a shock, and the ranch seemed a sanctuary. But now I'm not sure…"

"Maybe you've outgrown them," he said quietly.

"Outgrown loyalty, pride of family?" she said dryly. "No, I was brought up to believe that you stick by your own."

He raised his head and looked directly into her eyes, his face a hard mask of resolve. "I'm not going to let it go, you know. Arnie was a fellow game warden. And he was my friend. I'll find out who killed him."

Glancing down, she saw that his hands were clenched so tightly that white showed along the ridges of his knuckles. Sadly she realized what he meant. No matter what the sheriff did, Brad would not give up the hunt. He was obsessed with one idea, and she wondered again what was really behind his need for vengeance.

"And you suspect that the trail will lead to a Carmichael."

He shrugged. "When it comes to flirting with the wrong

side of the law and walking over other people, it usually does.''

It seemed so obviously unfair that she stared at him wordlessly. He returned her look, his dark eyes unreadable. As she looked into their smoldering depths, unable to break away, she saw the black flint soften to a warm gray, and her breath caught in her throat. Although he didn't move, the rock-hard muscles of his face loosened, rearranging themselves into an expression of desire. Slowly, very slowly, so slowly that she was almost unaware of movement, he cupped her chin within his palm.

She trembled with anticipation as he turned her face until it was so near his own that she felt his breath burn against her cheek. The scent of his sun-warmed skin filled her nostrils, filled all of her, and just before she closed her eyes she saw his long dark lashes framing his magnetic eyes. She was still trembling like a captured bird as he lowered his head and claimed her lips, softly at first, then with an intensity that aroused every cell in her body.

Her entire being seemed to center in that kiss as his lips, firm and demanding, met hers in a burst of fire. A searing fire, yet one that did not so much burn as enliven her every nerve to aching awareness. She had never known one could be oblivious to so much, while so intensely, throbbingly alive. She opened her lips to his hungry demand, needing him, wanting him, inviting him into the velvet softness of her mouth.

Desperately, as though in the grip of something stronger than himself, he pulled her body against the hard muscles of his chest. She felt the rapid pounding of his heart, and frantic to have him even closer, she raised her hand to entangle her fingers in the thick hair at the back of his neck. Its springy texture beneath her questing fingers was an entrancing thread in the fierce, sensual tapestry they were weaving between them. So was the feel of each separate finger of his hand against her back, his breath coming hotly against her tingling skin, the incoherent moans that escaped them like unconscious pleas for union. She was drowning and she didn't want to be saved.

Suddenly he stiffened, and then, with a seemingly tremendous effort, he pulled away. She gave a little whimper; his absence making her feel naked, stripped, a leafless tree trembling in a winter wind. With a wordless question, her eyes met his.

She saw him struggle as he held himself rigid, every muscle taut with the effort of control. His eyes met hers, then looked away.

"I'm sorry, Ramsey." His voice was rough with emotion. "I didn't mean to—I— Oh, hell!"

Without another word he rose abruptly, then stalked away into the surrounding brush as Ramsey, openmouthed, watched him go.

When her breath had returned to normal and her trembling lessened, she was able to smile, though somewhat grimly. She felt as though she had been through an explosion. There was no denying the strong physical attraction between them, but it was obviously an attraction that neither wanted to foster! Whatever his body demanded, his mind rejected her. And she was glad.

Ramsey knew that it wasn't just Brad's resentment of her family that caused her to shrink from the feelings the kiss had ignited. She was glad that he'd had the strength to pull away before they'd gone too far to retreat. She didn't want to be involved with anyone just now, and certainly not Brad. She sensed something in him that frightened her, something dark that hid deep in the recesses of his soul. Something tormented. There was a hard and unforgiving facet to his nature, a core of aloneness that she suspected was unbreachable, in spite of momentary lapses such as the one that had just occurred.

Perhaps, she thought, that was why he was still unmarried. There was a part of him that could never admit anyone else into his inner being, never allow anyone to see into his heart.

On legs that were still a bit tremulous, she rose, dusted off her jeans absently and walked toward her horse.

The man who had been watching inched farther back into the brush that bordered the overflow from the spring, the heels of his western boots sinking soundlessly into the damp moss of the streambed. A scowl twisted his face, and his eyes smoldered with anger. Why had she come back? Why now?

She was much too friendly with the game warden. All that talk about old school friends, and they couldn't even keep their hands off each other. It was bad enough that she was here, snooping around, digging into things best left covered, but if she got in too thick with Chillicott it might become a real problem.

He waited a long time, motionless as a boulder, until he was sure that both she and the warden were gone. Then he strode to a nearby stand of cottonwoods and untied his horse, springing lightly into the elaborately tooled saddle. With a nudge of his boot, he urged the horse into a light canter.

What bad luck that Ramsey was back. Ramsey, the princess who could do no wrong. His face darkened. He wished he knew what the old woman had told her, but he hadn't been able to hear a thing through the heavy door. Then his lips twisted in a mirthless grin. It couldn't be much; the old woman didn't know anything.

But one thing was sure. Things were too far along to let her snooping around jeopardize his plans. It had taken too many years, too much effort, too much eating dirt, to lose it all now. His lips tightened and he dug his spurs viciously into the side of the horse. She could always be eliminated.

Chapter 3

Brad dismounted and opened the gate of the horse trailer, then gave the brown gelding a sharp slap on the rump. The horse, with a defiant twist of his head, jumped into the trailer. Brad closed the tailgate, walked around and stepped up into the cab of the pickup, slamming the door viciously. With a roar of the engine, he pulled off the shoulder back onto the gravel road and headed toward Tyler.

The trip hadn't been a total waste of time. He hadn't learned anything about who had killed Arnie, he thought, a muscle twitching in the corner of his clenched jaw, but he had certainly learned something about Ramsey Carmichael Delacroix. If he had ever doubted she would go to any lengths to help her precious family, he did not doubt it now.

In his mind, he reenacted the scene at Three Tree Spring. He had arrived just a few minutes before Ramsey and had waited, hidden in the thick growth of pine and aspen that encircled the spring, as she tied her horse and made a thorough search of the glen. He had seen her stoop to pick up something, and watched her shove it in her pocket as he confronted her, but he had no idea what she'd found. Something that would incriminate her family, he had no doubt.

He had been about to demand that she show it to him when the unexpected sexual explosion had occurred between them, and he had momentarily forgotten everything but the feel of her responsive body in his arms. Caught in his need, drowning in his passionate reaction to her beauty, he'd been unable even to think of what her surreptitious action might have meant.

But he'd recovered in time, he thought grimly, although just barely. Even with his arms about her pliant form, her body straining against his in seeming sweet desire, he'd remembered he couldn't trust her. She had rushed to the spring to get there before he did, she had hidden something that could possibly lead him to the gunman. She hadn't changed from the spoiled princess she had been when they were younger.

Although he hadn't realized then that she was spoiled. He'd just known he could never aspire to anyone so far above him. She had been as unattainable as she was desirable. Only now was he beginning to realize what she was really like. Her family was still her first priority; they could do no wrong.

He wondered if her dramatic response to his embrace had been genuine. It had certainly been unexpected, but no more so than his own unaccountable need. Perhaps she suspected he'd seen her pick up something and had distracted him in the best way she knew. If so, it had almost worked. It had taken every ounce of willpower he had to pull away from her.

With his mind a battleground of frustrated emotion and suspicion, Brad hardly noticed the thirty-mile drive to Tyler until he hit the paved road a couple of miles out of town. Maybe Ramsey was right about one thing: perhaps he should let the sheriff handle the entire mess. He couldn't be objective about the Carmichaels. Not about Jacob and Jeff, Karl and Bud, and certainly not about Ramsey! Involuntarily he rubbed his hand over his lips, as though to wipe away the vestiges of her kiss, but he was still uncomfortably aware of the softness of her lips against his own.

It was well past quitting time, and he wondered if he should just go on home, then changed his mind. Nothing was waiting for him there. He pulled into his space in front of the small cinder-block building that housed the Jade County office of the Idaho Fish and Game Department, carefully not looking at the vacant space alongside him. Arnie used to park there, and it might be a while before Brad could look with equanimity at that empty space.

He strode into the office, barely acknowledging the greeting of Ginnie, the part-time secretary, who sat typing in the front room. She was working very late; everyone had an added load these days. He entered his own office, and settled down at his desk. Sighing, he saw that his in-basket was piled high. Another change, another reminder of Arnie's absence. The older man, nearing retirement, had usually done most of the paperwork, while Brad did the fieldwork. It was just Arnie's bad luck that he'd been making one of his infrequent inspections and had come upon the poacher.

And my good luck, Brad thought, anger tightening his lips. It could as easily have been he who came upon the poacher and he doubted that the end result would have been any different. A game warden would be dead.

A door slammed in the front office, after which he heard the murmur of his secretary's greeting. Looking up as the door of his inner office opened, his frown eased, and he smiled a sincere welcome.

"Hello, Sheriff."

Sheriff Thorenson, a heavy, balding man whose broad shoulders were balanced by a large paunch, looked like the stereotype of the good-ole-boy lawman who would shoot first and ask questions later. Brad wasn't fooled; he knew that the sheriff's appearance masked a sensitive, intelligent mind and a compassionate nature.

Thorenson pulled a chair up in front of Brad's desk and regarded him thoughtfully.

"Saw you coming into town. Out late, aren't you? Isn't this supposed to be your day off?"

Brad grinned and shrugged. "With Arnie gone, I don't have a day off. But I doubt that you're concerned about my hours. I suppose you want to know where I've been."

"Nope." Sheriff Thorenson leaned back in his chair, tilting until the front legs left the floor. "I've got a good idea where you've been. Find anything we missed?"

Brad hesitated a fraction of a second. Ramsey had found something, something she thought significant enough to hide, but he wouldn't mention it until he knew what it was. "No…"

"Well, I'm glad you looked," Thorenson said. "I can always use help—especially yours. I don't mind telling you I don't like this thing one bit." He scowled, and returned the chair to its four legs. "Why would somebody kill Arnie just because he found him skinning out an illegal deer? There'd be a fine, sure. But is that worth killing a man for?"

Brad managed to convey his bitterness in a shrug. "Maybe to some people."

Thorenson gave him a keen look. "You still thinking about the Carmichaels?"

"Who else?" Brad demanded. "You know as well as I do that they don't think any law applies to them. You know they kill deer anytime they take it in their heads to do it!"

"Hmm." Sheriff Thorenson rubbed his chin, while staring thoughtfully at a fly buzzing in the window behind Brad's head. "Could be. But it doesn't sound right, somehow. Poaching is one thing, killing a man is another. Old Jacob Carmichael just *might* kill someone if he thought he had provocation, but I can't see him sneaking around like that. If he did it, he'd own up."

Brad snorted. "An honest lawbreaker? How do you think he acquired all that ranchland?"

"You have to understand the old man's code," Thorenson said slowly. "I've known Jacob for years. He would have been right at home in the West of one hundred years ago, when men grabbed land when they could and defended it from all corners, however they could. They didn't mind fighting, but they didn't bushwhack. Not the honorable ones."

A muscle twitched in Brad's jaw, but he didn't reply. Then he shrugged, as though tired of the argument, and rose restlessly from his chair, turning his back to stare sightlessly out the window. "Anyway," he finally said, swinging around to look at Thorenson, "Jacob's not the only Carmichael. There are three other men at the Floating Eagle. Karl's last name may not technically be Carmichael, that's the only difference. They're all one bunch."

Now it was the sheriff's turn to hesitate. Then he gave a deep sigh. "I know. But I can't see any of them doing it, either. Bud doesn't have the guts. He's been so scared of his old man all his life that he doesn't move unless he's told to. Karl Powers is a tough man, and Jeff is smart and determined, but I can't see either of them actually killing someone to get out of a fine for poaching."

He rose and paced a couple of times around the room, a scowl on his heavy face. "I think we've got to look for somebody else. Some outsider, maybe..."

His face wore a baffled expression as he turned to Brad. "I'd like your help on this, Brad, but I hope you'll remember one thing."

Brad merely raised an eyebrow, and the sheriff continued firmly. "Don't go off half-cocked. You may not be able to be objective about the Carmichaels. Remember there are other possibilities."

Conveniently overlooking that he had thought the same thing himself a few minutes ago, Brad put a trace of indignation in his voice. "What makes you think I can't be objective?"

Instead of answering his question directly, Thorenson

gave him a thoughtful look. "I understand the girl is back. Ramsey. Have you seen her?"

Brad knew his face didn't betray a thing, even to the sheriff's observant eyes. He'd had a lot of practice keeping his emotions—or at least the appearance of his emotions—under control. "I saw her."

"Didn't you used to be kinda sweet on her?"

Brad raised a dark, heavy eyebrow. "Me and half the boys in high school," he said dryly. "But I'm a big boy now."

"Maybe none of us ever get that big."

"She means nothing to me now," Brad reiterated.

The sheriff didn't appear convinced, but he stood and shoved the chair back against the wall. "Well, as I said, I welcome your help. But be careful, Brad."

"Careful?"

"Yes, careful. There's no evidence at all that the Carmichaels had anything to do with Arnie getting shot—but there's something strange going on out at that ranch."

"Strange? Like what?"

"I don't know," the sheriff said slowly. "I hear things—rumors, hints. And we all know the ranch is losing money. Why would that be?" He reached for the door and swung it open, then paused and gave Brad a direct look. "Try to stay out of trouble."

The door closed behind the sheriff and Brad sat back down at his desk. For a long moment, he stared unseeingly at the dark green blotter in front of him. Stay out of trouble. It was a little late for that warning. He might be able to investigate the shooting and keep out of danger from the killer. But what of the other danger?

He hadn't been exactly honest with the sheriff. Ramsey's image flashed before him: hazel eyes, so deep he could drown in them, staring up at him in surprise. Could those eyes actually hide a scheming nature? When he had pulled away from their kiss he had seen bewilderment and pain in her face. At least, he thought that was what he had seen.

Was she such a consummate actress? But she must be; how else could he explain her actions? It wasn't reasonable that sexual passion had flared so quickly between them.

His lips twisted in a mirthless grin. How could he ever stay out of trouble where Ramsey was concerned?

Ramsey ran lightly up the stairs to change for dinner, very much aware of the silver conch still in her jeans pocket. Why hadn't she told Brad about it? She hadn't really meant to suppress evidence, but to be honest, her own reaction to him had, for the moment, taken precedence over her concern with the murder. Her action in hiding the conch had been automatic; she had been startled by his abrupt appearance. She would undoubtedly have told him about it later when she'd had time to think about it. He hadn't given her much of a chance, stalking off like an angry bear.

She paused at the door to her room, arrested by the sound of running footsteps coming toward her down the hall.

"Stevie!" She turned to gather the small, squirming boy in her arms, then reluctantly released him. "Did you have a good day?"

"You bet!" He lifted his little face to hers, his blue eyes dancing with excitement. His skin was lightly sunburned and heavily streaked with dust, and there was a three-cornered tear in his once-white T-shirt. "Karl let me ride Dumpy! He said I did so good that in a few days I can even ride Star!"

"That good?" She smiled fondly into his eager face. He certainly looked like he'd had fun, if you could judge by his disheveled appearance. It was good to see him acting like a normal eight-year-old. At least for the moment his defensive manner and simmering anger were gone. Perhaps her idea in bringing him to the ranch had been the right one after all.

She glanced down at his rumpled jeans and dusty boots, and then rubbed his blond head affectionately. "Well,

Stevie, right now you'd better wash up and change your clothes. Dinner will be in a few minutes.''

He nodded, but he didn't move away. ''You know what else Karl said?''

''No. What else did Karl say?'' She felt a twinge of amusement at the glowing excitement in Stevie's eyes.

''He said I can go with him whenever I want! He'll teach me lots of things! Roping! Rounding up the cows!''

''That's great, Stevie. Now wash up,'' she murmured, pivoting him around and giving him a little push down the hall toward his bedroom. She watched him go, his little back ramrod straight, his head high, as he hurried away from her, and a sharp pain caught in her throat. He was such a wonderful little boy. She had wanted him to have a male role model, but it hurt to be left behind so willingly. Being a parent is learning how to let go, she reminded herself firmly.

Then she frowned, suddenly uneasy, as she opened the door to her bedroom. It *was* great, wasn't it, that Karl was taking an interest in Stevie? Wasn't that the reason she had brought Stevie home, to give him a chance to know his family? She herself might think Karl a trifle macho, and possibly not too bright, but he was an integral part of the Floating Eagle, just as much as she or Jeff or Bud. He'd been here nearly as long, and obviously felt the same way about the ranch and about old Jacob as she did. If she were worried by the pride and awe in Stevie's voice when he spoke of the man, it was probably because she was slightly jealous.

Dinner that night was a quiet affair. Everyone seemed subdued by the recent events, involved in their own thoughts, and there was little of the banter Ramsey remembered. Stevie sat by Karl, watching the dark, powerful man with hero-worshiping eyes. Uncle Bud hardly looked up from his plate. Delia had asked for a tray in her room, and Jacob was so quiet he was almost morose. Only Jeff was his usual witty, affectionate self.

''Well, Ramsey,'' he said, winking and lifting his fork in

a mock salute, "I must say you certainly add a touch of class to this place." His amused gaze swept around the table. "As you can see, we're not much for conversation when we're alone."

She smiled back, grateful that he was lightening the mood. Jeff hadn't changed much since they were kids. He still had a lean, restless look about him, was always ready with a quick quip. As usual, his hair was neatly combed, his clothes immaculate. Unlike the other men, he occasionally dressed in something other than jeans, and tonight he looked handsome and confident in a white linen dress shirt and chino trousers.

"You always did make up for anyone else's lack of conversation," she teased. "For which I've always been grateful."

"That's true," he said equably. "I never knew why strong, silent men are so much admired. From my observation, they are usually silent because they have very little to say."

He grinned disarmingly. "Although that might not be the case with our old friend, Brad. I suspect there's something simmering under that granite exterior! He probably has plenty to say!"

"I take it you haven't been close for a while. You used to be friends."

"I'm not sure we were. Or if he hung around me to see you." He gave her a keen glance. "You sure talked to him long enough the other day."

She merely smiled, and turned her attention to her food, feeling suddenly uncomfortable. Was Jeff fishing subtly for information, trying to get her to discuss her meeting with Brad? Just as she was reluctant to discuss her family with Brad, always feeling she must go to their defense, she found she didn't want to talk to them about Brad, either. Either way, she felt slightly disloyal. Why couldn't things be simple?

Uncle Bud lifted his blond head from his scrutiny of his

plate. "Anybody know what he's up to? I'm getting jumpy. I hate to keep looking over my shoulder for the game warden."

Jacob gave him a stern glance. "That will do, Bud. No one has any reason to be concerned. Don't exaggerate."

Ramsey watched Bud flush and silently devote himself to his dinner, and she felt a pang of sympathy for the man. He'd said only what the others were thinking. He was so easily cowed by Jacob, seeming to breathe only when his father gave him permission. As a child, Ramsey used to wonder if Bud would ever rebel, but she could see he never had.

"I saw Brad today," she said quietly. "I was out riding and ran into him."

"Just happened to run into him?" Jeff said, a laugh in his voice.

Jacob shot Ramsey a quick glance, his old eyes suddenly suspicious. "Ran into him, Ramsey? Was he on Carmichael land?"

"No, I was over on the national forest," she said slowly, deciding she wouldn't volunteer that she had actually been at the site of Arnie Parkins's murder. Her grandfather would surely believe she had no business mixing into it, and he would be right.

"Well, be careful," the old man said, giving her a worried glance. "Didn't used to be anything to harm a person on Carmichael land, but things are changing. All these strangers hunting and fishing. No idea who they are. And now murder. I can't believe it." He shook his white head in obvious bewilderment. "I don't like the thought of Chillicott snooping around, either."

"Are you worried about going out alone?" Jeff asked, his blue eyes solicitous. "After all, someone was shot; I could ride with you, Ramsey."

"Oh, no, of course I'm not worried," Ramsey said hastily. "Whatever happened had nothing to do with me. And you have work to do."

The meal resumed, everyone glumly silent. Ramsey sighed, picking at the perfectly broiled steak that she knew Martha had prepared in her honor. Why did this incident have to happen now, when she so desperately needed to find comfort and relaxation at the Floating Eagle? She had thought of the ranch as an always available refuge, a retreat to the safety of childhood, and her grandfather was actually warning her to be careful!

She thought of Brad, warning her of the same thing, and frowned. There was something going on, a murderer at large, but she didn't see how it affected her. She had been away so long she was nearly a stranger, in no way involved in the murky undercurrents.

Her grandfather broke the lengthening silence. "I think you ought to stay away from Brad Chillicott, Ramsey." His pale blue eyes fastened sternly on her face. "Seems strange to me he was just wandering around and *happened* to run into you. He might have had another motive."

Ramsey flushed. She knew Brad had a motive other than a simple desire to see her. He wanted to be sure she didn't search the murder site before he did! But that wasn't what her grandfather meant, she knew. "What do you mean, another motive?"

Jacob seemed slightly uncomfortable; he twisted his fork in his hand, choosing his words, but the direct look from fierce blue eyes didn't waver. "After what you heard last night, you know he don't think much of any of us. Considers us lawbreakers. Criminals! One-track mind, the boy's got. He might think you're the way to get to us..."

"I—I doubt I'll be seeing him." Not if she had a brain in her head, she wouldn't be seeing him. Only a fool would let herself in for that flood of sexual chemistry she felt every time she got near the man. What was the basis for her exaggerated response? Her own need and vulnerability? How could she feel that sexual attraction for a man who was merely an old acquaintance from high-school days?

Whatever was causing the reaction, she agreed with her

grandfather; Brad was trouble, although they had different reasons for thinking so.

She would stay away; in spite of the undeniable chemistry, she didn't want to start anything with a man like Brad. Even if he weren't pursuing a vendetta against her family, he wasn't the type of man she wanted, not for the long term, and that was the only way Ramsey wanted a man. She wasn't about to start anything when she would be going back to San Francisco in a few weeks, back to her real life. In her vulnerable state, an affair with a man like Brad could be shattering.

She didn't even know this adult Brad. She felt estranged from the shy boy of her memory. She sensed a flintiness, an inflexibility, to his character that was the exact antithesis to her own nature. His control had broken for a moment today, but he had hurriedly erected the barrier around his emotions.

For a moment she wondered what had happened to put that shell around him.

The next morning Ramsey drove along the road toward Tyler, fighting an impulse to turn the pickup around and scurry back to the Floating Eagle. Last night her decision to stay away from Brad had seemed reasonable and justified. Today, in the light of morning, it seemed merely cowardly. She was overreacting to a sexual impulse, letting it dictate her actions. She *needed* to see Brad to be sure that in his zeal he didn't manufacture evidence against the Carmichaels. She owed her family that.

As she approached the little town, she realized Tyler had changed very little since she was a teenager. A sign still proclaimed population 1050. She thought the number was the same when she left years ago. It was situated on a flat spot in the bend of the river, and consisted of a cluster of brick-and-frame buildings along several narrow streets, their outlines softened by dozens of sycamores and elms.

She spotted the Fish and Game building as she drove into

the outskirts of Tyler, and swung into the empty space beside Brad's pickup. She was glad she had caught him in the office. She really had to talk to him before misunderstandings compounded themselves.

After a great deal of thought, she had decided that she would tell him about the silver conch she had found. She might have a hard time explaining the reason she had kept silent until now, but it was better to get it over with. She couldn't suppress evidence; besides, it didn't point to a member of her family any more than it pointed to anyone else in the community.

She clenched her jaw as she stepped out onto the hardtop. It was necessary that she talk to Brad; it was quite clear that he planned to implicate her family if he could, whether they were guilty or not, and she wasn't going to allow it. Whatever his reasons for hating the Carmichaels, he had no right to use this tragedy to get back at them.

She thrust open the door and smiled at the young woman seated behind the receptionist's desk, noting briefly that she had a narrow, pleasant face and alert blue eyes. "Hello, I'm Ramsey Delacroix. Is Brad Chillicott in?"

The woman's blue eyes widened with curiosity, and she started to get up from her chair. "I'll see—"

Before she could finish the sentence the door behind her swung open and Brad lounged in the doorway. There was a smile on his hard, lean face, but to Ramsey, it didn't seem particularly welcoming.

"Hello, Ramsey. This is a surprise."

She drew herself up to her full height. Who would have thought that Brad, humble, worshipful Brad, could come this close to intimidating her? "I think we need to talk," she said quietly.

His eyes met hers in a deep, searching gaze, then he smiled. She saw some of the rigidity leave his muscular form, and a flicker of warmth enter his slate-colored eyes. She relaxed a little, realizing only then how tense she had been.

"I think you're probably right," he said. "Want some coffee?" He gave the woman at the desk a warm smile. "I'll be over at the coffee shop, Ginnie, in case anything turns up."

They walked silently along the narrow sidewalk, arms nearly touching. Ramsey was acutely aware of his tall form striding along beside her, and out of the corner of her eye she saw the hard set of his jaw. What was it with Brad? How did he keep her continually off base, so welcoming and friendly one minute, harsh and unapproachable the next? How could he kiss her as he had done, and then treat her with cool courtesy? Well, that was what she hoped to find out.

When they were seated at a corner booth in the coffee shop, cups of the dark, steaming liquid in front of them, Brad finally spoke.

"What did you want to talk about, Ramsey?"

His eyes were so remote that she could almost believe yesterday had never happened. Or that he had once told her he'd had a crush on her since he was a young boy. She had to force herself to face him squarely.

"That's part of it, Brad. Your attitude. You seemed genuinely glad to see me the other day. Even more than glad," she said firmly, refusing to let her eyes drop from his face. "Now I'm a stranger again, a Carmichael whom you obviously dislike. What have I—what have any of us—done to you?"

"Did you really come all the way in here to find out why I didn't continue the seduction scene?"

She flushed at the sardonic tone in his voice. "No. I assume you came to your senses—as I did!"

At his lifted eyebrow, she hurried on. "Brad, for some reason you seem determined to find a Carmichael guilty of Arnie's murder. I want to tell you, you might as well look elsewhere. There's nothing at all to tie my family to it but your own preconceived notions."

"No?" His voice was cold. "Then why did you bother to hide whatever you found at Three Tree Spring?"

Her eyes widened in shock and surprise. Brad had seen her hide the silver conch. Could that be why he had acted so strangely, at first so passionate, then pulling away with insulting swiftness? By hiding that bit of evidence, she had only increased his suspicion of her and her family.

She had planned to volunteer the fact that she had found it, enlist his sympathy and trust. Now he would believe she would have continued to hide it if he hadn't called her on it. Any trust she had hoped to establish was negated by the fact that he was the one who first mentioned catching her in the act of concealing evidence.

It might be too late to allay his suspicions, but she had to try.

She took a deep, shaky breath, fumbled in her pocket, and then stretched out her arm toward him, the conch lying in the palm of her hand. "This was a few feet away in the bushes."

He frowned as he reached over to touch the shining object. "A conch? That doesn't tell us too much."

His fingers brushed against hers as he took the conch from her hand, and she had to fight to keep from flinching away from the warmth of his touch. A current of awareness ran up her arm, sending shivers of sexual excitement through her body. Had she been honest with herself? Had she really wanted only to discuss the situation with Brad, deflect his single-minded pursuit, or had she been inexorably drawn to him, needing to see him again?

"It certainly doesn't point the finger at a Carmichael," she said, more sharply than she had intended.

"So why did you hide it?" His eyes bored into her's with angry intensity.

"I didn't mean to hide it; it was just a reaction. Then, when I might have told you, we—we—" she floundered into silence.

She saw the dark flush on his face and felt a flash of

triumph; he hadn't forgotten. He was remembering the same thing she was, and it was affecting him.

Their eyes held each other until Ramsey, with a tremendous effort, managed to look away. She glanced out the window at the street, trying to regain control of her ridiculous emotions. Whatever the reason for that explosion, it wouldn't happen again.

Her eye was caught by a pickup pausing at the stop sign in front of the coffee shop. From where they sat, the street was only a few feet away. She wouldn't even have noticed if the woman driving the vehicle hadn't looked so harried. Almost frightened. She was staring straight ahead, jaw clenched, shoulders rigid. There was something familiar about her, too.

Ramsey turned quickly to Brad. "Who is that in the pickup?"

He turned quickly, then frowned. "Ella Parkins."

"The game warden's wife?" No wonder she had seemed familiar. Ramsey had seen Ella Parkins occasionally years ago when she had been Ella Kirkpatrick, and she and Ramsey's Uncle Bud had dated for a year or so. She should have recognized her—the woman hadn't changed that much. Even from the glimpse she'd had of her, Ramsey could see Ella had retained her delicate blond beauty, her large eyes and classic profile.

Brad was still staring thoughtfully after the pickup as it turned a corner in a shower of gravel and headed out of town. "Wonder where she's going?"

Ramsey started to shrug off the question, then paused. On the surface, there was no reason to think anything was unusual. But there had been the frightened, almost desperate, expression on the woman's face that had first caught her attention. Perhaps something *was* wrong.

"Did you say Arnie was nearly ready to retire?"

"In a year," Brad replied.

"Then he must have been nearly sixty," Ramsey said slowly.

"Sixty-four," Brad said absently, still staring out the window.

Ella, even with her face contorted in fear or grief, hadn't looked a day over forty. Ramsey suddenly remembered that her Uncle Bud, now in his forties, had been only a few years older than the woman when they were dating.

Brad, as though coming to a decision, rose hastily and reached for the check. "Let's see where she's going."

Ramsey scrambled after him, but by the time they reached his pickup and pulled out onto the street, the woman was out of sight.

"We'll never catch her," Ramsey said, holding on to the dash as they hurtled along the road.

"Don't want to catch her," Brad said cheerfully. "I'm just a little curious as to where she's going in such a hurry."

"But how will you find her? She could be anywhere."

"Not exactly." He steered expertly around a large rock that had fallen into the road from the steep bank. "We know she took this turn. The only place this road goes is along the lake."

They drove for several miles, both immersed in their own speculations. Ramsey thought they were probably on a wild-goose chase. There was no reason in the world why a recently widowed woman shouldn't go for a drive, and the despairing expression that had bothered her was also perfectly understandable. She probably just wanted to be alone. Undoubtedly they would soon come upon Ella, intrude on her grief and feel like fools.

She tensed as they turned a bend and saw the woman's pickup parked off the road a few hundred yards ahead of them. Ramsey froze, her breath catching in her throat, as she focused in on another vehicle parked close beside it. A quarter-ton truck, black with silver strips. She didn't dare look at Brad's face.

She recognized that pickup. She had seen it this morning; it had been one of the two parked side by side in the Carmichael garage.

Chapter 4

Brad drove on about a quarter of a mile past the two pick-ups, then maneuvered his truck off the road onto the narrow shoulder. He ran along the shoulder for several feet, then pulled off into an opening in a grove of willow and aspen. When he finally pulled to a stop, the loden-green vehicle was almost hidden among dense foliage.

Ramsey opened the door and jumped out onto the ground, balancing herself as the heels of her western boots sunk slightly into the moss and meadow grass. At another time she would have noticed and appreciated the minty fragrance rising from the crushed green mat, but now she could only think of one thing. The pickup truck parked alongside Ella Parkins's. The pickup she had recognized.

She had no idea who was driving it. Jeff had his own red sporty coupe, old Jacob often drove his luxury sedan and there were two pickups kept for use by anyone at the ranch. She had one.

She felt Brad's sardonic gaze on her face, aware that her shock was apparent; she could never hide any emotion. He must have recognized the pickup also. She remembered that in this country everyone was as familiar with the vehicle a person drove as with the person himself. It was painfully obvious that someone from the Floating Eagle ranch was meeting the widow of the slain game warden.

Wordlessly, Brad reached for her hand and propelled her swiftly through the thick brush, backtracking until they had reached a point nearly opposite the two parked pickups. Although she tried not to make a sound, Ramsey could hear the beat of her heart pounding in her ears. To their left, nearly hidden by the fringe of green trees and shrubs, was Beaver Lake, and in the silence she could hear the soft, relentless lapping of water along the shoreline. A rustle of leaves betrayed an occasional bird or tree squirrel, and a slight breeze set the aspen leaves to quivering and murmuring, but otherwise all was quiet. So quiet, Ramsey could hear herself breathe.

As they crept along, she realized she was familiar with the place. She recalled that just ahead, a path reached down from the narrow road to connect with a ramshackle pier built out into the shallow water. She wondered if the rickety structure was still standing after all these years. It had branched out from a tiny glade where an outcropping of flat granite boulders made a convenient picnic table. In her high-school days, this secluded spot had been a well-known place for what was then called making out.

Brad paused, looked up at the road where the pickups, barely visible through the green screen, were parked, then down at the moist ground. A faint path was apparent, and Ramsey made out two sets of footprints in the spongy earth.

Putting his hand lightly on her shoulder and giving her a warning glance, Brad moved to the side of the trail where their own footprints would not show, and inched stealthily forward.

He moved like a predator, Ramsey thought, silently following. His lean, rangy body emanated tension; the bunched muscles of his back rippled through the thin material of his olive-green shirt, and the twill pants stretched tightly over his slim hips as he moved forward. Not a branch cracked beneath his feet, not a leaf rustled. He was probably used to this relentless stalking of prey, to the dismay of many a poacher.

He motioned her to stop, then pushed aside a low-hanging willow branch. Hardly breathing, apprehensive as to what she would see, Ramsey gazed out into the open area at the two figures.

A wave of shock mingled with stinging disappointment as she recognized the two people. Ella, of course, but she hadn't expected to see the man who held the woman tightly in his arms. Ramsey sucked in her breath and clutched Brad's arm, her fingers digging into the muscles beneath his shirt.

Uncle Bud.

The two people, oblivious of the onlookers and of everything except themselves, were standing at the edge of the lake, enfolded in each other's arms. Ella's blond head was pressed against Bud's chest, and Ramsey and Brad were close enough to see that her eyes were tightly closed, her face streaked with tears. Bud, a grim expression on his face, brushed her hair with his lips. Then the couple pulled slightly apart, and Ramsey saw that Bud was murmuring something to the obviously unhappy woman.

Suddenly stiffening, Bud looked up from Ella and peered sharply around at the encircling trees, and Ramsey instinctively drew back farther into the gloom. Had Bud been alerted by some sound, or did he sense their presence? He and Ella obviously didn't want to be seen; there was something furtive and frightened in the way Bud's eyes darted around the enclosed glade.

Then, apparently feeling he had been unduly alarmed, he turned back to Ella. He stroked her back as he held her slender body firmly against his. Although Ramsey strained to hear what the couple said, only the low murmur of voices reached her ears. Their actions told her more than enough.

This was a rendezvous of lovers, lovers who had gone to great pains to keep their meeting secret.

Ramsey tried to resist the obvious conclusion. Bud and Ella had loved each other when they were much younger; she remembered that. She had never known why they had stopped seeing each other, and she had been slightly surprised when she learned, from one of her grandmother's letters, that Ella had married someone else. At the time, however, she'd had her own problems, and she'd given Ella's surprising marriage very little thought.

Now she had to think about what this meeting signified, and she didn't like the conclusion she came to. Bud and Ella had loved each other, Ella had married Arnie Parkins and now Arnie Parkins was dead. Was this meeting just an old friend comforting a grieving widow, or was it something sinister Ramsey didn't even want to think about?

Brad put his arm around her waist and pulled her farther back into the concealing foliage as the other couple turned and, hand in hand, heads down, started back up the path to the road. They passed so close she could have reached out and touched them, but they were conscious only of each other. Ramsey saw that she had not been mistaken in thinking Ella was frightened of something. The aftermath of fear was in her wide china-blue eyes, her face was pale and her hand gripped Bud's as though he were a lifeline.

Neither Brad nor Ramsey spoke until they heard the sound of engines starting, and then the squeal of tires. Still Brad remained motionless, his hand lightly on her shoulder until, after only a minute or so, they heard the sound of the returning vehicles. Bud and Ella had apparently driven on until they found a wide place to turn around, and were now heading back to town.

As the sound of the motors faded, Ramsey slumped against the trunk of an aspen, staring at the ground, refusing to meet Brad's eyes. Finally, when he said nothing, she lifted her head slowly and met his somber gaze. Taken aback at his expression, she gazed at him in silence. She had expected to see triumph, vindication of his theories, but instead there was a glint of sympathy in his dark eyes.

He put his arm gently around her waist and drew her out into the clearing where her uncle and Ella had so recently stood. She sank down upon a boulder, and he squatted beside her.

"Aren't you going to say, 'I told you so'?" she asked when the silence lengthened.

"Why?" He lifted a dark eyebrow in the quizzical gesture she had come to associate with him.

"You've said all along a Carmichael was mixed up in this," she said bitterly. "Uncle Bud meeting Ella should clinch it."

"I don't see why," he said slowly, breaking off a blossoming head of clover and crumbling it absently between his fingers. "Aren't you jumping to conclusions yourself?"

At her startled look, he gave her a slow, sweet smile. For a moment she couldn't look away from his face. She hadn't seen that smile for years, but the memory of it came flooding back, when she would look up from an algebra text and catch Brad's eyes, or when he would inexplicably be standing by her locker when she arrived between classes, that smile lit up the darkness of his face, revealing warmth and tenderness.

Suddenly she realized she had missed that smile.

She jerked her attention back to the present situation. "I'm sure there must be a reasonable explanation for Bud and Ella being together," she said slowly, "but I thought you would jump immediately to a connection between them and Arnie's—death."

His expression regained its old guarded look. "I haven't changed my opinion. I still think the Carmichaels are in this thing up to their necks. I'm just not sure it's Bud."

"Does it matter which one it is, as long as you get a Carmichael? Why the vendetta, Brad?"

He rose and turned away from her, his thumbs shoved in his front pockets, his eyes gazing out across the lake. She thought he wasn't going to answer, but finally he turned back, a thoughtful expression on his lean face.

"Is that how you see it, a vendetta?"

"Isn't it?"

"I hope not. It's just that I've had a lot of experience with your family, Ramsey."

"Why do you take it so personally? Sure, they may poach a little. I don't condone it. But you act like they are delibᵧ ᵼely trying to hurt *you*."

His eyes darkened, and she wondered what he was thinking. Certainly she could never tell from his expression; she would know only what he chose to tell her.

"I've seen them hurt others," he said briefly. "Old Jacob stepped on a few toes acquiring the Floating Eagle."

"He's had it for years," she protested. "That's ancient history."

"Not so ancient," Brad replied. "He expanded it, remember. Acquired a few acres here and there, as other ranchers couldn't meet his competition."

"Well, of course. That's just common business practice…"

"Of course." He gave her a wry grin, but she thought she detected a deep sadness in his eyes.

"Did you really have a crush on me in high school?" she asked suddenly. Immediately, blushing, she wished she could recall the words. They sounded as though she were fishing. Had they been hovering on the edge of her subconscious all the time?

He laughed and reached for her hand. "The worst. Come on, Ramsey, we'd better be getting out of here."

She didn't move, still searching his face. "You never said anything."

"What could I say?" The lines around his mouth hardened. "You and I didn't exactly move in the same social circles. The granddaughter of the county's leading rancher, and the son of the town's leading alcoholic."

"I—didn't know that about your father."

"No reason you should. He died when I was about fourteen. He never could adjust to town life, although we lived there from the time I was eight or nine. Just killed himself slowly, I guess." His tone was completely matter-of-fact. A person would have had to be watching him intently—as Ramsey was—to see the muscle twitch in his firm jaw.

"Your mother?" Ramsey said softly.

"Oh, she never was much good without Dad. She didn't die until a few years ago, though."

Ramsey felt a surge of sympathy, not so much for the hard, unemotional man standing beside her as for the lonely, unhappy boy he had been. She was beginning to understand the hard shell around his emotions.

"I'm sorry I didn't know you better then," she said impulsively.

"No use digging into the past," he said brusquely.

Ramsey still held his eyes. He might say there was no use digging into the past, but it was affecting them both. It colored the way they related to each other—he couldn't separate her from her family. She felt intuitively the past held the key to Brad's unwavering disapproval of the Carmichaels.

"We'd better get going," he said again, his voice impatient, whether with himself or Ramsey, she had no idea.

Ramsey nodded, and started after him as he strode along the path to the road. Was he running from the past? From her? There was no indication that he even remembered what had happened between them yesterday when they had burst into simultaneous flame. He obviously was taking no chances of anything like that reoccurring. His infrequent touches all had been light and nearly impersonal, although they had nevertheless sent little shivers along her spine. He was willing to admit he had once had a case of puppy love, but he apparently considered such emotions part of the past.

If that was his decision, she certainly would go along with it. Finding Uncle Bud here had shaken her implicit faith that her family was uninvolved in Arnie's death. Oh, she certainly didn't think one of them was guilty of actually shooting him, but there was still some mystery at the Floating Eagle. She thought of her grandmother's anxiety, the inexplicable absences of the men from the ranch. A cold wind seemed to blow across her body, leaving her shaking. Sides were being chosen here, and she knew which side she had to be on.

She hurried, catching Brad just as he reached the road and together they walked toward the place where he had hidden the pickup. She spotted it when they were still a few feet away, although it was so well hidden she might have passed it if she hadn't known where to look. She dropped behind as Brad strode into the little opening.

She saw him stop abruptly and heard an explosive sound escape his lips. "Damn!"

Hurrying up beside him, she found him glaring at the pickup, hands on hips, a thunderous look on his lean face. She followed his gaze, and gasped.

"The tires!"

"Slashed," he agreed.

Ramsey stared incredulously at the shredded rubber. Was Brad thinking the same thing she was? Bud and Ella had driven up this way before turning around for town.

"Uncle Bud?" she whispered.

He shrugged. "Not necessarily. I don't think they were gone long enough to do this."

"How long would it take to slash tires?"

"You've got a point." He grinned. "But it could have been anyone. Anyone seeing the pickup. Game wardens aren't always loved," he said dryly. "This could be considered a hazard of the business."

"But we didn't hear another car drive by, and this is a dead-end road."

"Someone could already have been here. Or maybe they walked across the ridge from the main road. It could have been anyone."

Ramsey watched dolefully as Brad made a quick inspec-

tion. The motor was intact. The spongy green moss held
slight indentations of her footprints and of Brad's, as well
as another set. It was no help. The prints could have been
made by any man in Jade County. Including, Ramsey
thought with a shiver, Uncle Bud.

And if it had not been him, who *had* seen the partially
hidden pickup? Ramsey and Brad had followed Ella; had
someone followed them, parking far enough away so they
didn't hear the sound of the motor? It would have been
difficult, but not impossible, to see the truck when merely
driving by on the road.

The pickup, all four tires flat, looked strangely misshapen,
and Ramsey gave Brad a worried look. "How will we get
back to town?"

His frown was erased by a devilish grin. "We'll walk,
princess. Carmichaels do walk, don't they?"

It was almost dusk when they finally left the gravel behind and reached the pavement that meant they were nearing
Tyler. Ramsey had long since lost count of the time and the
miles. Her feet were on fire, her muscles ached and the grit
on her face felt a foot deep. The ten-mile drive to Beaver
Lake had taken only a few minutes; the ten-mile walk back
was endless.

She had hoped someone would pick them up, but the road
to Beaver Lake was not heavily traveled. Bud and Ella had
picked the site for their rendezvous well. Ramsey and Brad
had trudged along without seeing another car. Ramsey was
limping, and there was a catch in her side as she stepped
up on the pavement and limped toward her own pickup,
which she had parked in front of the Fish and Game building
earlier that day.

She gave Brad a questioning look. "How long will it take
you to get some tires? Shall I drive you back?"

He ran his hand through his dark hair and grinned down
at her. They had talked some during the walk into town—
at least, before Ramsey became so exhausted—and had de-

veloped a little more camaraderie. Now his expression was concerned.

"You aren't doing any driving for a while—not until you pull those boots off and rest a bit," he said.

She looked down her jeans-clad legs to the dusty western boots with their one-inch heels. They weren't made for hiking, and the thought of pulling them off and wriggling her cramped toes was the most seductive thought she'd had in years.

Before she could reply, Brad took her arm and propelled her along a path that led behind the Fish and Games structure toward another small building. He opened a door and they were in the small foyer of a fourplex apartment building.

He smiled at her puzzled expression. "I don't believe in living far from work. It saves on commute time."

He ushered her into a small, sparsely furnished apartment, and with a groan, Ramsey flung herself down on the beige sofa that took up almost all the space of one wall. She lay back and closed her eyes as Brad knelt in front of her and pulled off each boot.

Waving her toes in ecstasy, she gave a deep sigh. "Oh, that feels good. But I'll never get them back on."

"Not for a while," he agreed, gently rubbing the soles of her feet and massaging her toes with strong, yet gentle fingers. "Why don't you take a shower, and I'll fix us something to eat."

Ramsey remembered she had last eaten at breakfast, and it was now early evening. A cool shower, food—it sounded idyllic. She nodded happily, and Brad took her hand and pulled her to her feet.

"The bathroom is through that door, clean towels in the drawer."

Almost too tired to stand, Ramsey stripped off her jeans and shirt, stepped out of the lacy silk bra and panties and turned the shower to hot. For long, delicious minutes she stood there, letting the water cascade over her tired muscles until the worst of the ache was gone. She leaned back, closing her eyes, feeling the water caress her face, run over her firm breasts, down to her flat abdomen and gently curved hips. Pure heaven.

Finally, realizing that the hot water might be limited and that Brad would undoubtedly want to shower off the dust, she quickly shampooed her hair, turned the water to a brisk, invigorating temperature, then stepped out to towel herself dry. When she returned to the living room, wrapped in one of Brad's white terry robes, she felt almost completely rejuvenated.

At the sound of the bathroom door opening, Brad turned from the stove and froze in midmotion. His eyes took her in slowly, moving from her damp hair that fell over her shoulders, lingered on her face, moist and clean and shining, down over the robe that she had tied firmly around her narrow waist, but which still fell open to reveal the tender valley between her high, firm breasts. He let out a long, low breath.

They stared wordlessly at each other; she could see her effect on him, and it started a thrill of excitement tingling all along her spine. His eyes, almost black, devoured her hungrily, and his hand tightened convulsively around the skillet he was holding.

She didn't want to, she tried to keep her eyes away, but she couldn't help it. Her gaze traveled down his hard lean body to the bulge showing prominently in his twill pants.

Her skin felt hot; she swallowed, and finally managed to look away.

"If you'll keep an eye on this steak I'm broiling," he said, his voice a husky whisper, "I'll take a quick shower."

She nodded, and he walked by her, exaggeratedly careful not to brush against her. Her throat still dry, she checked the steaks sizzling under the broiler, then began to set the table. Any activity would help keep her mind off his lean, rangy body, with the water pouring down over his broad shoulders, running through the dark hair on his muscular chest, over his hips...

As she set two plates on the small table, she glanced around the apartment. Somehow it didn't fit her preconception of the way Brad would live. The place consisted of a living room, bathroom and a kitchen-dining area, with presumably a bedroom somewhere. It was starkly furnished with only the necessities, and was strangely bare of ornamentation or the little personal items that would tell an observer something about the person who lived there.

She hadn't thought much about how Brad would live, but she realized that on some unconscious level she had expected comfortable surroundings. A touch of art and beauty. This apartment was almost monastic. She had wondered if his hard surface might be only a façade for an inner softness. Now she suspected the flint went all the way through to the core.

Her thoughts were interrupted by Brad's return. His promise of a quick shower had been kept. He had slipped into a clean pair of faded jeans and wore a white knit shirt that accentuated his bronzed skin, glistening from the shower. His dark, thick hair, still wet, was slicked back from his high forehead, his face clean shaven. He wasn't exactly handsome, she thought; his nose was slightly crooked, his jaw squared too harshly, but he exuded a vibrant, compelling energy that made him extremely attractive.

His wide-spaced, intelligent eyes returned her appraisal, and he grinned slowly. "Do I smell steak burning?"

She gasped and quickly turned to retrieve the two steaks from the broiler. "I guess they're done," she said lamely. "Extremely well done."

"Just singed a little."

They worked together in the tiny kitchen, by mutual unspoken agreement being extremely careful not to touch, and soon sat down to salad, steak and microwaved baked potatoes. Dinner was over too soon, leaving an uncomfortable silence. Brad stacked the dishes as Ramsey walked into the living room.

"I suppose I should be getting home."

Certainly she should, but she made no move to go. The sexual tension that had sparked between them for the past few days escalated until she could feel it pounding in every cell. She didn't know what she wanted. Certainly she didn't want Brad to take her in his arms, bring his warm, tender, demanding mouth down on hers, dig his fingers deep into her yielding flesh as he held her against his hard body—of course she didn't!

She didn't move as he came slowly toward her. He put his hands on her shoulders and stood looking down into her eyes. Her face was turned upward, his lips were inches away. Without volition, her own lips parted softly, and a shudder went through her body. As though moving through deep water, she put her arms around his shoulders, feeling the muscles of his back ripple through the thin knit shirt. He slid his warm hands down over her arms, on over her waist, until they were flat against the enticing curve just below the small of her back.

He pulled her against his taut body, and her robe fell partially open. She felt the knit material of his shirt against her flesh, the stiff denim of his jeans rubbing against her tender skin, and her knees turned to water. She couldn't have moved away from his descending mouth, his mouth that found hers and lingered like an enraptured butterfly, then captured her lips with the force of desperation, if she had wanted to. And she didn't want to.

He deepened the kiss, demanding everything she had to give. Rationality fled, thought subsided, as she opened her lips to his fierce quest—inviting, welcoming, pleading. She pressed closer, reveling in the feel of the warm length of his body against her own responsive flesh, acutely aware of the pool of desire forming in her lower abdomen like molten honey.

The rigidity of his body against her hips left her in no

doubt as to the strength of his own desire. Every bone in her body seemed to melt, to flow in a sweet, sensual current, as though to merge with his.

When he finally pulled his lips away she couldn't stop the faint cry of loss that came to her lips. Surprised and shaken, she stared up into his enigmatic face. Seeing his set, smoldering expression, she tried to get her emotions under control, to put a mask over her vulnerability.

With a rueful smile, he lifted his hand to tousle her hair as he might have caressed a child, or, she thought, anger replacing her recent passion, a favorite horse. Then his hand dropped heavily to his side, and he eased back slightly. His actions left her in no doubt that he regretted the impulse that had put them in each other's arms.

"I'll get dressed," she said stiffly, turning toward the bathroom. She had been silly to put herself in a position where she could be humiliated again, she thought, her face flaming. The kiss had seemed so inevitable, and she had responded so completely, forgetting the insurmountable problems that stood between them. Brad, obviously, had not forgotten.

"Ramsey—"

"It's all right," she said, keeping her head averted. "I understand."

"Do you? I shouldn't have done that. I certainly enjoyed it," he said, his mouth twisting in a wry grin, "but—"

She turned with a tight smile. "But you plan to put one of my relatives in jail."

Before he could reply, she moved toward him, her pleading eyes on his face, and put her hand lightly on his arm. "Brad, it's not your problem. Can't you let the sheriff handle it? It's his duty, not yours."

His lips tightened, and his dark eyes met hers squarely. He didn't move, but something inside him seemed to inch away. "My friend was killed."

"Then let me help you," she said impulsively. "Seeing Uncle Bud and Ella together made me realize there may be something going on I'm unaware of. Not that I believe any of my family killed Arnie, but I'm as interested as you are in finding out what really happened. To prove they are innocent.''

He started to protest, but she hurried on. ''You need me. Admit it. Grandpa will find a way to keep you off the Floating Eagle, unless I help you.'' And if I stay close to you, she thought, I'll be sure you don't try any tricks. You won't unfairly implicate any of my family.

He thought it over, and finally smiled. ''Okay. Deal.''

A few minutes later, Brad stood on the path of his apartment, scowling as he watched the taillights of Ramsey's pickup disappear into the dusky evening. He wasn't feeling very happy with himself. In fact, he was feeling like a dolt and a fool. He'd seen the hurt in her eyes when he released her from the kiss, and he felt as though he'd been beating up on a puppy. But he'd had no choice. He had to stop then before he was beyond stopping. And that would have hurt her worse.

He'd been determined to keep things on an impersonal basis between them, but the devastating force of his attraction to Ramsey always caught him off balance. No matter that he vowed each time he wasn't going to kiss her, was going to keep his distance, he ended up with his arms around her.

And that couldn't happen; it wouldn't work. It was much too dangerous. It was obvious that the feeling he'd had for her as a young boy hadn't gone away at all; in fact, it had intensified. It was also obvious that nothing could come of it, and he'd be left even more alone than before.

He remembered the guilty look in her eyes when he had demanded she show him the conch she had found at the site of the murder, and how reluctantly she had handed it over. She must have a pretty good idea of who had lost that conch. She had come to town for one reason: to distract him from his search, and she had nearly succeeded.

He would have to be very sure that today's passionate

episode was never repeated. He might desire her still, but he wasn't a kid anymore. He had gotten along without her for years, and he could continue to do so. Until she'd shown up unexpectedly at the ranch, he hadn't even thought of her for years. Weeks, anyway. He didn't even know the mature Ramsey, the Ramsey who was now a woman, and no longer the young girl of his memories.

His response to her was probably based on what he used to feel, a holdover from the time when she had been the center of his dreams, his inspiration when things got too painful in the real world. He was trying to recapture the innocence and rapture of youth. The adult man had to keep her at arm's length; he couldn't trust her. For all her swift, fiery response, she was a Carmichael, and he knew where her loyalties lay.

His hands clenched and a muscle twitched in his set jaw. But God, how sweet, how unbearably sweet, she felt in his arms.

Frowning, he turned and walked back into his apartment, thinking over the day. He didn't feel quite as nonchalant about the slashed tires as he had pretended to Ramsey. Game wardens might not be universally loved, but in his experience, they were seldom attacked.

Until recently, he amended, slamming his fist absently against the arm of a nearby chair. Until Arnie.

No, he decided, he wasn't blinded by his distrust of the family; even Sheriff Thorenson felt something wasn't quite right at the Floating Eagle. He would bet his life that one of the Carmichaels was somehow involved in the shooting.

His frown deepened and a sharp spasm of fear reached deep into his gut. He had agreed very easily to let Ramsey assist in the investigation, but not for the reason she thought. He doubted that old Jacob could keep him off the ranch, but he wanted a reason to stay close to Ramsey, one she would accept. He wanted to keep an eye on her.

Ramsey might try to shield her family, but he didn't think she would ever do anything dishonest herself. That could present a problem to someone. Poking around alone, she might stumble on to something someone wished to keep hidden. If he were right, someone at the Floating Eagle must be desperate, desperate enough to strike out in any direction.

He needed an excuse to be with her as much as he could; it was just possible that she might be in danger herself.

Chapter 5

Ramsey pulled into the garage and stepped lightly from the pickup, leaving the keys, as always, in the ignition. She was still seething from her recent encounter with Brad, but she had to admit that much of her anger was with herself. How had she managed to put herself in a position where she could be humiliated and rejected again?

She had been lulled right into it, had let down her guard. Everything had seemed to flow along so naturally and inevitably: the soothing shower after the grueling walk, the camaraderie over dinner, the admiring look she'd seen in his eyes. She hadn't imagined that look, and it had set her pulse racing.

She certainly hadn't intended to let the situation get out of hand, although she'd been under no illusions as to her strong physical attraction to Brad. He simply radiated sex appeal. She also knew the attraction was a simple chemical reaction, probably accentuated by her loneliness and her deep sense of hurt at Paul's betrayal. Nothing serious could develop between her and Brad—a childhood friend, and a person whose future was pointed in a direction opposite to hers. She was also repelled by what she sensed in his character: a dark and almost ruthless quality, a capacity for revenge, that almost frightened her.

Ramsey knew if she ever fell in love again, she would take her time and be very sure of what she was getting into. She would find a man with whom she could share the same interests, a man who'd uphold the same values. A man who valued loyalty and family as she did. She wouldn't be swept away into a current of sensuality like a susceptible schoolgirl.

She should have been the one to pull away, the one to realize first how untenable the situation was. But she hadn't pulled away, and she deserved his abrupt retreat. He must think she was desperate! Perhaps it was just as well she'd been so harshly rejected. They would be seeing a lot of each other since he had agreed to accept her help, and she didn't want a repetition of this afternoon's scene. She had been warned.

She didn't regret her offer to help Brad track down the guilty person, since it meant she could keep an eye on him. She had no idea, however, how to go about the search; she didn't think he did, either. He was going ahead on grit and determination.

Satisfied that she had put the episode in perspective, she glanced around the spacious garage, not surprised to find all the other vehicles gone: Jeff's red coupe, the other ranch pickup truck, even the sedan her grandfather sometimes drove to town. Her eyes were thoughtful as she surveyed the empty spaces; apparently everyone at the ranch had business elsewhere.

Did that business include slashing Brad's tires? The thought leaped into her mind, and she as quickly rejected it. Brad had pointed out that Uncle Bud hadn't had time to disable the Fish and Game pickup, and among her family Uncle Bud was certainly the only possibility. To think anything else was disloyal and ridiculous. She had been infected by Brad's suspicious mind. It was probably a disgruntled hunter as he'd said, performing a wanton act of destruction.

She left the garage and began walking the short distance to the ranch house, feeling some of her tension dissolve. Light shone out of the front windows, pouring warmth on the path in front of her. At least she wouldn't have to face Uncle Bud for a while. She always found it hard to dissemble, and she certainly wasn't going to confront him.

As she neared the front door, she heard the scramble of feet and braced herself for the two dogs that came tumbling off the veranda, barking a frantic welcome. Smiling, she put out her hand and patted the nearest head. "Hello, Bogus." Another link to her childhood. There had always been a succession of lean black cattle dogs named Bogus. This one licking her hand was probably a grandson or great-grandson of the original.

She gave each of the dogs a final pat, dodging their eager tongues, and entered the living room just as Martha bustled out of the kitchen to meet her.

"Will you want any supper, Ramsey? I've left some hot soup on the stove."

"Oh, Martha, I'm afraid I've already eaten. I hope you didn't wait around just for me." Ramsey felt a pang of guilt; she should have called. Martha came in every day, but she lived a mile or so away, and usually walked home after the supper dishes were done. Her husband could have picked her up, or one of the Carmichaels would have been glad to drive her, but, except in the bad weather, the woman always maintained she needed the walking after a day of housework. Kept her bones from getting stiff. Now Ramsey was afraid the woman had waited for her instead of leaving at her usual time. "Has everyone else already eaten?"

Martha shook her head disapprovingly. "I don't know what's going on around here. No one showed up for supper except Stevie." A beaming smile spread over her round face, giving her the appearance of an elderly cherub. "Now that boy is a wonder. He takes to ranch life like a duck to water. You shouldn't have kept him away so long, Ramsey.''

''I know—'' Ramsey sighed, thinking she had indeed been selfish not to bring Stevie to the ranch before now. She hadn't really kept him away, though; it was Paul who had disapproved, and she hadn't wanted to rock the boat. On their infrequent vacations, her ex-husband had always opted for more sophisticated surroundings: a Greek island, a villa in the south of France, and she had never made an issue of it, wanting to keep the peace. She'd always thought, next year I'll take Stevie to the ranch, but next year had never seemed to come.

''Anyway, Stevie isn't here, either,'' Martha said, breaking into her painful thoughts. ''He went for a ride right after his supper. Probably meeting Karl somewhere. Those two sure hit it off.''

Ramsey frowned slightly, thinking of Stevie out riding in the dusk, then relaxed. It was dark, but there was a moon out; Stevie wouldn't get lost. There was nothing on the ranch to hurt him. She remembered how she had felt as a child, riding alone in the night, a little scared, a little self-important and very grownup. He would probably return very soon, whether or not he had gone to meet Karl.

Martha turned away toward the kitchen, unfastening her apron and slipping it over her head as she went. ''I'll be off, then,'' she said, looking back over her shoulder. ''You'd better go up and see your grandma. She's been asking for you.''

Ramsey ran lightly up the stairs and down the hall, knocked softly at her grandmother's door, then turned the knob and peeked in.

''Are you awake, Gram?''

''Come in, Ramsey.'' Her grandmother was sitting in an armchair by an open window, a book open on her lap, but from the bemused expression on her face, Ramsey wondered whether she had actually been reading. More likely she had been looking out the window, watching for her family to come home. Although the night was warm, the older woman had a shawl around her shoulders to ward off the evening breeze that softly fluttered the white curtains and ruffled her thin hair in a gentle caress.

At the sight, Ramsey felt a catch in her throat; Delia's hair had become so white since she had last visited the ranch, another indication of her grandmother's increasing fragility. She had always been a vibrant, energetic woman, but age and worry were leaving their mark. Ramsey pressed her lips together in a determined line; she wouldn't leave Delia alone so long again.

"How are you, darling? Are you feeling all right?"

"Oh, I'm fine, really." Her grandmother smiled up sweetly into her face. "It's just a little heart condition, Ramsey. I do very well as long as I take my medicine and don't exert myself too much. Or get too excited." She made a wry face. "Fat chance of that. I'm getting bored with nothing to do and everyone gone so much."

Ramsey leaned down and hugged her grandmother's frail shoulders, then kissed her pale cheek. The skin felt cool against her lips, and she caught the faint fragrance of lilacs. "So where is everyone?"

"Jacob said he had some business in town," Delia said slowly, a slight frown on her face. Ramsey guessed her grandfather hadn't told his wife what that business was, and it worried her.

"The others?"

Delia shrugged. "Bud left a short time after you did, and then Jeff left in that ridiculous little car of his. Karl rode off somewhere about the same time. No one has come back yet."

Ramsey sank down in the flowered armchair opposite her grandmother and leaned her head back slowly against the cushion, waiting for the comfort and reassurance she had always found in this room to seep into her tired body. She was home. As a frightened child, grieving for her parents, bewildered by the changes in her life, she had often sought sanctuary with her grandmother, and had always found the love and security she needed.

But the comfort didn't come. She wasn't a child anymore, she thought uneasily, watching her grandmother's face through half-closed eyes. Delia was worried; perhaps it was time for her to lean on Ramsey instead of the other way around.

"You look tired, Gram," she said softly. "Shall I help you back into bed?"

Delia gave her a disdainful look. "I certainly can walk to my bed!" She rose, teetered slightly and, with a sheepish look, accepted Ramsey's arm. When she was all settled in, pillow plumped behind her head, the light coverlet over her shoulders, Ramsey sat on the side of the bed holding her delicate hand.

"Being here with you brings back so many memories, Grandma. Things I'd nearly forgotten. I'm glad I'm home."

"You belong here, Ramsey," Delia said softly.

Did she belong here, Ramsey wondered. She didn't think so, not anymore. She loved the Floating Eagle and everyone in it, but she had long since chosen another life. She enjoyed her work, her friends in Berkeley, and the Floating Eagle could only be a part of her past, although a past that had given her a sense of worth and security that had been the unyielding base on which everything else had been built. No, when classes started again this fall, she would go back to her job, rebuild her life. All she needed was a respite, time to reevaluate her life, to see who she was without Paul.

"You never did say exactly why you are so worried," she said, squeezing Delia's hand. "Have you told me everything you know?"

Instead of answering, Delia asked a question of her own. "You've been here a few days now, Ramsey. How does everything seem to you?"

Absently, Ramsey bit her lip, turning her answer over in her mind. On the surface, she couldn't see that much had changed; at least, nothing had changed that couldn't be explained by the deep uneasiness that had gripped them all after Arnie Parkins's death. She had fallen easily into the same banter, the same joking ways of relating, that she had known as a young girl. Was she imagining that everyone seemed a little tense, watchful? The jokes forced? But why wouldn't they be? The shooting must have been a shock to them all.

"Grandma," she said suddenly, "whatever happened between Uncle Bud and Ella? I thought they were going to be married."

Delia sighed, and her fingers tightened around Ramsey's hand. "Poor Bud. I wished sometimes he had a little more of your father's fire and determination, and that your father had had a little more of Bud's gentleness."

This wasn't the first time Ramsey had heard comparisons made between her father and his younger brother. She hadn't thought much about it as a child, but as she grew older she'd suspected it must have been difficult for Bud to always be compared to his older brother. Even as a child, he must have lived in his brother's shadow, always second, and after his brother died, of course, there had been no hope at all of competing. Her father, faults forgotten, had become more golden with the years, while Bud had lost what little color he'd had.

"Nevertheless, I think Jacob was wrong," Delia said. "I told him so, but he wouldn't listen."

"Wrong?" Ramsey turned sharply to look at her grandmother's face. She didn't recall ever hearing Delia use that word about Jacob. "How was he wrong?"

"Bud felt so bad about it," Delia continued softly, as though speaking to herself. "Maybe Ella was too young, and maybe her family wasn't the best, but Jacob should have let Bud make up his own mind."

"Grandpa broke them up?"

"He told Bud he had to stop seeing her." Delia sighed. "He threatened to cut Bud off without a cent, said he couldn't stay at the Floating Eagle—"

"And Bud went along with it! I can't believe it. I never thought he cared that much about the ranch. Or money."

"I don't think he did," Delia answered. "But her folks got in on it, too. Bud and Jacob had a terrible row, and Bud left. Didn't come back for a couple of years. I've always thought Ella's folks were to blame as much as Jacob. They were always pressuring her to marry Arnie. Said he was more settled…"

"I never knew any of that…" How many other cracks were there in the serene, loving facade of the Floating Eagle?

"I didn't see any reason to tell you. There wasn't anything you could do but worry. Then Bud came back, and Ella was already married…" Delia's voice trailed away.

The purr of a motor ended the discussion. Rising, Ramsey went to the window and saw Jacob's car entering the garage. A few minutes later, they heard the old man's boots on the stairs, and Ramsey opened the door for him.

As he stood there, his rawboned frame nearly filling the doorway, Ramsey used the opportunity to study him. Had she really noticed the changes in him since she returned home, or was she still seeing him in the haze of memory? But the rock of her childhood was still there. Age hadn't weakened him; it had set him in concrete. With his craggy features—strong, prominent nose, jutting chin, probing blue eyes—he still cut an imposing figure.

His expression softened to tenderness as his pale blue eyes met her wide hazel ones. He put his hand gently on her shoulder and squeezed, then looked away, almost embarrassed. Gestures of affection didn't come easily to Jacob, but they were sincere. Ramsey felt tears spring to her eyes. Impulsively, she stepped forward and hugged his giant frame, and he ran his callused hand softly over her hair.

In that moment, Ramsey knew that the love and affection that had flowed so strongly between them when she was a child were still there. She could still turn to Jacob.

Disengaging herself, she watched the old man walk to the

bed and gently take his wife's hand, then lean down to place his lips on her mouth. There was such tenderness in the intimate gesture that Ramsey felt as though she were observing something meant for the two alone. It was love like this she wanted, love that lasted, love that united two people, but still left room for others. This was what being a family meant, she thought, her throat suddenly tight.

Then the moment was over; Delia looked at her husband and set her own delicate jaw. "Jacob, we have to talk."

Ramsey started edging toward the door but her grandmother motioned her to stay. "No, this concerns you, too, Ramsey. What is going on, Jacob? Why won't you tell me?"

When her husband remained silent, the little woman spoke more fiercely. "Don't pretend. I know when you're worried about something. Why are you shutting me out?"

"Okay, okay." Jacob sat down on the bed and gave her a tender smile. "I guess I have been a little preoccupied, but it's nothing for you to worry about. You know the Floating Eagle is losing money, has been for a few years."

"Is that all you're worried about? We've had hard times before."

"I know." He sighed. "Karl reports there are a few cattle missing, too."

"Strayed away?"

"Probably. Hard to keep track of them when they are over on the national forest."

Ramsey knew that the public grazing land of the national forest was important to the Floating Eagle. The ranch had a government permit to graze a certain amount of cattle on the public land and, since there were no fences, it was a job to keep them rounded up.

As though to forestall any more questions, her grandfather turned to Ramsey. "I haven't had any time to really talk to you since you've been home, Ramsey. Everything okay?"

"Just fine."

He gave her a keen look. "I'm glad of that. Stevie likes it here, too. Karl says he's a regular cowboy."

Karl again. She ignored the quick flash of jealousy. "Yes, Stevie seems to enjoy riding."

"Soon as I have a minute, maybe you and I could ride around the ranch. I don't do enough of it anymore. The younger men have taken over the work, and I don't have much reason to be in the saddle."

"I'd love to." She approached the bed and bent over to kiss the two old people. "For now, I want to go out and wait for Stevie and be sure that young man gets to bed on time."

Ramsey bolted upright in her narrow bed and clutched the blanket to her chest, her heart hammering. What had wakened her? Her pulse slowing, she looked carefully around the room. The early-morning sun flooded in the open window and fingered the entwined red and white roses on the faded wallpaper; it turned the white wicker bed and dresser to glowing gold, and lay in a bar on the braided burgundy rug. Everything looked just as it always had.

Glancing at her watch, she saw that it was nearly eight o'clock, and swung her feet over the side of the bed into soft slippers. She should be thankful for whatever had wakened her, otherwise she might have slept until noon!

As she reached for her robe the sound came again, and she froze. Now she recognized it: the hard, staccato sound of pistol shots.

Dropping her robe, she reached for her jeans and shirt, and shoved her feet into her western boots. The shots had come from somewhere out in the yard. She would check on Stevie and be sure he wasn't frightened, then go see what was going on.

She ran down the hall to his room and pushed open the door. He'd been so tired from his ride yesterday that when she tucked him in last night she'd been sure he'd sleep all day. Now, glancing at his rumpled bed, her breath caught in her throat. Empty.

The sound of shots came again, sending uneasy vibrations all along her spine, and she went swiftly down the stairs and out the back door. From the steps she could see two figures out near the corral and she walked quickly toward them, her lips tightening. Even from a distance of a hundred yards, she recognized Karl and Stevie.

She was within a few feet of the two when Stevie turned and saw her. His face broke into a wide, excited smile. "Mom, it's about time you woke up! Look, Karl's teaching me to shoot."

Her heart froze with fear and indignation as she saw the heavy black pistol in Stevie's small hand. With a grin in her direction, he threw back his shoulders, took a wide-legged stance and pointed the gun at a target tacked to the corral railing. "Watch!"

The pistol made a frightening sound, and Ramsey saw a puff of dust rise a few feet to the right of the target. Instinctively she moved forward, but Karl, a smile on his bronzed face, took the gun from Stevie's hand as he ran a broad palm across the small boy's blond hair.

"You need a little more practice, partner. Look, hold it like this." Very carefully, Karl raised the gun, then lowered it on the target, and squeezed the trigger. There was a sharp retort, and a hole appeared in the bull's-eye of the target.

"Stevie! Go to the house!"

Startled, Stevie turned to his mother. "Why?"

"Just go! I'll talk to you later."

He shot her a fiercely angry look, then turned and trudged away, his stiff spine clearly showing his indignation.

Ramsey waited until the boy was out of earshot, then whirled to confront Karl. He was lounging against the railing of the corral, an amused smile on his broad face. She met his eyes angrily. "Karl, don't you think you should have asked me before you taught Stevie to shoot?"

He regarded her intently, and she stared back. He was a

powerfully built man, wearing the usual jeans, blue chambray shirt, western boots and hat. His naturally dark skin was deeply bronzed and weathered, and his straight black hair and strongly chiseled features announced his part-Indian heritage. An orphan befriended by Jacob when he was a teenager, he had been a part of the Floating Eagle as long as Ramsey could remember. He had taught her to ride. She knew Jacob thought of him as a son, and that the affection was returned.

She hadn't seen Karl for a long time, and an unwilling thought popped into her head. Had he changed? She had adored him as a young girl; he was just the type to be a hero to a child of a certain age. She couldn't blame Stevie for regarding him as a pied piper; she had done the same.

She took a deep breath. "Karl, maybe I came on a little strong. It's just that I think Stevie is too young to be learning to shoot."

"Best time to start," Karl said, his black eyes unreadable.

A flash of anger brightened her cheeks. "I'm not sure I want him to start at all."

He gave her a slow, lazy grin. "Now, Ramsey, you haven't forgotten your raisings, have you? Everybody around here knows how to handle a gun. Has to. If Stevie is going to be a rancher—"

"He's not!" she broke in. "I'll thank you to let me decide what my child should be taught!"

"Sure." Karl shrugged, but from the expression in his dark eyes, she thought he was laughing at her. She was under no illusions that he would respect her request, but she suspected he still thought of her as a young girl. Karl generally did what he wanted to do.

Shoving her hands in her pockets, Ramsey turned away and started back to the house. She was ambivalent about the encounter with Karl. He had a point. Hardly anyone in the country would understand her reluctance to let Stevie learn to shoot. Almost every pickup had a rifle rack, almost every saddle sported a gun carrier. Pistols were commonplace.

She had never liked them, and her years in California had hardened her attitude. No matter what people argued, she firmly believed that pistols were for killing people. They encouraged violence. They intensified fear of the stranger. If everyone in Idaho carried his pistol for killing snakes, as they all maintained, she doubted there would be a rattlesnake left in the country.

Karl had said Stevie needed to learn to shoot if he were going to stay on the ranch. Did she want that kind of life for Stevie? She had returned to the Floating Eagle, seeing it almost as a giant feather bed, something to cushion and protect her from reality. But violence was here, too.

Stevie was waiting for her on the porch; he kept his blond head averted and thrust out his lower lip, idly tossing pebbles at a bantam hen that clucked around his feet. The chicken, not overly concerned by the boy's aim, dodged when necessary, and continued scratching in the kitchen herb garden.

Sitting down on the step beside the small boy, Ramsey put one arm around his narrow shoulders. "Mad at me?" she whispered, flinching as he inched away from her embrace.

When he didn't answer, she put her hand under his chin and turned his head until she could look into his eyes—blue eyes that blazed with anger and hurt.

"I'm sorry I yelled at you. But I think you're too young to learn to shoot," she said softly, still cupping his chin in her hand.

"Karl doesn't think so!"

She sighed and released him. "Karl isn't your mother."

"But he knows everything! How to ride, how to rope a cow! How to shoot! He's a real man!"

The implication was clear. She wasn't even a man, so how would she know what a boy should learn? She ruffled his hair and smiled. "Stevie, I think it's great that Karl is teaching you all those neat things. Except the gun. I want your promise that you won't target practice."

"Karl says—"

"Stevie."

He stared stubbornly at the ground, his little chin set in a defiant manner.

"Okay, Stevie?"

"All right," he finally said. "Now can I go back and see Karl? We're going to ride over to the national forest today. He says there may be some strays over there. We're going to round them up!"

"I guess so—" Before the words were completely out of her mouth, Stevie was gone, racing toward the barn. She smiled after him ruefully. This was what she had hoped for; Stevie had found a male role model, a hero to emulate. She knew how important that was for a boy. Karl was a good, solid, dependable man, not too imaginative, perhaps, but he certainly performed his duties as ranch foreman splendidly.

And did she really want Stevie emulating him?

She sat on the porch, elbows propped on her knees, hands under her chin, as she stared sightlessly into the distance. Horses neighed, dogs barked, all the sounds of a working ranch swirled around her in a cacophony of sound, to which she was completely oblivious. She didn't even hear the sound of a motor, or the crunch of footsteps on gravel, until they were right beside her.

"Hello, Ramsey." His voice was deep and warm, and stirred something inside her chest. She looked up quickly.

"Brad!" She jumped to her feet, hastily brushing off her jeans. "What are you doing here!"

He smiled, a slow, easy smile that started in his dark eyes and spread over his lean, bronzed face. "Don't you remember?"

"Remember? Remember what?" Was he going to make some reference to the scene between them yesterday? Wasn't it enough that he had made a fool of her, without coming out here so early to rub it in?

He put one booted foot on the step and lounged against

a wooden pillar that supported the porch as his eyes traveled over her. His smile broadened, and he lifted a dark eyebrow.

"Didn't we agree yesterday that we would investigate Arnie's murder together?"

"Yes..."

"Well, then," he said, "let's investigate."

"How? Brad, I know I said I wanted to help you, but frankly, I haven't the slightest idea where to start. Have you?"

"No, I suppose not. But I think the Floating Eagle is as good a place to start as any."

She gave him an exasperated look. "So that's it. You know very well Jacob would send you right back to town unless you had a reason to be here." She raised her head in quick challenge, her eyes flashing. "So you came to see me."

"I thought we might take a little ride around the place," he admitted.

She approved of the idea. When he was with her, he wouldn't be out manufacturing or misinterpreting evidence, and he'd find absolutely nothing incriminating on the Carmichael ranch. "Fine. You'll have to wait until I've had coffee," she said, moving toward the kitchen door. "How about a cup while you're waiting?"

"Suits me." He followed her into the ranch kitchen, where Martha was standing over the sink, rinsing dishes. The woman raised her head, gray curls bobbing, and reached for the coffeepot.

"Where is everyone?" Ramsey asked, sitting down at the pine trestle table and accepting a cup of the steaming liquid.

"You're still on city time," Martha said. "Everybody's been up and about for hours."

She moved away and busied herself around the kitchen, while Brad and Ramsey chatted. After the first few awkward minutes, he was surprisingly easy to talk to. As a young boy, he had seemed practically tongue-tied, but now he conversed on a wide range of subjects. Ramsey nearly forgot they were antagonists as she leaned forward, eager to make a point.

The watcher moved back farther into the shadow of an outbuilding, and his eyes narrowed. The game warden's pickup with the horse trailer behind it was still parked in front of the house, and the horse in the trailer was saddled. Chillicott must plan on going for a ride with her, although they hadn't come out of the house yet.

He took a handkerchief from his pocket and wiped the cold sweat from his forehead. He had to do something; he couldn't let them keep stirring things up. Bad luck that they wouldn't drop it; bad luck for both of them. They probably wouldn't find out anything, but after all this time and work, this sweat and anguish, he couldn't take a chance.

He'd hoped Ramsey would have headed back to the city long before this. He didn't look forward to doing what he would have to do if she stayed, but what was his alternative? Now that she was so thick with the game warden, who knew how long she'd stay? She was stuck on that uniformed prig, if he could judge by the way her eyes lit up when anyone mentioned his name.

His lips thinned in anger and his face darkened. Maybe she would still leave. Maybe she needed a little encouragement.

Chapter 6

The day was as nearly perfect as a June day in the high country of Idaho was likely to get, Brad thought, flicking his horse lightly with the tip of the reins and cantering after Ramsey. Not one cloud marred the deep, endless blue of the sky. To the north, high mountain peaks, still covered with snow that defied the summer sun, jutted aggressively into the cerulean cover. Stands of pine and cedar pushed close to the trail and stretched long branches out to brush against his chaps. Their crisp, minty fragrance mixed with the scent of the wild roses and syringa that floated in on the light breeze, and Brad took a deep breath. Although they had ridden several miles into the mountains, by glancing over his shoulder Brad could still make out the outlines of the buildings of the Floating Eagle below them; they reminded him of a series of miniature log cabins.

Ahead of him, her body swaying lightly to the rhythm of her spirited horse, was Ramsey, and the sight of her was probably what made the day seem so special, he admitted silently. Her hair, the color reminding him of a field of autumn corn, was tied back from her face with a wide blue ribbon, leaving a portion of her white neck enticingly bare. He had suggested a wide-brimmed hat, but she had grinned, telling him she would depend on sunscreen. Whatever she had put on didn't mask the warm, healthy glow of her complexion. He watched her shoulders, broad for a woman, and her slender back move sensuously under the silken material of her shirt, and then dropped his eyes to the curve of her hips, just visible above the cantle of her saddle. He felt the heat building in his body, and winced. The day wasn't that hot; it was the nearness of Ramsey that caused the tightening in his throat, the warmth under his skin.

A high, wailing screech pierced the silence, and he took his gaze off the woman in front of him to look up into the sky where a red-tailed hawk was wheeling and dipping in lazy circles. As he watched, the raptor seemed to freeze in midair, then drop with incredible velocity on some unsuspecting quarry.

The casual, unexpected violence broke into his peaceful mood, making him slightly uneasy. Could you ever tell what lay under any surface? Noticing that the trail had widened slightly, he spurred the large brown gelding, an action designed to alert rather than inflict pain, and rode up beside Ramsey.

"Enjoying yourself?"

She turned a smiling face toward him; her eyes, he saw, reflecting the green forest surrounding them, sparkled with excitement.

"Oh, yes! This was a wonderful idea; I feel like a kid on the first day of vacation."

She neck-reined Amber around a small outcropping of granite that narrowed the trail for a few feet, then turned back to Brad, her smile growing more doubtful.

"I'm not sure, though, about this investigating we're supposed to be doing. What are we looking for?"

He didn't know, either, but this wasn't exactly the time to admit it. He'd tossed most of the night, trying to reject the insidious suspicion that Ramsey was somehow in danger at the ranch. On the surface, it was a ridiculous notion. She was the golden princess, the returning prodigal daughter, beloved by all.

Not all, something kept whispering in his sleepless mind. Not all.

When morning came, he knew immediately that he had to keep an eye on her, and he didn't want to waste a minute. Whether it was because he was worried about her, or because the nerves of his body still carried the imprint of their passionate embrace, he wasn't sure, but it was imperative that he be with her. Her suggestion that they work together in investigating the murder had provided a perfect excuse. No one was likely to try anything when he was around to protect her. They'd better not.

But now she was asking what they were investigating, what they were looking for. He had no idea, he just hoped to bump into something that might trigger an idea. The sheriff was still trying to trace the bullet found in Arnie's body, but he didn't hold out much hope. More and more Thorenson was inclined to suspect an outsider—a casual hunter just passing through. And if the killer did live on the Carmichael ranch, he wasn't likely to come out and announce himself.

"Just keep your eyes open," he said shortly.

She rode silently for a few moments, apparently giving herself over to the mesmerizing movement of the horse. An easy feeling of friendship, independent of speech, seemed to be growing between them. Like a flower greeting the morning light, she slanted her face upward and closed her eyes, letting the warm sun caress her face.

"I wonder why we never rode together before," she finally said. "When I look back to high school, it seems you were always around someplace, but we never did anything together. I don't mean dating, just goofing around together like a lot of the kids did."

''For one thing, I didn't have a horse.'' He said the words more sharply than he intended.

Her eyes flew open. ''Didn't have a horse? You could have borrowed one—''

''Not from a Carmichael,'' he said quietly.

She jerked the reins impatiently, and he thought she was going to challenge him. Tensed, he waited for her questions, but she merely shrugged.

''Maybe we should stay off the subject of the Carmichaels for a while—just catch up on old times. What's been happening in your life, anyway?'' She gave him a keen glance. ''For instance, why aren't you married?''

He had his answer ready; it was the one he saved for just such occasions. ''I never found the right woman, I guess.'' None that measured up to you, he could have added. You spoiled me for anyone else. He still didn't know how much of that youthful worship had been because of Ramsey herself, and how much was based on what she represented, but whatever the cause, it had burrowed deep inside him, carved out an indelible niche in his heart. The fact that it was hopeless only seemed to make it stronger.

She opened her mouth to speak, and he broke in quickly to forestall her question. ''What about you, Ramsey? Delia told me when you got married.'' He could still feel the pain that he'd felt then, duller now, but still a pervasive ache. ''I'm sorry about what happened. Did you love him?''

''Of course!'' Her answer came much too quickly, he thought. ''We had a good marriage, until...'' Her voice trailed away.

''Until?''

She looked straight ahead. ''I was going to say we had a good marriage until the divorce, but I guess that couldn't be, could it? Or there wouldn't have been a divorce. There always seemed to be something missing, for both of us, I think. I've been thinking a lot about it lately. Perhaps the marriage was like an agreement between partners.''

''That doesn't sound very exciting,'' he murmured.

"I'm not sure I wanted it to be exciting," she said slowly. "I don't know how much you've heard about my parents. Delia says my dad liked living in the fast lane, and I guess my mother did, too. By all reports, they were wildly in love. So much so that I was an afterthought. Excess baggage. I didn't see them very often, and most of what I remember before I was six years old was a succession of housekeepers. When my parents died in an accident, they were halfway around the world from me. I—I remember how frightened I was."

"That's when you came to live with your grandparents?"

"Yes. I can still remember how I was trembling when I opened the door of the apartment in San Francisco. The current housekeeper had stepped out. And there they were, Delia and Jacob. They looked bigger than life. Solid as rocks. And they just picked me up and hugged me like they'd never let me go."

"You hadn't had much hugging before then," he ventured.

She gave a soft little laugh that tore at his heart. "Not much. I was always more or less alone. Then they took me back to the ranch, and for the first time I had a real family. Uncle Bud. Jeff. Karl." She turned and gave him a defiant look. "It was like waking up in heaven..."

He felt a swift stab of pain; he knew what being alone was.

"And Paul?"

"When I met him, he seemed just what I needed. Safe. Reliable. I distrusted all the talk about being swept off your feet by love, and I certainly didn't want to emulate my parents. They were always talking about being crazily in love, couldn't live without each other. But they could live without me." Even now, the ancient hurt colored her voice. "I always wanted children, but I decided early I'd never put my child through what my parents put me through."

Her mouth twisted in a wry grin. "Instead, I put Stevie through a divorce and the loss of one parent."

He had no answer for her obvious guilt, though he didn't think it justified, and they rode silently for a few minutes.

"I'm not sure I understand," Brad finally said. "You seem to distrust love; weren't your grandparents in love?"

"That was different," she said. "They had room for others: me, Jeff, Karl, whatever stray might wander in. They are a tight unit, but it doesn't keep other people out. As a youngster I felt they were rocks. Stable, always there for me, someone to turn to if I ever needed them."

She chewed her lip thoughtfully, turning her next words over in her mind. "I think now that what I saw as stability in Paul was just the lack of deep emotion."

"So you decided that the frenzy of romantic love wasn't to be trusted," Brad said, giving her a wry grin.

"Even though my divorce was traumatic, I learned something," she replied. "I think I was right in what I wanted; I just didn't know how to recognize it."

"Now you think you could?"

"I think so," she said slowly. "I want what my grandparents have. They have the same values, the same goals. They are always there for each other, and yet they don't exclude the rest of us. They've always been there when I needed them." She took a deep breath. "Just as I'll always be there for them."

"You make them sound so picture perfect," he said dryly. "You don't think they might have been a little giddy when they were younger? Maybe even occasional slaves of passion?"

"I think they always had a firm, loyal relationship," she said a little tartly.

"You don't think you can have both? The wild ecstasy, the firm devotion?"

She gave him a quick look, then grinned. "You're a poet, Mr. Chillicott. I remember that about you. You always showed us all up in English class, too! Anyway, we're much too serious for a day like this. Come on, I'll race you to the creek!"

As she spurred her horse ahead, Brad saw that the trail had widened into a beautiful little alpine meadow and that the trees had thinned out, leaving a wide expanse of clover and meadow grass. Pine Creek was about a mile in front of them, a narrow ribbon bordered with willows; he could hear the faint murmur of water running over rock. He spurred his horse and took off after Ramsey.

She rode well, he thought, watching her hair fly out behind her as she hunched over the saddle horn and urged her horse on with her knees. He loosened the reins and felt his horse stretch out beneath him, gaining on Ramsey in powerful strides. It was a heady, exhilarating feeling, one of the few times he felt carefree. Brad loved the rush of speed, the sound of hooves beating on soft ground, the feel of his body adapting to the smooth-flowing motion. He threw back his head with an exultant laugh and urged the gelding on.

She glanced over her shoulder, saw him gaining, grinned wickedly and murmured something to her horse. Amber increased her stride, hurtling over the soft ground like a brown arrow.

Brad grinned, thrilling to the surge of controlled power as his horse covered the ground in huge strides. They were neck and neck as they came up to the streambed, and Brad finally pulled up on the bridle. His horse reared, snorted, then halted as he patted his shoulder.

Ramsey waited to pull up until the last possible minute, and Brad's breath caught in his throat. Amber finally came to a stop only a foot from the rushing stream.

"I won!" she shouted.

He thought it was a tie, but he certainly wasn't going to dispute her, not with the color glowing in her cheeks, her eyes sparkling, her deep breaths making her high, rounded breasts rise and fall deliciously beneath her blue silk shirt. In fact, he would undoubtedly agree with anything she said.

She leaned forward to stroke Amber's sweaty neck. That action might have saved her life.

Brad heard the whine of a bullet. Instinctively he reached

over and grabbed her around the waist, pulling her from the saddle. They tumbled together onto the ground, and he half pushed her, half carried her into some thick, low-lying bushes that fringed the stream.

He glanced at her anxiously. "Are you hurt?" he whispered, his own voice sounding harsh in his ears.

Her eyes were enormous in her white face and her breath came in sharp gasps as she clung to him. "Brad—what was that?"

"A shot," he said tersely, pulling her back farther into the seclusion of the brush. With one arm still around her waist, his other hand went to his holster and rested lightly on the handle of his pistol. He peered out into the open meadow. Where had the shot come from?

There was only one possibility—a thicket of fir and aspen a hundred yards away. The grove was thick enough to conceal a man and was at the edge of the meadow with the forest stretching unbroken behind it, making a perfect shelter.

The person who fired the rifle might still be there, or he could have disappeared into the forest without being seen. If he were still waiting, Brad didn't want to take a chance on moving. Not with Ramsey beside him. Not until he knew who had been the target.

They huddled together, their breathing shallow, muscles tense, until Brad thought he would explode with the waiting. Had he been alone he would have taken a chance, scouted out another route to the thicket, and either surprised the assailant or made sure that he was gone. He couldn't take a chance with Ramsey.

She was still tightly folded against his body, her face almost hidden against his chest, as they peeked out into the meadow. He felt her heart pounding through her silk shirt, and he tightened his grip around her waist. Were they up against someone who merely wanted to frighten them, or someone who was just a bad shot? Offhand, he couldn't think of a reason for the attack.

There was always the possibility that it was just a stray bullet, although that did seem more of a coincidence than he could believe. Had they stumbled on someone with something to hide? Had someone followed them? Most important, who was the target—he or Ramsey?

She was recovering from her fright now; he felt her heart beat slow and her muscles relax. She took a few deep breaths, then turned her face to whisper to him. He was surprised that even under the circumstances he was keenly aware of the faint, haunting scent of roses rising from her warm skin, and of the clean, fresh fragrance of her hair. He flinched a little as her breath, warm and moist, touched his skin.

Her lips, half-open, were very near his ear. "Are we investigating now?" she whispered. "Is this how we do it, hiding in the bushes?" He swore there was a chuckle in her voice.

He nearly laughed aloud, but he drew back far enough to give her a severe look. "This is serious; you could have been killed."

"Or you could have been."

He hesitated. "Maybe not." He still watched the thicket with narrowed eyes. "Maybe we're just getting a message to stay away. I didn't notice it before, but we are close to the old forest service road." He was speaking as much to himself as to her. "I don't think it's likely we were followed—I kept my eyes open. More likely somebody came up this road, and decided they didn't want us so close..."

As if to underscore his words, he heard the faint sound of a motor, and listened intently until it died away. He relaxed slightly, feeling the tension flow from his muscles. Something told him the assailant had just driven away. They would stay here a while longer to be sure, and then ride back...

She twisted slightly, bringing his hand that had been on her waist up to her rib cage. His thumb touched the softness of her breast and a shiver ran through his body. Like a man in a trance, he moved his hand until he held the sweetness of her entire breast in his palm. Even through her silk shirt he felt its texture, soft as a summer cloud, springy as moist meadow grass. He heard the sharp intake of her breath and knew it matched his own.

He didn't dare move. The air around him thickened, became charged with a dazzling radiance of pure sexual energy. He couldn't breathe. The only thing that would help would be to melt into her arms, hold her body, warm and pliant and soft with desire, against his own hard need.

He turned toward her, easing her backward until she lay on the soft, springy grass. He leaned above her, his mouth poised to capture her lips and never let her go. He was conscious of the ache in his loins as his manhood sought blindly to surge through the material that separated them.

With a movement he doubted had been conscious on her part, she moved under him until they were touching all along the length of their bodies. He held her even more tightly, hardly aware of what he was doing.

Suddenly he felt her stiffen beneath him. For a long moment she held herself rigid, and he heard her deep, painful gasps; then she wiggled free from under him and sat up, brushing the leaves from her hair.

He felt a wave of disappointment mixed with relief; one of them had managed to keep control. However, the relief hadn't reached his loins yet! He inched into a more comfortable position as he watched her face.

She didn't meet his eyes, and wild regret tore at him. This wasn't what he had intended; he hadn't meant to let himself get out of control. Had he hurt her again?

She turned her cool hazel eyes toward him, a half smile on her face, and now it was confusion that threatened to overcome him. She didn't appear to be hurt—just amused.

"I've heard that danger is a great aphrodisiac," she said, rising smoothly to her feet. "This is my first actual experience of it, but I'd say they were right."

He rose, too, a muscle twitching in his set jaw. He wanted

to say something, but anything he could think of would only worsen the situation. Whatever the situation was. Was there a possibility she had lured him on to punish him for the way he'd treated her before?

"I'd better go see if our man is gone," he finally said. Without waiting for a reply, he thrashed out of the brush, careful not to look at her.

He saw at once that there was no one in the thicket, although from the trampled grasses it was obvious someone had been there. He made a quick survey, and picked up a spent rifle casing. There was nothing more to be found, but he couldn't go back just yet, back and face those cool, assessing eyes.

He had to come up with another plan for keeping her safe, that was easy to see. He had thought he could kid her along into thinking they were sleuthing while he kept an eye on her. Now it appeared that she was in as much, if not more, danger with him than without him. Not to mention, from him!

He stumbled on a cedar root and swore briefly. Obviously he had been the only one to feel that compelling surge of desire, that desperate intensity. She had smiled so coolly, had recovered her poise so completely. In charge. Just like the Carmichael she was.

He was going to stop seeing her; why torture himself? He would try to throw a scare into her and convince her not to leave the ranch house, while he kept trying to find out what was going on. He hoped it would work. But he was going to stay away from her.

She heard the sound of approaching footsteps, but Ramsey didn't look up from her position on the bench in the rose garden. The garden was overgrown now that Delia couldn't tend it, but it still provided a convenient haven. She had been sitting here for the past hour, ever since she and Brad had returned from their ride, and she still didn't feel any better. He had immediately loaded his horse and drove off down the road; she had occupied herself by muttering and tearing petals off roses, then scattering them absently in front of her.

She wasted little time on conjecture about the rifle shot; it was the other trauma that occupied her mind. At least *she* had been the one to pull away this time, although she hadn't thought she would be able to. The man was a walking sex bomb! She blushed, remembering how she had wanted to tear away the constricting clothing, feel him hot and ready against her moist skin, envelop him in the sweetness of her femininity. Somehow she had managed to remember the times before when he had pulled away, leaving her humiliated and rejected, and she had made a supreme effort.

It was worth it to see the surprise and shock on his face!

A tremor ran down her spine, and she jerked angrily at the white rose. What was happening to her? Could she actually be falling in love with him? He wasn't at all the kind of man she wanted; he was hard and morose and judgmental. And, she admitted, remembering their conversation, caring and compassionate.

"A penny for your thoughts."

She looked up to see Jeff standing beside her, and gave him a wan smile. "That's about all they're worth."

Lifting an eyebrow, he sat down beside her and slid his arm along the bench, letting it rest lightly on her shoulder. "Want to talk?"

"Maybe later, Jeff." She looked miserably at the ground.

He rose and took her hand, pulling her up beside him.

"Well, I can't let you just sit here and sulk. Come on. I've got something to show you."

He set a brisk pace, and she hurried along beside him, glad to have something to distract her thoughts. It was one of the strengths of an extended family, she thought; someone was always there when you needed them.

They walked about half a mile along a little path nearly obliterated by ancient fruit trees: apples, pears, plums, most now in blossom. She recognized the old fruit orchard where she and Jeff had played as children, and wasn't really surprised when he stopped in front of a small wooden structure. She remembered it had been an old packing shed, but she saw that it had been extensively remodeled. Newly painted siding, a new shingle roof, shuttered windows, all told her someone had spent a lot of time and effort restoring the old place.

Jeff smiled at the expectant look on her face, and turned the key in the lock. Stepping aside, he motioned her ahead of him.

For a moment, she was speechless. The room was a riot of color. Skylights in the roof let in huge washes of light, light that illuminated dozens of paintings. She moved slowly from one to the other as she took in this facet of Jeff she had never suspected. Painted in a representational style, the canvases had a vitality that impressed her. Western scenes mostly, they depicted old-time cowboys doing backbreaking ranch work; Indians, faces remote and withdrawn, an ancient people looking lost in modern garb; lonely, abandoned houses standing against stark defoliated mountains.

"They're beautiful…" That wasn't quite the word; they were also disturbing. He had created a hard, lonely landscape.

"I think I have a talent," he said evenly. "Of course, I could use a few lessons."

She shook her head, still amazed at this unknown side of Jeff. "When did you start painting?"

"I've done it for years."

"Have you ever exhibited?"

"I'm nearly ready for that." He gave her a grin, and the old, witty Jeff was back. "If the world is ready for me."

"What does Grandpa think?"

His smile broadened. "You know Jacob. I love the old boy, but he's stuck in the Paleozoic. If it isn't connected with the land, forget it. It's effete, not something a man would do." He gave her a wink. "I doubt he even knows what I do here."

"But you must spend a lot of time—"

"It doesn't take much time to keep the books for the Floating Eagle," he said cheerfully, steering her out the door and locking it behind them. "That's my main job. I ride over and look for cattle once in a while, but both Jacob and I know I'm more at home pouring over a ledger than flogging a horse!"

They chatted until they reached the ranch house. Dinner was ready, Ramsey saw, and for once nearly everyone was gathered for it. As she took her seat, she stole a glance at Uncle Bud. He looked just as usual, with his bland expression and diffident manner. She couldn't believe this was the same man who had held Ella so passionately. Karl and Stevie talked mainly to each other, and she thought she saw real affection in the man's dark face as he teased the small boy. Jeff talked lightly about cattle, about the possibility of a storm, and yet only a few moments ago he had shown her a side of himself that apparently no one else at the table realized existed.

Looking around at her assembled family, she felt a slight stirring of apprehension. Almost disorientation. Were they all hiding secrets of some kind?

Jacob interrupted her train of thought. He had been quiet most of the meal, and now he turned to Ramsey, cutting off Jeff in the middle of a sentence.

"Ramsey, I was looking for you earlier. Where were you all day?"

The table was suddenly silent, making her reply seem louder than she had expected. "I went for a ride with Brad Chillicott."

The old man's face darkened. "I thought I warned you about him."

"But you didn't give me a good reason," Ramsey insisted.

"Isn't the fact that he's out to put us in jail a good reason?"

"He's wants to find out who killed Arnie Parkins," she protested. "I can't see anything wrong with that."

She wondered if Bud's face had actually paled, or whether it was a trick of the light. Karl, glowering, stared at his plate, and the mocking smile Jeff usually wore was absent. "Unless someone has something to hide," she added defiantly.

Jacob's fist struck the table, rattling the dishes. "Don't talk like that! Don't forget you're a Carmichael."

She faced him, eyes blazing, her jaw as square as his. "At least it wasn't Brad who shot at us today."

Old Jacob looked stricken; Ramsey thought he actually seemed to shrink. "Somebody shot at you? Who?"

"I don't know," she answered. The group around the table was abnormally quiet. "Maybe just a random shot."

"Well, that settles it," Jacob said. "Don't ride off with Brad anymore, or by yourself, either. Stay near the house. I don't want you hurt."

Ramsey started to protest, but thought better of it. Here on the Floating Eagle she was strangely still a child. And she agreed with Jacob that there was danger. She just didn't know where it was coming from.

Jacob sighed and rose heavily from the table. "Ramsey, it's good to have you home—you and the boy. I've missed you. It's time we had a talk. A serious talk. That's why I tried to find you today."

Everyone else studied their plates with exaggerated interest as Ramsey threw her grandfather a questioning look. "Now?"

"No, not now. This will take a while. Come to my office in the morning." They all watched the erect old figure stride majestically from the room.

Later that evening, as Ramsey sat on Delia's bed for the chat that had become a nightly habit, she wondered what Jacob wanted to talk to her about. Something serious, he'd said, and it must be if the talk was to take place in his office. The room at the foot of the stairs, small, bleak, functional, was where all formal discussions took place. Her feelings about it were ambivalent. She remembered being summoned when she'd got one of her infrequent *C*s on her report card; when Jacob had decided it was time for her to have her first horse; when he'd tried to persuade her not to accept the scholarship that meant she would be leaving the Floating Eagle. What was it this time?

"Do you know what Jacob wants to talk to me about?" she asked suddenly.

"I might." Delia smiled a soft, secret smile and stroked Ramsey's hand. "But I'll let him tell you."

"Come on, darling. Just a hint?" she coaxed.

"Just a hint," Delia said firmly. "It has to do with you and Stevie—and the Floating Eagle."

She knew she'd get nothing more out of Delia; she'd have to wait until morning. Why did Jacob want to talk to her about the ranch? If the ranch were losing money, he would be frantic, but there was nothing she could do about it, no advice she could give. She knew the place meant everything to him. It was a major sorrow of his life that his older son had died and that his granddaughter had never wanted to live on the ranch.

For the first time, she faced the fact that her grandfather was mortal. When he died, what would happen to the Floating Eagle? Possibly he would leave it to Bud, although he'd never bothered to hide his disappointment with his younger son. What about Karl and Jeff, who had no blood claim, but who were firmly in her grandfather's affection? Perhaps it would be sold and the proceeds divided, although she knew Jacob would hate that.

Before Ramsey could frame her next question to her grandmother, she thought she heard a faint sound at the door. Out of habit, she had closed it when she came in to talk to Delia, but now she thought she heard a soft scuffling sound outside. It was as much intuition as hearing that made her wonder if someone were standing out there eavesdropping. She listened intently, but heard nothing else. She must have imagined it. Why would someone be crouching outside the door? What secrets could they hope to hear?

She rose and kissed Delia lightly on the forehead, whisked back to her childhood by the faint fragrance of her grandmother's perfume. It meant security. Unquestioning love.

"I'll just have to wait until he tells me, then," she said cheerfully. "Now you go to sleep. It's late. I'll see you in the morning."

Closing Delia's door softly behind her, she stepped out into the darkened hall. As had become routine with her, she would just run downstairs to tell the others good-night, then go to Stevie's room to tuck him in and give him a kiss he would pretend to ignore. Still, he was becoming more affectionate, less defensive. She hoped his hurt was lessening.

The hallway seemed darker than she remembered. Puzzled, she glanced up and saw that the light globe in the ceiling must have burned out, leaving the length of the hall in darkness. It didn't matter. She had gone up and down the stairs so often she could have done it with her eyes shut.

She paused for a moment, her hand on the stairway banister. The light at the bottom of the stairs seemed to have gone out, too, leaving a pool of blackness beneath her. Odd. She seemed to remember that everything had been well lit when she entered her grandmother's room. Someone must have turned the lights off. Possibly one of the men, thinking everyone in bed.

With her hand lightly on the railing, she moved quickly down the stairway. She would turn the lights on as soon as she reached the landing. There was no reason for that little tickle of fear that was making the hair rise along her arms.

Suddenly her toe caught in something stretched tautly across the stair step. Her heart nearly stopped, then raced in terror. A wire! The knowledge came instantaneously with her lurch forward. She reached desperately for the banister, caught it, felt her hand slide helplessly along the smooth surface. Her fingernails scratched into the polished wood as she tried wildly to break her fall.

Panic tightened her chest in a painful vise. A scream rose in her throat as she pitched headlong into the well of darkness at the foot of the stairs.

Chapter 7

She was vaguely aware of arms cradling her body, of anxious, excited voices, and opened her eyes as she struggled to sit up. The pain that accompanied the movement lanced through her ankle, and she gasped, sinking back into the strong arms.

"She's coming around." She recognized Jacob's harsh voice as though coming from afar, and realized it was he who was holding her against his hard chest.

"Mom! Mom! Are you all right?" Stevie's thin young voice was squeaky with panic, and she managed to turn her head toward him. He was kneeling on the floor beside her, his small face white, his eyes wide with shock. Instinctively she reached out to touch his cheek.

"I'm all right. Don't worry," she faltered, her voice a whisper.

Slowly she became completely aware of her surroundings. Her grandfather, kneeling on the floor at the foot of the stairs, held her tightly in his arms as his old eyes anxiously searched her face. In a semicircle above her, their faces wearing identical expressions of shock and worry, Jeff, Karl and Uncle Bud stared down at her prostrate form.

Gingerly she moved again. The pain wasn't so bad this time. Her muscles felt bruised, and there was a definite ache in her ankle, but she didn't think it was broken. Probably sprained. Her head ached, as though she had bumped it during the fall. Aside from that, she didn't seem to be seriously hurt.

As she made an abortive attempt to sit up, Karl bent down and plucked her from old Jacob's arms as though she were a feather. Without a word, he carried her to the living room and placed her on the couch, while Stevie hurriedly put a pillow beneath her head and Jacob gently straightened her legs, observing, she knew, for cuts or broken bones.

"How badly are you hurt?" There was a quaver in the old man's voice that Ramsey didn't recall ever having heard before.

"I—I think I'm all right," she answered. "Shook up, and my left ankle hurts…"

Immediately, Jacob's hands closed around her ankle, testing, probing, and in spite of her pain, Ramsey felt a sense of well-being. His touch reminded her of all the times she had come running with a skinned knee, a scratched leg, and her grandfather had made it well.

"Hmm," he said finally. "Nothing broken, far as I can see. Maybe a sprain. We'll bandage it, and I think you can put a little weight on it." He grinned at her, trying to camouflage his concern. "Don't think you'll be dancing in the next day or two, though."

He turned to Stevie. "Go upstairs to Grandma, Stevie. She'll be wanting to know what all the fuss is about. Tell her everything's okay, and I'll be up in a few minutes."

As Stevie scurried away, Jacob turned his piercing eyes back to Ramsey. "What happened, girl?"

She managed to shrug and gave him a slight smile. "I guess I fell down the stairs."

"I know that." He snorted. "What happened? You've been up and down those stairs since you were a kid."

Ramsey looked around at the assembled men: Karl, remote as a winter peak, stared blankly down at her. If she had not remembered the gentleness in his hands when he placed her on the couch, she would think he might even dislike her. Jeff's face was as white as Stevie's had been, and there was a tense, tight line around his sensitive mouth. Uncle Bud, she thought, looked as though he might burst into tears any minute.

She took a deep breath. It didn't seem possible, but could one of these people—one of these men whom she had loved since childhood—have turned out all the lights and placed a wire across the stairs? They all knew her habits. It had become routine for her to spend a few minutes with Delia, then go back downstairs to say good-night to everyone before tucking Stevie in and going to her room. And there had been someone listening at the door while she talked to Delia, she remembered. She was nearly sure of it. Had that person heard something that forced him to take a drastic step?

Her grandfather was waiting for her reply, and she wasn't sure what to say. She wasn't sure enough to accuse anyone of anything. Perhaps it had all been a coincidence. An accident.

"I—I'm not sure what happened," she finally said. "When I came out of Delia's room, all the lights were out. And I tripped coming down the stairs. Tripped over something. A wire, I think..."

Her grandfather spun around and left the room, leaving her alone with the three men. Karl lounged against the fireplace mantel, his eyes still hooded, while Uncle Bud sank into a nearby armchair and stared at his hands clenched on his knees. Only Jeff still stood above her, one eyebrow lifted slightly as he watched her face. Of the three men, she thought, he seemed to be the only one who recognized the significance of what she had just said. To stumble over a wire, it would have had to be stretched across the stair.

Unless they were all consummate actors! She didn't know what to believe anymore. Seeing Bud with Ella had shaken her. The shot that had been fired at her and Brad had further weakened her belief that her family was a strong, unbreachable unit. Not that she had any reason to believe one of them had fired the rifle, but she suddenly realized, remembering the expression on Brad's face when he gazed up at the thicket, that *he* believed a Carmichael may have pulled the trigger!

But if one of the men had actually stretched a wire across the stairs...

She rejected the thought angrily. Brad Chillicott's only reason for thinking one of her family had fired the shot was because he thought them capable of anything! He had some twisted need to find them guilty of something! Even if one of them was somehow mixed up in the shooting, they would never hurt *her*.

She was glad when her grandfather strode back into the room and she could get her mind off her useless ruminations.

He held two light globes in one hand. "Burned out," he said with disgust. "Seems when one globe goes, they all go." His other hand held a toy guitar, which he placed on the end table by the couch. Ramsey recognized it as one Stevie had insisted on bringing with him when they came to the Floating Eagle. "I guess this is what you stumbled over," Jacob continued. "Your son had better be more careful in putting his toys away."

Some of the tension seemed to drain from the room. Jeff's rigid shoulders relaxed, and Uncle Bud gave a small sigh. Even Karl's expressionless features softened a little. It was an accident, an explanation they were all eager to accept, Ramsey realized.

Old Jacob sighed as he reached out to smooth Ramsey's hair. "I think it's time you got to bed, young lady. You'll be stiff in the morning."

Karl moved towards her, lifted her in his arms and carried

her quickly up the stairs. The others gathered around when she was deposited on her bed, then all said good-night and drifted from the room. Finally the door closed on old Jacob, and she was alone.

Her nightdress, a thin drift of pale blue silk, was under her pillow, and she had no difficulty slipping from her clothes and putting it on. Gingerly, aware of every sore spot on her body, she slid between the cool, fragrant sheets, and wiggled her toes. Miraculously she had escaped serious injury. Even her ankle seemed better, and she thought she'd be able to walk on it in the morning.

But it might not have turned out that way, she thought, her heart pounding. She had taken a bad fall. Was it really an accident? Jacob had found no evidence of anything wrong. The light globes were burned out, not unscrewed or turned off. The lights could have failed at any time. And there was the wire she thought she'd felt in front of her foot. Could it really have been a toy, left thoughtlessly by a small boy? Had her toe caught in one of the strings? It had been so dark she couldn't actually see what she had stumbled over.

Somehow it seemed everything was just too much of a coincidence, especially coming on top of everything else that had happened recently. Both lights going out at once, a toy just happening to be where she would fall over it. But was the other possibility any more believable? If a wire had been strung across the stairs, it would still have been there when Jacob went back to search.

Then a thought sent a cold chill down her back. She didn't know how long she had been unconscious. Everyone's attention had been focused on her. Someone could have removed the wire then without anyone noticing, and substituted the toy. Or later, when Karl carried her to the couch, someone could have lagged behind...

But if it hadn't been an accident, if someone had deliberately tried to harm her, why? She turned her head into her pillow, swallowing to keep back the tears. She couldn't keep on thinking *someone*. The only person who could possibly have tried to harm her tonight was one of her own family. And that was impossible. She knew her own family!

It was true that Karl was often brusque and morose, and his hooded eyes gave nothing away, and maybe he was angry because she had stopped him from teaching Stevie to shoot. Still, she didn't doubt he was fond of her. She had only to remember the gentleness in his huge arms as he carried her up the stairs. And Uncle Bud—Bud had always loved her. Unless—unless he had somehow found out she had seen him with Ella, and he would go to any lengths to hide the relationship.

Her mind rebelled at the next logical step. That would mean that he was somehow involved with Arnie Parkins's death, and knowing sweet, gentle Bud, that wasn't possible.

Jeff had no reason at all to harm her. Of all the men, he was closest to her own age, and they had been playmates as children, often banding together against the adults. He had come to the Floating Eagle before she did, and after an initial period of childish jealousy, he had become her champion. He was as close as a brother could be to her. His quick wit and urbane conversation had always been a delight. There might be facets to his personality she had never suspected, she thought, remembering his strangely disturbing paintings, but their own relationship had always been solidly loving and supportive.

She tossed restlessly, willing herself to think of something else. The house was silent around her, so silent she could hear the wind whining softly around the eaves, and she supposed everyone had gone to bed. How many were still awake, as she was, staring sightlessly into darkness?

For the first time she was experiencing a profound uneasiness hovering over her and the Floating Eagle. A faint sense of distrust and forboding. A sense that someone wished her ill.

What about Brad, she wondered, his image coming unbidden into her consciousness. Had his suspicions communicated themselves to her, and was she more susceptible to doubts than she should have been? What was he doing now? Was he, too, lying awake, tossing on his bed, possibly thinking of her? Or was he completely obsessed by his need to bring someone to justice for the murder of his partner? Was it hate, not desire, that kept him awake?

She wished now she had never come back to the Floating Eagle, never met Brad again, never felt his kiss reverberating through her entire body, his hands awakening delicious sensations that she had never believed existed. Even now, just thinking of him, her breath quickened, and her pulse throbbed in her temples. Her breasts tingled, and she felt a yearning ache in her hardening nipples. A rush of warmth spread through her body, and her limbs felt heavy and languorous. She could almost feel his hot breath on her cheek, and the moist hair on his broad chest, as she moved against him....

She bit her lip in frustration. It wasn't safe to think about Brad, either. She knew she was physically attracted to him, she didn't need the divine scintillation of warmth all through her body to tell her that! But all that vibrant masculinity, that virile charm, was a trap. She had made one mistake in her life where men were concerned. She wouldn't make another. If she were a different kind of woman she might make love to him, try to get him out of her system, but she wasn't that kind. She could never take physical love lightly, and for the two of them, there could never be more. Very soon, she would leave the Floating Eagle and go back to her real life, leaving Brad to his own different future.

She almost wished she had not stayed as long as she had. It was necessary to come back to see Delia, of course, but there was no reason she had to stay. Things weren't turning out at all as she had hoped. Her refuge was eroding, her sanctuary wasn't the citadel she had expected. Karl as a role model for Stevie caused her uneasiness. She had mixed feelings about a compelling man who seemed bent on persecuting her family. She hadn't been any help at all in finding out what was worrying Jacob, as Delia had hoped.

Maybe she could find out tomorrow, when they had the talk that he said was going to be a serious one. Delia had admitted that it had something to do with her and Stevie and the ranch.

Suddenly she tensed, and her eyes opened wide in the darkness. There had been someone outside her grandmother's door when Delia had said that. Someone knew that Jacob planned something concerning her and the ranch and Stevie. Was that someone afraid of what that might be? Afraid enough to try to harm her? Or at least frighten her away?

Ramsey awoke the next morning with a few sore muscles and a swollen ankle, but found that she was able to hobble about without too much difficulty. Her sleep had been restless, broken by disturbing dreams, and she hoped that her coming conversation with her grandfather would alleviate some of her concerns. Although the coming discussion seemed quite routine on the surface, she had sensed an urgency in the old man's summons. She had no idea what he wanted to talk about that involved her and Stevie and the ranch, but she thought, from his attitude and her grandmother's hints, that it might be an enlightening discussion. Maybe she would even find out what was worrying him.

A glance at her watch confirmed her feeling that she was up earlier than usual, and she decided to look in on Delia before going down to breakfast. She knew Delia had been told of her fall, and she wanted to reassure the old woman that she was all right.

To her surprise, Delia was already up, sitting at the window and looking out over the front yard of the ranch house. She turned at Ramsey's entrance, gave her an anxious smile and motioned her to a seat.

"Are you all right, dear? Jacob said you had quite a fall."

"I'm fine," Ramsey reassured her, dropping a kiss on her

grandmother's hair and seating herself beside her. "I've bandaged my ankle, and I can bear weight on it. I'm just a little curious, that's all, wondering what Granddad has to say to me. He made it sound like a summit meeting."

Delia frowned slightly. "I'm afraid it will have to wait, dear. Jacob had to leave early this morning."

"He did! He didn't say anything about it last night."

"He didn't know. He got a call late last night from a man in Nevada, said it was something urgent, so he left this morning before dawn."

"Why would someone from Nevada be calling Granddad at such an hour? And why would he leave in such a rush? What's it all about?"

Delia sighed, and carefully smoothed out the folds of her robe as she thought over her reply. "I don't know what it's all about," she said finally, "and Jacob didn't say anything else. That's what worries me. He just said he was going to drive over there and talk to the man. And that he'll talk to you when he gets back."

There was a frown on Delia's expressive face, and Ramsey knew she was concerned about Jacob's trip, especially since he had again shut her out. She hadn't the slightest idea of why the old man had hurried off. It was definitely out of character.

"How long will he be gone?"

"He didn't say. Now, dear," Delia said, putting one hand lightly on her granddaughter's arm, "why don't you rest today? That fall isn't to be taken lightly, you know. You may be more shaken up than you think."

There didn't seem to be much of an alternative; she didn't feel up to riding. For the next few hours, Ramsey wandered aimlessly around the house and yard, at a loss as to how to fill the time. She soon gave up on reading. Speculation about her grandfather's trip was useless; she suspected it was connected with whatever had been worrying the old man for so long, but that didn't help. There was no one around the ranch to talk to except Martha; all the men had effectively vanished. She knew Karl often rode over the ranch, making sure that everything was all right, and Stevie might be with him. Uncle Bud and Jeff probably also had their duties that took them away from the house.

She wandered idly out to the barn, wincing a little, but telling herself that inactivity was worse for her ankle than walking on it. She was still a few feet away when the door opened and Stevie came bursting out.

"Hi, Mom! I'm glad you're up. I wanted to come up to see you earlier, but Martha said you had to sleep."

She gave him a quick hug, pulling his blond head close to her chest, and was relieved when he didn't immediately pull away.

"What are you doing out here by yourself?"

"I've been playing with the new colt, waiting for you to get up."

"You must have got up with the chickens. I thought you'd be out someplace with Karl."

"He said I'd better stay home, today," Stevie answered. "Someone has to look after you."

Ramsey hid a smile. That was uncharacteristic of Karl. Was he really concerned about her, or was he up to something and didn't want the company of a small, talkative boy?

"That's great, partner," she said. "We haven't had a day together for quite a while. What would you like to do?"

He thought it over, his small face serious with the importance of the choice. "I think I'd like a hamburger," he finally said.

Ramsey concealed a grin. Martha wouldn't like that, after all her pains to provide everything a small boy would want! But she didn't mind at all; it sounded like a marvelous idea. As far as she knew, the nearest drive-in was in Tyler. So was Brad, although she didn't voice that thought even to herself. A short time later the two of them were in the ranch pickup and driving down the road toward the small town.

Although she had told herself sternly that Brad didn't figure at all in her decision to come to town, she couldn't help feeling a sharp pang of disappointment as she passed the Fish and Game building and saw that his pickup was gone. She drove on past, down the narrow main street lined with shops, and stopped in front of the drive-in.

Stevie was out of the truck like a rocket. "Let's eat inside!"

"Mind if I join you?"

At the sound of the familiar voice, Ramsey turned, her heart jumping up inside her chest. The loden-green pickup had pulled up beside them and Brad opened the door and jumped out onto the parking lot.

"Brad." Her voice didn't betray her keen pleasure at the sight of him. "Sure, come along. I didn't see your truck and I thought—"

"I'm glad you looked for it." He grinned. "Means you were thinking of me."

"Not necessarily," she said coolly. "I just happened to notice as I drove by. I'm not unobservant, you know."

"Nor am I," he said, his eyes going over her face and slender form with obvious appreciation. She felt herself flushing at the intimacy of the look, and stood a little straighter. Nevertheless, she was glad she'd put on an emerald-green silk shirt that contrasted nicely with her golden hair.

"How did you know we were here?"

"The traffic's not that heavy on main street," he said cheerfully. "I was in the coffee shop and saw you drive by." His eyes left her and went to the small boy who was standing beside her. "This must be Stevie," he said with a friendly grin.

Stevie inched closer to Ramsey, a scowl on his face. Ramsey wondered why; it was unusual for him to take an instant dislike to anyone. "Yes, this is my son, Stevie. Stevie, Brad Chillicott."

Brad put out his hand and the small boy continued to glare, his eyes flicking over the green uniform. "I know who he is," he muttered. "He's the game warden."

"Stevie! Mind your manners!"

At the command, Stevie put out his hand and shook Brad's briefly, but there was no mistaking his reluctance.

"Don't you like game wardens, son?" Brad's eyes were amused.

"Karl says you like to pick on people," Stevie muttered.

Ramsey met Brad's eyes briefly above Stevie's head, then he knelt beside the boy until their eyes were level. "Well, I don't think I pick on anybody but the bad guys."

"*We're* not bad! Karl says you'd like to put us in jail!"

Brad sighed. "Stevie, I only bother people who break the law. Do you like to fish?"

"Yes..."

"Well, I help protect the fish. And the deer. Sometimes weaker things need help to survive."

Stevie still wasn't convinced, but Ramsey could see he was weakening. Apparently Brad had a charm that even small boys weren't immune to.

"Would you like to go fishing with me someday?" Brad asked. "I sure know where there are some good holes. Some pretty big fish live there."

"How big?" Stevie demanded.

"Oh, about so long." Brad spread out his hands and Ramsey fell back, letting the two walk on ahead of her to the counter. She was seething with exasperation at Karl. She would talk to him about the ideas he was putting in Stevie's head. She certainly didn't want to raise a son with no respect for the law. Apparently Stevie soaked up everything Karl said. What else was he teaching him on those long rides together?

She sighed as she watched the two ahead of her. They were talking animatedly, Stevie obviously having forgotten his recent animosity; his small face glowed. She wouldn't have suspected it, but Brad had a way with kids. His reticence and dark intensity were apparently reserved only for adults, she thought wryly. His expression, looking down at

Stevie, seemed almost wistful. Did he miss having children of his own?

They sat down at a table with their double-cheeseburgers and milk shakes, and the conversation became general. Brad treated Stevie with respect and consideration, Ramsey saw, listening to his comments, never patronizing. She hardly knew how it happened, but a date was set for Brad to take Stevie fishing. She felt a quick pang of regret. She had been looking for a role model for her son, and Brad certainly epitomized much of what she had looked for—strong, honest, empathetic to a small boy. She thought of the dark, relentless side of his nature, his fierce hatreds, his capacity to nourish anger, and sighed. He was a complex man, and she wasn't going to be around long enough even to scratch the surface of his personality.

She returned her attention to the conversation in time to catch Brad's question to Stevie.

"Why aren't you out riding today, Stevie? Your Mom tells me you're real good on a horse."

Stevie's chest swelled importantly. "I couldn't go today. I had to stay home and take care of Mom."

"Oh?" Brad's head jerked up and he gave Ramsey a keen look. "Why was that?"

"'Cause she fell last night," Stevie said through a huge bite of hamburger.

"Don't talk with your mouth full," Ramsey said automatically.

"Fell!" Brad's mouth tightened and he glared at Ramsey. "What happened?"

"It—it was just an accident," she said lamely. She didn't want to involve Brad in her own growing suspicions. He was suspicious enough without hearing anything else.

Stevie's eyes grew wide. "The lights were out," he said. "It was real dark. Mom tripped on something and fell on the stairs."

"What did you trip on?" Brad said sharply.

She didn't meet his eyes. "I thought it was a wire, but I guess I was mistaken. Jacob didn't find anything but a toy."

"Why was it so dark you didn't see it?"

"The light globes burned out."

"All at once?" His tone was frankly skeptical. Then his eyes darkened. "How badly were you hurt?"

"Not bad. Just a wrenched ankle." She moved her foot from under the table. "I have a bandage on it, but I'm not sure it's necessary."

He leaned over and took her foot in his hand, his fingers going softly over the bandage and touching the bare flesh of her leg. She was reminded of the way she had once seen someone hold a frightened bird in his hand—carefully and gently. Even so, she winced slightly at his probing fingers.

"Still pretty sore?" The tenderness in his voice contrasted with the hard set of his mouth as his eyes sought hers.

"Not bad now," she replied. It was true enough; the pain in her ankle was almost forgotten in the surge of sensation that coursed through her at the touch of his fingers on her skin. She wondered if her response showed in her face, and dropped her eyes. For a moment she felt an invisible bond between them, a force that held them together as securely as the strongest rope.

Then Stevie broke the spell. "Come on, Mom," he said, jumping up from the table. "Let's go buy me a cowboy hat. Karl said I needed one."

She smiled and got up from the table. "Want to come along?" she asked Brad.

"Sure. I can take a break."

For an hour or so they wandered along the main street of Tyler, watching Stevie try on western garb, and finally outfitting him in a new Stetson hat, new boots and a western-style cowboy shirt. Brad insisted on buying him a pair of spurs, and admonished him seriously that they weren't to be used roughly. When they finally returned to the pickup, Stevie was strutting and jingling like an old-time westerner.

Ramsey couldn't remember when she had felt so content. The time was idyllic as she momentarily forgot her fears and forebodings. Had she and Paul ever done anything like this with Stevie? They had both been so busy, but they had certainly managed to see that he got to his soccer games, his swimming lessons. He couldn't be called deprived! But an idle hour spent with the three of them just loafing around had never seemed to happen.

Brad gave her a quick glance. "You're limping a little. Feeling worse?"

"I think I've had enough walking for now." She gave him a warm smile as he opened the door of the pickup, then turned to put his hands on her waist and lift her up lightly into the seat. He reached across her and tousled Stevie's head, then stepped back as Ramsey started the engine and drove out of the lot.

She saw him in the rearview mirror, looking after them, and she thought his expression looked somehow forlorn. Then she turned a corner and he was lost from sight.

Brad stood at the curb watching them until the pickup was out of view. Even then, he stared at the empty street, disconcerted by his abrupt sense of loss. He'd felt surprisingly at ease with Stevie, and the boy, after the initial hostility, had seemed to like him, too. He hadn't realized how much he missed having kids until now. He guessed he'd never really thought about it. A wife usually comes before kids, he thought, his mouth twisting in a wry smile, and he'd never come close to finding one of those. But Stevie was sure a son a man could be proud of. He thought of the unknown Paul and snorted with contempt. The man must be crazy.

He thought of Ramsey's accident the night before, and his jaw clenched convulsively. He didn't doubt for a minute that the accident had been staged. Did they want to hurt her or just frighten her away? Whatever they had hoped for, it had changed the situation as far as he was concerned.

When Ramsey had suggested that they investigate the shooting of Arnie together, he had agreed because he thought it would be a way to keep an eye on her, and he'd had a nagging suspicion that she was in danger. Then he had decided it wasn't a good idea and had made up his mind to stay away from Ramsey; the situation between them was much too explosive. He knew they were very close to an irrevocable step. He didn't take physical intimacy lightly, and he suspected that, with Ramsey, such an act would indelibly change his life. Nothing could come of it; even if she weren't a Carmichael, she would be leaving soon and he would be left lonelier than before.

He had planned to keep to his resolve. If she had been alone today, he might not have dropped everything he was doing when he saw her driving through town and rushed out to meet her, but he'd realized her son was a good chaperon. It had seemed safe.

Now, though, it was different. He had thought before that she might be in danger from someone at the Carmichael ranch, but the idea was difficult to accept, even for him, who would put very little past that crew. Still, the idea had lacked reality. She was, after all, the beloved granddaughter of the old pirate. The slashed tires and the random shot could have been meant for him instead of her. Now, however, he had no doubt at all. The "accident" was much too coincidental. Someone at the ranch must be getting desperate to go that far.

He walked over to his pickup, took the rifle down, examined it carefully and replaced it on the rack. His hand dropped to the handle of his pistol, and his fingers tightened around it. His plans were already fully formed in his mind. From now on, he would be at the Carmichael ranch every day. If he could be openly with Ramsey, he would; if not, he would be near, but out of sight. If he could have thought of an excuse, he would have slept outside her door! He would protect her as much as he could.

He pulled the pistol from his holster, flipped out the clip to check the bullets, then reloaded and shoved the gun back. He would be ready.

Chapter 8

The excited barking of the dogs and the heavy tromp of boots on the veranda was Ramsey's first indication that her grandfather had returned. She dropped the magazine she had been idly leafing through, rose hastily from her chair and went to meet him.

Her first thought when he came through the door was that he had aged considerably in the two days he had been gone. A swift uneasiness tightened her chest as she watched his approach. His shoulders were slumped as though under a heavy weight and his eyes weren't flashing the old fire. His rough-hewn face, though, cracked into a smile when he saw Ramsey.

"Grandpa," she said, stepping quickly forward and giving him a swift hug. "It's good to see you back."

"Good to be back." He grunted, accepting her embrace, then going past her to the living room and sinking wearily into a chair. "Too much driving for an old man."

It was an opening she wasn't going to miss. Maybe he was evasive with his wife and preferred to keep his problems to himself, but he could hardly ignore a direct question. "Delia said you drove over to Nevada. What were you doing there?"

He concentrated on kicking off his boots and settling back comfortably into the chair before he finally raised his eyes to hers. He might be tired and worried, she realized then, but a keen intelligence and firm resolve still shone through his eyes. He was no pushover.

"Little business to attend to."

She stuck out her chin in an expression that looked much like his. "Out of state? What kind of business?"

He chuckled. "Nosy, aren't you?"

"Grandpa," she said firmly, standing and facing him, hands on hips, "something is going on around here. Delia is worried sick. I just want to help, but I can't unless I know what's happening. What are you so worried about?"

For a minute she thought he wasn't going to answer. Then he heaved a deep sigh. "Suppose you might as well know. I didn't want to worry Delia, she being so poorly these days. But I'm worried about losing the Floating Eagle."

"Worried about losing the Floating Eagle! But it's the biggest ranch in the county!"

"Land and cattle ain't everything," he said morosely. "You need a cash flow. And for the past several years we've been taking in less and less. Even been borrowing at the bank."

"But why? The economy isn't that bad—"

"I don't know why," he said shortly. "It's true we've been plagued with a few strays wandering over on the forest, and turning up missing. But that's normal. With an operation this big, you expect to lose some..."

He shifted in his seat and stared at the empty fireplace. Ramsey suspected he was talking to himself now.

"I had a call from the manager of a cattle sales yard in Nevada. Fellow I used to know. He said a few steers with the Floating Eagle brand were turning up over there, and I went over to check on it.'' He sighed. ''There weren't many. Not enough by themselves to account for our losses.''

''Do you know how many you're missing?''

''Not really. Seems to be quite a few, according to the records. But I've no idea what's happening to them. Karl spends half his time riding over on the forest to see if he can find out anything, but there's nothing.''

Karl! Vague suspicions she had about Karl intensified. He was absent so much of the time, seemed to drift on and off the ranch continually. Was he really looking for the answer to the missing cattle? Or was he doing something much more sinister?

''I've been waiting for our 'serious' talk,'' she said lightly. ''Is this it?''

He grinned, then the look of defeat came back over his face. ''No, but it will have to wait. There are a few things I have to sort out first... Where is everybody?'' he asked abruptly, and she knew that the moment of intimacy was over.

''I think they're all here,'' she replied. ''I saw Jeff in the office working on the books earlier; I think he's still around. Karl was in the corral teaching Stevie to rope, the last I saw. Bud—''

Jacob rose heavily, and pushed his feet into his boots. ''Tell Jeff and Karl I want to see them.'' He strode off toward the office before she could finish her sentence.

As she went to find the men, she thought about the obvious omission in Jacob's command for attendance. He hadn't cared where Bud was; Bud was not involved in the meeting. As usual, his son was either forgotten by Jacob, or dismissed as inconsequential. Was Bud used to such summary contempt from his father by now, or did it still hurt?

Well, they were both excluded, she thought after the three men had retreated to the office and shut the door. She wasn't going to get anything more out of her grandfather, although she suspected he hadn't told her everything. But that didn't mean she had to accept it passively, as Bud had always done.

She walked out to the neglected rose garden, and started pulling weeds vigorously. Doing something with her hands always helped her think. And she needed to think, and think clearly, pierce through the rosy haze that always seemed to color her ideas about her family and the Floating Eagle. She was tired of being a patsy. She had refused to accept it for a long while, but now she had to face it; something was drastically wrong.

For an instant Brad's image, dark and intense and accusing, flashed before her eyes. She wouldn't accept his version of her family, either. The Carmichaels might be in trouble, but they were not evil. She thought of her offer to help Brad investigate Arnie's murder, and smiled wryly. He had no more idea of what to look for than she did; all he was doing was floundering around. If anything was going to be done, she would have to do it. She was at least more objective than he was.

Putting aside emotion and preconceived ideas, what did she actually know? A man had been murdered, and she had been the subject of frightening attacks. She was almost sure of it, as much as the thought pained her. Somehow, the incidents must be related.

She sat back on her heels and stared thoughtfully into the distance. What did she have to go on? The conch that had been lost at the site of the murder; was it conceivable that someone had seen her pick it up? There was Uncle Bud's secret meeting with Ella, and then they had found the slashed tires. Did that mean her presence and Brad's had been discovered? Then there was the shot that could have been meant for either her or Brad, or might merely have been an attempt to scare them off. And finally, her own fall down the stairs. She could accept now that someone at the ranch must have arranged it, although it was probably an attempt to frighten, not seriously injure, her.

She could understand why Brad might be in danger, but

why her? Was her presence at the ranch posing a threat to someone?

A wave of pure sorrow washed over her. She had come so far in the past few days, from a fierce insistence on the innocence of everyone at the ranch to a grudging acceptance that someone there might not be what he appeared to be. But when she thought of each person individually, the thought was still untenable. Even if she were right, she still loved each and every one of them. Because of the past, she owed them loyalty; she would help them if she could.

She had kept her head in the sand long enough; it was time to make a few inquiries. She rose, dusted off her knees and started toward the house. Uncle Bud was alone; she would start with him.

At her tentative knock on his open door, he turned from the window where he had been standing, looking out over the summer pasture, and gave her his familiar sweet smile. Her heart constricted; not Uncle Bud. He had always been so open and loving, there couldn't be a duplicitous bone in his body. Certainly not a violent one. Then she thought of his blond head bent over Ella's, his hand caressing the woman's back, and squared her shoulders with resolve.

"Mind if I come in?"

"Of course not." He moved from the window and motioned her to a chair beside his bed. She looked quickly around the room. It was neat and pleasantly furnished with a bed, a comfortable chair, a table placed beside the window, a few bookshelves. It was a nice room, but was it enough for an adult man?

"I'm glad you came," he continued, sitting down on the bed beside her. "We never seem to have time to talk since you've been home."

"Maybe you'd like to drive into town for dinner tonight," she said impulsively. "Just the two of us."

He flushed slightly. "I'd like to. But—but I have to go someplace later on..."

"Going to meet a girlfriend?" she teased, hoping he didn't hear the tension in her tone.

"Now who would be interested in an old crock like me?" he said lightly.

"You seem to be gone a lot," she said, watching his face for any telltale expression.

He shrugged. "As you've probably noticed, I'm not too necessary around here. I'm not much of a rancher, I guess."

"Why do you stay here?" she asked suddenly. "Don't you resent the way Jacob treats you?"

His smile was soft and wistful. "Oh, you get used to anything. I did leave once, you know. Stayed away a couple of years."

"I—I heard that. Where did you go?"

"Oh, I rodeoed around a little. Down through Arizona, New Mexico, living on prize money. But it wasn't any good. There was too much here I missed. Not only the ranch... I finally decided to come back." His expression was so sad she wanted to jump up and try to comfort him. She knew very well what had drawn him back to the ranch. And what was apparently keeping him here.

As though he regretted his remark, he smiled broadly and rose from the bed. "Are you interested in rodeos? The Navajo have some of the best. I won first in bronco riding at one of them."

She was touched by the pride in his voice. It was unusual for Uncle Bud to come in first in anything. "I'm very interested."

He rose and took a photo album from a shelf above his bed. "Then here's a picture you might like." He chuckled as he flipped the album open. "Here I am with the trophy."

Ramsey stared at the picture, and sucked in her breath. It was a younger Bud, but his face had the same guileless look as he held up a silver belt buckle to the camera. It wasn't the belt, though, that caused her heart to pound against her chest. He was wearing a black Navajo hat with a silver conch hatband.

As she stared at the picture, she was aware of a phone ringing and then Martha's voice calling up the stairs. "For you, Ramsey."

It was a welcome interruption. As she went down the stairs, her mind was busy with what she had just learned. A case could certainly be made against Uncle Bud. His love for Ella, the murdered husband, and perhaps he had seen Ramsey and Brad when they were spying on him. That would certainly account for the slashed tires, the shot, her plunge down the stairs. The Navajo hat, while not conclusive by itself, certainly cast a shadow of suspicion his way.

But as logical as it was, her mind refused to accept it. Not her Uncle Bud. He would never hurt her. Her thoughts were a confused mixture of doubt and sadness as she picked up the phone.

"Ramsey?"

His voice came deep and warm across the line, almost like a physical caress. It reverberated throughout her body, and she caught her breath, then said softly, "Hello, Brad."

"I wondered what you were doing today. Want to go for a ride?"

She played for time while she decided how to answer the question. "Don't you ever work? What will the department think if you take a woman riding?"

He laughed. "I wish it were a simple date, but the truth is, I have to be up that way, anyway. I'm going to ride over on Cottonwood Creek and put up some signs. Thought I might just look around some while I was doing it. Want to come along?"

She hesitated, and his voice was more insistent. "Hey, I thought we agreed to investigate together. You want to be sure I don't manufacture any evidence, don't you?"

That had certainly been her motive at one time, but her recent talk with Uncle Bud had changed things. Brad might not have to manufacture anything! If he knew what she suspected about Uncle Bud, he might go straight to the sheriff. Whether Bud were guilty or not, there might be enough evidence to cause his arrest. And she couldn't, wouldn't, let that happen! If he were actually guilty of murder, she wouldn't shield him, of course. She couldn't condone that. But that was by no means proven, and she didn't want Brad any closer on the scent.

"I can't make it today, Brad," she said, trying to keep her voice even. "I—I promised Delia I'd sit with her."

"Oh." She could almost feel his disappointment as the pause lengthened. Then he spoke sharply. "You are sure you plan to be with Delia all day?"

"Certain," she said, a little irritated at his question. It was really no concern of his.

"Well, I guess that's all right," he said, and she realized from the tone of his voice that it had been concern for her that had prompted his rather macho attitude.

"I'm sorry I can't go with you," she said.

"Well, it's not absolutely necessary that I go today," he said slowly. "I'll call tomorrow."

Her hand was shaking as she put down the phone. The thought of being with Brad was terribly seductive, but too much to risk. He was much too clever at knowing exactly what was on her mind, and she doubted she could keep her suspicions about Uncle Bud from him. Besides, that wasn't the greatest risk. His presence made her feel like tinder, and he was the match.

Brad put down the phone and turned to find Sheriff Thorenson standing in the doorway with a big grin on his face.

"Turned you down, did she?"

Brad gave him a stiff smile. "What can I do for you, Sheriff?"

Unoffended, the sheriff ambled in and sat down in the chair opposite Brad's desk and heaved a big sigh. "I tell you, Brad, I don't like it one bit. Don't like to have an unsolved murder around, but it's beginning to look like that's what it is. I'm wondering more than ever if Arnie didn't just happen on a random poacher, and the man who shot him is long gone.''

"Maybe," Brad said tersely. "It just doesn't feel right, though."

"I know," the sheriff said slowly. "I been thinking about your hunch that the Carmichaels are involved, but I can't come up with a thing. Old Jacob's getting pretty worried about something, though."

Brad's head shot up. "How do you know?"

"He was over in Nevada yesterday. I understand he found some of his strays in a sales ring. And the bank just called me. He's made an appointment to see Old Man Tanner."

Brad nodded thoughtfully. Old Man Tanner, as Frank Tanner was called by nearly everyone, was Tyler's only banker, a contemporary of Jacob's. Jacob Carmichael always refused to deal with anyone else, although Frank Tanner had turned most of the day-to-day business over to his son at least five years ago. "When is he going to see him?"

"Tanner's on a trip to the coast, and won't be back for a few days. I understand Jacob didn't like the delay, but he's waiting until then."

"Probably wants another loan," Brad said.

"I suppose." Thorenson rose heavily from his chair. "Guess you haven't come up with anything?"

At Brad's regretful nod, he ambled out the door, closing it softly behind him. Brad stared at his in-basket. Things were getting a bit out of hand here. There were several overdue reports he'd already had calls on this morning. He couldn't afford the time for too many wild-goose chases on the Carmichael land, especially since he had no idea what he was looking for.

But things seemed to be heating up. He could have sworn there was an almost frightened tone in Ramsey's voice when she had told him she couldn't ride with him today. And Jacob had actually found some of his strayed or stolen steers. Although he had known cattle were disappearing from the range, it was the first time Brad had heard of any actually showing up later.

At least Ramsey would be at the ranch house, safe if she stayed with Delia, and he could look things over without interference. He decided to put up those signs after all.

Ramsey walked purposefully toward the barn, glad to be occupied with a mission. The men had stayed inside the office for over an hour, and then Karl and Jeff had both saddled up and ridden off. She'd seen Uncle Bud do the same a few minutes later, though he rode in an opposite direction. For once, Stevie was happily employed inside the house with Martha, learning to bake his favorite kind of cookies, and Jacob was talking to Delia. There was no one to question her actions.

She had a fleeting moment of regret that she hadn't taken Brad up on his offer, but stifled it immediately. She would be better off by herself. Still, it was probably a wild-goose chase. If cattle were being rustled from the Floating Eagle and Karl couldn't find out how it was being accomplished, how could she hope to? On the other hand, perhaps Karl wasn't looking very hard.

She stepped into the gloom of the barn and saw Amber waiting as usual. Karl usually brought the horse in from the corral and put her in the stall since he knew Ramsey rode almost every day. She was surprised to see the horse was saddled, though. That was something she usually did herself.

She untied the halter and led Amber out into the yard, then bridled her and swung up into the saddle. Settling her foot into the stirrup, she winced a little. Her ankle was still slightly tender, but it didn't hamper her movements.

She kept Amber to a brisk walk until they passed the boundary of the Floating Eagle and rode over onto forest service land. The demarcation was not easy to see, although there was a three-strand barbed-wire fence that was supposed to mark the separation of public and private land. At a glance, she saw that it was down in several places, offering no obstacle at all to the passage of cattle from the Floating Eagle to public land.

She wasn't surprised; no one on the Floating Eagle would have kept the fence up unless forced to do so. This way, cattle could pass freely over to the forest to graze. If told this was dishonest, and that he should run only the amount of cattle he had a permit for, old Jacob would probably have shrugged it off as meddling by environmentalists telling him what he could and couldn't do.

There would be changes made when the old man died, she thought a little sadly. Right now, the authorities were inclined to let Jacob get away with things they would never countenance from his heirs. He had been around so long he was nearly an institution.

She wondered where she should start looking, then supposed it didn't matter which way she went. The chances of her finding anything were slim, anyway. If cattle were being rustled, it certainly didn't happen every day. It would be pure luck if she found out anything at all.

She gave Amber her head, and leaned back in the saddle, tilted her face toward the warmth of the sun, content to go wherever the horse led. She didn't have a better idea, anyway. In spite of her somber mood, the forest began to work its magic on her, and she began looking around, smiling at the startled chirp of a bird that flew from the brush at Amber's feet, and chattering back at a pine squirrel that scolded her from a nearby limb.

The peace seeped into her. Berkeley seemed far away, another planet, perhaps. Her concerns there seemed superficial, petty, now that she was enfolded by the timeless aura of the elemental land. Why had she really left Idaho? Could she ever be happy anyplace else? She had read someplace of a theory that one absorbed the vibrations of the place where you were born or raised, and that you were always an alien in any other spot on earth.

The thought caught her off guard, and she instantly quelled it. Seeing a deer trail slope up the side of the mountain, she guided Amber along the faint track. She needed to get up higher where she could look around.

When she gained the top of the ridge, though, she saw nothing. The forest stretched around her, its greenery unbroken by any sign of roads or human activities. Although she had felt once or twice as though she were not alone, when she reached this vantage point, she could see how absurd that was. She was the only human being for miles around. She had wondered if she might run into Karl, and had decided if she did she would just tell him she was out for a ride, but there was no sign of him.

The realization that she was completely alone was somehow comforting; the thought of company would have made her uneasy. For two or three hours she rode through the forest, but saw absolutely nothing unusual.

Starting back home, she decided to go by way of Three Tree Spring. Not that she expected to find anything; the place had been thoroughly searched by nearly everyone, and it would be a stupid killer who returned there.

She was still a mile or so away when she heard the faint bawling of cattle. She reined in, listening intently, and it came again, along with the rhythmic throb of a motor. She must be very near the old forest service road.

She had to get a better look; this might be just what she was searching for. She dug her knees into Amber's flanks and struck her sharply with the quirt.

The horse lunged forward up the steep bank, and Ramsey grabbed for the horn. She felt the saddle twist beneath her, fall to the side, and she catapulted onto the forest floor. She gave a high, piercing scream as she landed with a heavy thud. Shaken, her mouth open in astonishment, she watched Amber clamber up the bank and disappear.

The sound pierced the quiet of the forest, and Brad was instantly alert. He froze against the trunk of the ponderosa pine against which he was leaning to watch his horse drink from the icy water of Three Tree Spring. For an instant he wasn't sure what the sound was. Every muscle tensed as he waited for it to come again. But all remained quiet, the silence echoing around him as though to mock him. He heard the moaning of the wind in the top of the pines, the gurgle of water from the stream falling to the placid pool, nothing more. He tightened his jaw, threw the reins over the brown gelding's head and leaped up into the saddle, his conscious mind accepting what his subconscious had been sure of. That had definitely been a scream.

It had to be Ramsey, he thought, deftly guiding his horse through the thick stand of timber and brush that caught at his twill pants. He had known where she was all day, although he'd never gotten close enough to her to be detected. He had cursed his suspicions, called himself a fool, but he hadn't been able to forget the strained note in her voice when he had called on the phone, and the more he thought of it the more certain he became that she had no intention at all of staying with Delia and out of trouble. She just wanted him out of the way.

He had hurried to be ahead of her, parked his trailer off the road in a stand of aspen and, keeping far back in the cover of the trees, had watched as she rode out from the ranch. Then he had guided the gelding along her trail.

He wasn't sure what she was up to. Seemingly she was riding at random, no apparent destination, and finally he decided reluctantly that she was just out for a ride. When she had turned and started for the ranch, he had given up the vigil and was resting his horse, preparatory to starting home himself. She hadn't seemed to be in any danger, no one except himself seemed to be following her, and he certainly didn't plan on letting her know that he was!

But that scream meant something was terribly wrong.

Urging his horse forward with his knees, he topped a slight rise and looked down into the tiny depression. His chest constricted and fear lanced through him as he saw her. He spurred the gelding frantically down the incline, ignoring the cloud of dust that rose from the animal's hooves as he scrambled for footing. She was sitting on the ground, her back propped against a tree, looking as forlorn as a doll that a peevish child had dropped.

Thank God she was conscious, he thought, a steel band tightening around his heart, but she looked so vulnerable with her eyes closed, her wheat-colored hair loose from its ribbon and falling over her dusty, tearstained face, that he had to swallow the huge lump in his throat. A wave of tenderness washed over him, so strong it was nearly painful.

He leaped from the horse and reached her in two strides, wordlessly pulling her close against his chest. Her pliant body was warm and yielding against him, and he held her as though he could never let go. My God, if anything happened to Ramsey, he wasn't sure what he would do! He held her so tightly that he felt her heart throbbing against his chest as he buried his face in her disordered hair. He took a deep, strangled breath. At that moment, he was incapable of saying anything at all.

Then, at her slight wince, he came partially to his senses. If she were badly hurt, the last thing she needed was to be manhandled. He released his grip and held her a little away so he could look into her face.

"Ramsey!" he choked. "Are you hurt?"

She pulled away slightly and gave an embarrassed little shrug. "I don't think so. Just my pride. And my ankle may be reinjured. It hurt when I tried to stand up."

Immediately he examined her ankle, running his fingers quickly over the delicate bone structure. Gently he moved her legs so they were straight in front of her, assessing them with his hands. Finally, satisfied with his examination, he gave her a reassuring smile.

"I think you're a lucky girl. Nothing seems to be broken."

He relaxed a little, relieved that she was apparently just scratched and shaken, and his smile changed to a wicked grin.

"You have to stop doing this kind of thing, Ramsey. Don't you know you could get hurt?"

She opened her mouth to protest, then returned his smile, raising her eyebrows in mock indignation. "Tell me about it! It's not as though I enjoy this! But I do seem to be accident-prone, don't I?"

"Let's say you have *some* kind of trouble!" He stroked her hair absently, his narrowed eyes never leaving her face. "What happened?"

"My fault, this time. I know better than to be so careless. I should have checked the cinch on the saddle before I got on. I usually do, but Amber was already in the stall, saddled, and I didn't bother. But the cinch must have been frayed. When she lunged forward unexpectedly, it broke." She spread her hands in a helpless gesture. "And you can see what happened to me."

"What happened to her?" He searched the clearing with a quick glance, but there was no horse.

"She took off like lightning. She was topping that embankment, the last I saw of her."

"Probably on her way home," Brad said thoughtfully. "That means there will be a search party out for you real soon."

Ramsey nodded. She knew that a riderless horse was certain to head for home, and that horses seemed to know unerringly in which direction to go. There would be consternation when Amber showed up, without a saddle. Everyone would know immediately that there had been an accident, and they would come to find her. It might take them a long while, though. She had replayed the possible scenarios as she lay back against the tree, and had shuddered at the thought of the oncoming darkness.

"I'm glad you found me," she whispered, leaning her head against Brad's hard chest. "I was beginning to get a little scared…"

He squeezed her shoulders roughly. It was all he could do to keep from lowering his head toward her pale face and kissing her trembling lips until her fright turned to something else, but he stopped himself in disgust. The woman was hurt, for God's sake. Maybe not seriously, but certainly shaken up and scared. He jerked his mind back from the delicious path it was taking.

"Where's the saddle?"

She pointed, and Brad turned his head and saw the saddle lying in the brush a few feet away.

Easing her gently back against the pine trunk, he came swiftly to his feet and strode to the saddle. His expression was thoughtful as he reached down to pick up the cinch. He stared at it for a long moment, glad that his back was to her, disabling her from seeing the expression on his face as he turned the cinch in his hand. His suspicion was correct. It hadn't seemed logical that the equipment on the Floating Eagle would be allowed to fall into disrepair. And the cinch was not frayed; it showed very little wear at all. But it had been expertly cut, leaving only a strand or two to hold the saddle on the horse. Any sharp, unexpected move, any hard gallop, would have broken it.

He turned to face her, carefully keeping his face expressionless. He didn't want her to see his fear, and it might be just as well if she didn't know right now that her fall had not been an accident.

What could he do? His jaw tightened as he pondered the implications. The horse had already been saddled and waiting. Only someone from the Floating Eagle could have done that—someone who wanted Ramsey to have an accident. He clenched his fists against the hot burst of anger that blazed through him, visions of what he would do to that person when he found him flashing through his mind. Ramsey had hurt no one. He thought her loyalty to that nest of scoundrels unwarranted, but he knew how much they meant to her.

He didn't know whether the person who arranged the accident had hoped to merely scare her or to actually injure her, but either way, she had an enemy. Until he knew who it was, there was no way he could take her back to the Floating Eagle.

Chapter 9

Ramsey shifted slightly until her back fit more comfortably against the tree and watched Brad stride toward her. His face was an expressionless mask, but she knew him well enough by now to read signs of anger in the set of his shoulders, the tightness of his lips. So he had figured out that the cinch had been cut. The knowledge made her more apprehensive than she already was.

After her first shock at being thrown from Amber had eased, she had thought of that possibility—no, probability—herself, and after she had dragged herself up off the ground and staggered against the tree, had considered walking over to examine the cinch. She was slightly dazed, still shaking from the fall, and the effort had seemed too great right at the time, but she could see, even from a distance of several feet, that the break in the cinch was sharp—not at all worn and frayed. The sight, and what it meant, had sent such a paroxysm of fear through her that she had huddled where she was, not knowing whether she was more afraid of spending the night alone in the darkness or facing a rescuer from the ranch.

She had heard the pounding of hooves a long way off, and when Brad had appeared over the brow of the hill, had sighed and closed her eyes with intense relief, even as she inwardly chastised herself. How far she had come from the woman she used to be when the sight of the enemy of her family, the man sworn to bring one of them to justice, brought a blessed sense of relief? How did it happen that she felt safer with him than with any of the men whom she had loved since childhood?

Yet he was still the enemy, and she had better remember that. The situation had escalated from a citation for poaching to arrest for murder. She couldn't betray them, even though someone at the ranch was apparently trying to discourage her from discovering the truth for some unfathomable reason; that didn't mean everyone at the Floating Eagle was equally culpable. Brad didn't make any such distinctions; they were all tarred with the same brush. Until she could find out what was going on, she didn't want to give Brad any more ammunition. She had tried to pass off the fall from the horse as an accident. Even if Brad suspected that wasn't true, she saw no reason to bring it out in the open. She would handle the problem within the family; Brad was much too biased to react in an objective manner.

But, oh, how good it had felt when he pressed her against his chest, buried his face in her hair. For one instant she had wanted nothing so much as to stay in his arms and forget about everything but the two of them.

Now, as he walked toward her, she started to struggle to her feet, but stopped when he held up his hand. "Wait a minute, Ramsey."

She sank back down, partly because of his command and partly because of the rush of dizziness. She didn't protest when he gently lifted her in his arms and carried her toward the horse that was grazing unconcernedly a few feet away. For an instant, she wondered why that horse hadn't bolted, too, then realized that, like most well-trained cattle horses, it wouldn't budge when its reins were lying on the ground.

He lifted her up into the saddle, then, putting his hand on the horn, shoved his foot in the stirrup and leaped up behind her. She felt his arms sliding around her waist as he reached for the reins and she leaned her head back against his muscled chest, closing her eyes with a sigh. For a few minutes she would relax, forget about everything—Arnie's murder, the conch, her *accidents*—safe in the strength of Brad's encircling arms.

She felt a soft shiver go through him, and his arms tensed slightly as she settled back against his chest. Through the thin material of her silk shirt she felt the shifting of his muscles as his body adjusted to the horse's gait. The warmth of his body burned through his light shirt; she took in his clean masculine scent, subtly combined with the smell of horseflesh and astringent pine. His shirt was open at the neck, and she could almost feel the springy curls of his dark chest hair against her back. Or she imagined she did.

As he neck-reined his horse, his arm tightened against her side and she felt his biceps brush against her breast, sending delicious chills all through her body. Suddenly the atmosphere was tense, loaded, heavy with tension. It was almost as though they were caught in a force field with sexual energy vibrating between them in strong, pulsating currents. She stiffened, suddenly finding it difficult to breathe.

She heard him catch his breath as his arms tightened convulsively around her. Then, as though making a supreme effort, he sighed and carefully moved his arm away, placing his strong, bronzed hand on the green twill pants that stretched tautly across his thigh. She might have thought he was impervious to the moment, but she saw his fingers clench and dig into the hard muscle. In spite of her sense of loss at the removal of his touch, she half smiled. He might be a master at keeping his emotions under control, but he wasn't perfect!

''Do you think Amber is home yet?'' she said, more to break the tension than because she really wanted an answer.

''I doubt it,'' he replied. ''We're several miles from the Floating Eagle. She'll be going fast, but I think it will take her at least an hour or two to reach the ranch.''

''Then maybe we'll meet them when they come looking for me.''

He hesitated, then spoke slowly. ''I think we won't go back just yet.''

She stiffened and twisted around so she could see his face. It told her nothing. ''What do you mean?''

''It's a long ride back,'' he said smoothly. ''You may be a little more shaken up than you think. There's nothing broken, but you could use a rest. There's a line cabin a short distance from here. I think we'll go there first, and be sure you're all right.''

She considered his face, then turned around and thought about his suggestion. She had forgotten the old line cabin, though she had come there occasionally with Jeff or Karl when she was a girl. It was called a line cabin because it was situated where it could be used when the men had to ride the fence line, a never-ending job on a ranch the size of the Floating Eagle. It was just a one-room shack, but it was kept supplied with the necessities, in case a man had work to complete and wanted to avoid the long ride to and from the ranch. She had never stayed overnight, but she knew the men occasionally did.

Neither spoke as the horse picked its way across the dried pine needles of the forest floor, then emerged onto a definite trail. The slow, rocking motion of the horse was hypnotic, and she allowed her head to rest lightly against Brad's chest, aware of the soft clop of the animal's hooves in the soft earth and of Brad's even breathing. By turning her head just a little she could even feel the thud of his heartbeat. She wished the ride wouldn't end. When it did, they would have to discuss a few things.

"Here it is." She thought his voice sounded suspiciously husky.

At Brad's words, she looked up the trail and saw the little weather-beaten cabin, nearly hidden by high chaparral and evergreens bending over it like a benediction. They rode up to the rail post beside the door and Brad swung down, dropping the reins to the ground, then reached up his arms to Ramsey. She slid from the horse and he held her briefly against his chest, then put his arm around her waist and guided her toward the worn step in front of the cabin. Ordinarily she might have resented his assumption that she was unable to walk by herself, but this was no ordinary time. She was grateful for his solicitous touch, even as she was acutely aware of his thigh brushing hers as they walked.

Brad looked down at the soft-packed earth by the door and his brow wrinkled. "Looks like the old place is still used occasionally; see the tracks?"

She nodded, her gaze following his to the footprints beside the cabin: large footprints, the western heel cutting sharply into the soft earth; beside them, a much smaller pair.

She half smiled, guessing instantly who had made them. So this was where Karl and Stevie occasionally came when they were out riding. Then her gaze sharpened as she saw the casing of a bullet beside the path, and lifting her eyes, saw a target posted to a tree several yards away. No wonder she hadn't heard any more pistol shots around the ranch. That didn't mean at all that Karl had given up on his determination to teach Stevie to shoot.

Her thoughts returned uneasily to her son. It wasn't like Stevie to brazenly disobey her, and to keep quiet about something like this. He knew she disapproved. The knowledge that Karl had such influence with Stevie suddenly seemed sinister. She would have to do something about it when she got back to the ranch.

Brad pushed open the door, and they walked together into the room. It hadn't changed much; it was really just a shell, with rough board walls and a planked floor, the surface marred with scuffs and chinks of countless boots. Two small uncurtained windows, the glass dulled from years of weather, let in some light. There was a wood stove squarely in the middle of the room with logs stacked beside it. A shelf along one wall held buckets and basins for water that she knew had to be carried from a nearby spring; there was a closed cupboard that probably held some meager staples. A rough table, flanked by two chairs, faced the stove, and a cot with a mattress and a few blankets was pushed snugly against another wall.

Brad, his arm still around her waist, moved her toward the cot and settled her gently. Disregarding her protests, he lifted her legs up onto the cot, put a pillow under her head and covered her with a light blanket.

"I'm not an invalid," she said softly, pushing the blanket down.

"Falls can be nasty things," he replied. "Just lie there for a moment, and I'll get a fire started and heat up a little water. If nothing else," he said, grinning and running his finger lightly across her cheek, "you can wash your face."

With a sigh, she leaned back on the pillow, aware of a few aches she hadn't noticed before. She was glad for the respite of the cabin; she didn't think she could face going home just yet, searching every familiar face for a clue, wondering what lay behind every concerned smile.

She closed her eyes and just drifted, vaguely aware of the heat on her face as Brad got the stove roaring, the creak of the door as he went for the water. When she finally opened her eyes he had dragged a chair up by the bed and was sitting beside her, a basin of water in one hand, a towel in the other.

"Now you just relax," he said, dipping the cloth in the water and drawing it slowly across her face.

"Brad, I'm not a baby, I can do it—"

Since her words had absolutely no effect she shut her mouth and gave herself over to the sensuous warmth of the water as Brad gently cleansed the dust from her face. Then he pushed back her sleeves and murmured something comforting as he saw the cuts and scratches on her arms and bathed them gently with the warm towel.

His ministrations were doing more than cleansing her dusty skin, and she decided she had better keep a hold on her body that was giving every sign of enjoying this all too much. Her skin felt flushed and tingling, and a soft, languorous feeling made moving seem too great an effort to even contemplate.

"You do this very well," she murmured. "Maybe you should have been a nurse."

His hand trembled slightly, but his grin was wicked. "Are you trying to tell me this is just what the doctor ordered?"

She knew she flushed slightly and hoped he hadn't noticed. "Some doctor! I don't think there's any problem with the part of me you're massaging now."

He continued to rub her arm gently with the soft cloth, then moved it down to caress each separate finger. "You can never tell where the pain will surface," he said, but she could see the grin lurking behind the serious facade. "Maybe we'd better check out your ankle."

He pulled off her boots, pushed her jeans up to bare her ankle, then bathed it gently, his fingers massaging and caressing her tender flesh. "It's a little swollen, I think."

"It doesn't feel like it," she said dreamily. "I think I may start purring any minute. When should we be starting home?"

"I think we'd better stay here for a couple of hours at least."

"They'll be worried about me," she said, but the protest sounded halfhearted, even to herself.

"Do them good,' he said brusquely, his hand gently massaging her tender ankle, an activity that was sending currents of sweet sensation up her leg. She should probably put a stop to it. She remembered the other times when wild passion had flamed between them, and knew it wouldn't take much of this kind of thing to kindle it again.

"Brad—are you sure it's a good idea for us to be here?"

"Probably not," he said, giving her a crooked grin.

She looked up into his face, so near that by moving only a few inches, she could have reached up and run her fingers over the hard plane of his jaw. Hardly realizing what she was doing, she did just that, moving the tips softly, lingeringly, over his cheek. He had shaved this morning, she realized, and now there was a slight roughness to his skin, and the texture sent little thrills of excitement racing along her arm.

His eyes were nearly black as he met her gaze, full of such longing that she was startled and suddenly afraid. In a minute there would be no turning back. Her throat felt tight, but she forced herself to speak as she quickly retrieved her hand and clenched it by her side. She struggled to a sitting position, breaking the intensity of the moment.

"Brad, we need to talk."

"Suits me," he said, leaning back in his chair, eyes suddenly hooded. "Any particular subject?"

"Yes." She gave him a direct look. "Us."

"Us?" He raised dark eyebrows wryly. "The Carmichael princess and the game warden?"

"Stop that! You know what I'm talking about. Besides, I didn't think you where a whiner!"

A tighter line around his mouth was the only indication that her shot had hit home. "A whiner?" he said thoughtfully. "Is that how you see it? You know as well as I do, Ramsey, that we're on opposite sides of the fence."

Of course she knew it. She just didn't like to think about it. "It seems strange how little I really know about you," she said softly. "Even though I've known you all my life."

"We didn't really know each other in high school," he said slowly. "I think you represented an illusion for me. When we were kids, it was like looking at something across a chasm. You can think you know what it's like, but until you touch it, feel it..." He broke off, apparently feeling he had gone too far.

"I don't remember that you always hated the Carmichaels," she insisted. "I'm certain you came out to the ranch a couple of times with Jeff."

"Maybe I wanted to see how the other half lived," he said lightly. Then his face became somber, and she knew the next words cost him some effort. "Maybe hatred isn't the right word for what I felt then, maybe it was—envy."

She felt that he had given her a rare and unexpected look into his heart. "Is it still?"

"No, not now." His tone was abrupt and she knew the barricade was up again. "As a kid, you people dazzled me. Then my dad died—I saw Jacob for what he really was— what they all were…" He stopped, and she knew from the look on his face that he regretted saying as much as he had.

"And me?" she asked, her throat tightening. "Do you think you saw me as I really was?"

"I have always seen you as you are, Ramsey," he said lightly, the serious discussion apparently over. "Beautiful— desirable—expensive. Too expensive for me."

His words hurt more than she would have expected. He made her sound like a shallow dilettante, and she retaliated sharply. "I think I'm changing my mind about you. I always thought of you as fair, compassionate. A person with depth."

For several seconds they stared at each other, eyes locked in challenge. Then Brad pushed back his chair and came briskly to his feet.

"Are you hungry, Ramsey?"

Recent events—the fall, Brad's tender caretaking, the near quarrel—had pushed hunger from her mind, but she realized she hadn't eaten since breakfast and it was now early evening. Also any diversion that would diffuse the tension between them was welcome. "Starved. But do you think there's anything to eat around here?"

"We'll soon see." He strode across the room and rummaged through the cupboard. He put two cans on the table, then pulled out a bottle of wine. "Hey, we're in luck. Can't say much for the taste of the person who stocked this cabin, though," he said, holding up the bottle and looking at the label.

Ramsey grinned at his disgusted look, and swung her legs over the side of the cot. "It couldn't have been Karl; he much prefers Scotch." Walking gingerly to the cupboard where she located a couple of tin plates and some plastic knives and forks, she placed them on the table beside the cans of tuna and smoked oysters.

As they speared oysters directly from the can and drank wine out of jelly glasses, the mood between them changed to a comfortable camaraderie; although Ramsey knew the sexual tension was still there, for the moment it lay dormant. If she'd thought anything else, the sinking feeling she got in her chest every time she watched Brad's well-shaped, competent hand lightly reach to spear a chunk of tuna or his eyes crinkle at the corners as he flashed her a brilliant white smile, she would have been disabused of that notion immediately.

"Ramsey," he mused, pouring each of them a second glass of wine. "Ramsey. That's an unusual name. It fits you, though."

"It was Delia's maiden name and my father's middle name," she answered. "I think it was his only concession to tradition. There was a time when I didn't care for it, but now I do." She raised her eyes to his. "What about your family, Brad? You've told me a little, but I'd like to know more."

He half smiled, twisting the jelly glass idly in his fingers, then set it down, wine untasted. She didn't miss the faint bitterness in his voice. "Oh, the Chillicotts were big on tradition, too. We've lived in Jade County as long as the Carmichaels."

"In Tyler?"

"No. My grandfather had a little ranch, my father—" He broke off and stood from the table. "Ramsey, I suppose we'd better be thinking about what to do with you. I really don't think you should go home—''

''Of course I'm going home.'' She stood too, and quickly cleared off the table.

''I'm not sure it's safe.''

She gave him a quick look. She wasn't sure it was safe, either, as preposterous as that thought would have been a few days ago, but she couldn't run away from it. And she couldn't admit her growing fears to Brad. ''Of course it's safe!'' she said firmly. ''We're talking about my home! And we'd better be going.''

His lips thinned into a stubborn line. ''But—''

''Brad, they'll be looking for me in an hour or so. We'd better meet them on the trail. It will save explanations.''

''I don't like it,'' he said slowly, coming toward her and standing close so that he could look down into her face. ''I don't want anything to happen to you, Ramsey.'' The words seemed torn out of him as he placed one hand lightly on her waist.

His obvious sincerity moved her deeply. She couldn't doubt the look of concern on his face. And something else, something compelling that she couldn't even name. Hardly aware of what she was doing, she moved closer until her breasts were barely touching the hard planes of his chest, feeling the nipples spring to life against the soft material of her shirt. Her hips were so close to his that the tiniest movement would join them. ''Nothing will happen to me,'' she said softly.

His dark head was only an inch or so away, his eyes holding her as securely as though she were tight in his arms. She watched the gray irises darken, then caught her breath at the sudden flare of passion in their black depths. As though of their own volition, his arms wrapped around her, his hands spread against her back, and he pulled her to him in a swift, fierce motion that elicited an instantaneous response.

With a low moan, she put her arms around the back of

his neck and tangled her fingers in his springy dark hair, mindlessly pulling his head down to meet her lips. His mouth found hers, and he captured its welcoming warmth like a victorious pirate, tasting, delving, making it his own. They clung together, passion melding their bodies perfectly and sweetly as surges of delicious sensation sang through her, turning her flesh to an exquisite quivering garden of pleasure.

With a harsh moan, he held her away slightly so that his dark eyes could look into hers. "Oh, Ramsey, I shouldn't be doing this. You're hurt!"

She raised a finger and ran it lovingly over his lips, laughing shakily when he nibbled the tip of her finger. "I'm not hurt," she said softly. "I feel fine. Just fine."

Still his eyes held hers in an intense question. "Are you sure, Ramsey? You know what this means. Another kiss, another caress, and we will have no choice." His voice broke, and his words vibrated right to the center of her being. "I want you so much," he whispered. "I can't stand another instant of this agony. The times we've been together before have been torture. Holding you in my arms, wanting you—you can't imagine how much I want you. And letting you go! I can't do it again. If you're not sure—"

In reply, she moved against his hard body and raised her hand to the back of his neck to bring his mouth again to hers. There was no room for thought, for questions, for doubts. There was only intense, overwhelming feeling and need. It was as though this encounter were fated, whatever the consequences. She moved her hips urgently against the rigidity of his body, rotating them slightly, no longer in command of her responses.

"Ramsey!" Releasing her lips, he called her name as though it were a prayer, and buried his face in her neck. She felt the heat from his body, the building desire that met her own. Then with a strangled gasp, he picked her up and carried her swiftly to the bed, laying her back against the pillow where he had so recently lavished her with tenderness and care. Now the dam had broken, and there was no stopping the force that hurtled through them both; emotion so long denied surged through them in a wild, relentless flood, shaking them and molding them to its desperate need.

She lifted her hips as he stripped the jeans from her body, helped him as he fumbled with the buttons of her shirt. Kneeling by the bed, his breath coming in ragged gasps, he paused to look at her, lying before him clad only in a lacy bra and bikini panties, wisps of material barely covering what lay beyond.

"My God, you're beautiful!"

He buried his head between her breasts in an agony of passion as his hands molded her body. Sexual need hardened her breasts, moistened the sweet center between her thighs, as her head tossed wildly on the pillow. "Brad," she whispered, "Brad," her voice conveyed the urgency of her need.

He stood and swiftly removed his clothes, leaving them where they fell, and for one timeless instant stood looking down at her. Her pulse pounded as she saw him poised naked above her. He was beautiful. Beautiful. His body was well formed and muscular, with broad shoulders, a deep chest covered with dark hair that spread over its wide planes, then narrowed to form a line down his ridged abdomen, widening again into the dark nest of his sexuality. A sexuality, she saw, that was springing urgently upward.

One instant he was poised above her, then next she surged to meet his downward thrust. Their coupling was wild, delirious, as passion urged them on into ever-spiraling heights of sensation, until they reached the pinnacle together.

Hot and moist, they clung together, ragged breathing easing, heartbeats slowing, the world around them gradually coming into focus. Finally Brad raised himself on one elbow and looked down into her face.

"You're wonderful, darling," he said softly. "Fabulous. I can't tell you how often I've thought about you, visualized you like this, but never, never could I have dreamed how perfect you are. I've never known it could be like this.''

She smiled languidly back at him, her body replete with satisfaction. She hadn't known it could be like this, either: a wild, mindless surge of ravening desire. She'd always thought she needed foreplay, tenderness, a little coaxing, but this was like a hurricane sweeping everything before it.

It left her a little sad, and she felt tears sliding down her cheeks. Perhaps it was depression, although the French phrase, which she couldn't recall at the moment, but which meant ''the little death,'' expressed it better.

Brad's fingers traced the path of the tears down her cheek. ''What's the matter?'' he said softly. ''Regrets?''

''No regrets.'' She gave him a warm smile. Her mood was something she couldn't explain, and she wouldn't try. She didn't regret the wild maelstrom that had carried her where she'd never been before, but she was a little frightened of the intensity of her response. All that passion couldn't have been entirely physical, not on her part. Even in the midst of the storm, she had felt a tenderness, a deep warmth, that she was very much afraid might be love, and the very thought terrified her.

She knew it was not reciprocated. There had been no tenderness in Brad's approach, just a wild, savage need, which she had met with equal fervor. She had been transported by his intensity, but even in the throes of sexual delirium, she had felt a barrier between them. He had given himself completely sexually, but she sensed he was holding part of himself back. And now, he told her how beautiful she was, how fabulous she was in bed, but not one word of love.

He pulled her close again and began nibbling her neck with quick, enticing little bites. Suddenly he stopped, his muscles tensing as he propped himself up on one elbow. ''Listen!''

In the quiet, she made out quite distinctly the jingle of bridle and the clatter of horses' hooves. Her heart froze in her chest and she made an unconscious movement to pull the blanket up over her naked body. She had forgotten all about the fact that the people from the Floating Eagle would be searching for her. "It's them! They're here!"

Brad leaped from the cot and pulled his pants on hastily, then reached for his shirt. "Hurry. You don't want them to find us like this."

She certainly didn't! The thought of her grandfather coming through the door and seeing his granddaughter naked and in the arms of a man he detested was enough to lend her speed she hadn't known she was capable of. She slipped into her shirt, her fingers taking an agonizingly long time with the buttons, then stepped into her jeans and boots, and shoved her lingerie into her pocket.

"I don't think we'll fool them for a minute," she said, ineffectually brushing her tousled hair back from her flushed face.

"Maybe not." Brad was grinning wryly. "But we'll try. If I know old Jacob, he'd rather find you hurt along the trail someplace than here with me."

She didn't answer; he was probably right. She took a deep breath as she heard the stomping of boots on the porch and watched the door swing inward. Then Jacob stood outlined in the doorway, his frame nearly filling the opening. He looked quickly around, his pale blue eyes taking in everything, and she saw the worry on his old face combine almost equally with outrage. He straightened to his full impressive height and stared at the two of them, his mouth set in a hard line, looking, Ramsey thought, like an avenging prophet. Karl and Jeff stood a couple of feet behind him, and Ramsey knew they, too, had seen her and Brad.

The mature woman, the woman who made her own decisions about sex, slipped away somewhere, leaving Ramsey feeling like the young girl who had sometimes faced this awesome justice after coming in too late from a date. Almost instinctively she reached for Brad's hand.

Jacob didn't miss the movement, and his shrewd old eyes flashed. "What's going on around here?" he demanded.

Chapter 10

If Brad hadn't been so concerned about Ramsey's reaction to her grandfather's abrupt appearance, he would have almost enjoyed the look on the old man's face. He swore he could hear the wheels turning in Jacob's mind as suspicion fought with relief. Why wasn't Ramsey lying hurt someplace, instead of sitting comfortably in the cabin? Most definitely comfortable. Had his granddaughter been compromised or rescued? Whichever it was, he obviously didn't relish the fact that Brad Chillicott was involved.

The other two men accompanying the old robber baron weren't any happier with the situation, he saw with wry amusement. Karl glowered first at Brad, then at Ramsey, like a pugnacious Doberman attack animal momentarily leashed, and even Jeff's usually unflappable countenance had a look of wary surprise. The presence of the men seemed to fill the small cabin to bursting, and their hostility was nearly palpable. Brad waited grimly to see who would attack first.

Jacob, apparently deciding to ignore Brad for the moment, strode across the short space to his granddaughter and put his hand on her shoulder, turning her to look anxiously into her face.

"Are you all right, girl? Your horse came in alone. We thought you'd been thrown."

"I'm all right. I was thrown—" Ramsey circled her arms around the old man's waist, and laid her golden head momentarily on his broad chest. "I'm sorry to worry you, Grandpa. We were planning on starting for the ranch right away."

"Are you hurt?"

"Not really—just a little shook up."

Jacob sighed with relief, but said nothing, the tight set of his mouth and his swift glance from her to Brad saying as plainly as words that she had a little explaining to do. Brad wondered if he should help her out, then decided to let her handle her own family herself. Anything he said would only add to the uncomfortable situation.

"Amber threw me," Ramsey said. "Brad happened by, and brought me here to the cabin to rest a bit before we started back." Brad wondered if anyone else noticed her faint blush.

"Threw you?" There was a puzzled frown on Jacob's face. "That horse is as gentle as a lamb."

Ramsey rubbed her thigh ruefully. "Tell her about it."

Brad caught Jeff's assessing look, and Karl's deepening scowl, but he merely shrugged. Why didn't Ramsey tell them about the slashed cinch? Unless, he thought, a tiny frown creasing his forehead, she wasn't as sure of her family's innocence as she let on.

"And ole Brad just happened by?" Jeff's tone was mocking. "You seem to turn up in the oddest places, Chillicott. Places you've no business to be."

"The national forest is public land, Jeff. Or are you trying to acquire it by running your cattle all over it?"

"It's lucky for me Brad happened by," Ramsey broke in,

but her comment didn't lessen the tension rising among the men.

Brad's glance at Jeff was cool and appraising. "Lucky for Ramsey, I guess. Perhaps not as lucky for someone else."

"What does that mean?"

"I think at least one of you knows."

Jeff took a half step forward, Brad tensed and moved to meet him. It would be so satisfying to smash a fist into that supercilious smile.

"Stop it, you two!" Ramsey said sharply.

Reluctantly Brad let his fist drop slowly to his side as Jacob thrust himself quickly between the two men.

"Enough of that!" Jacob barked harshly. "I'm in no mood for puzzles, Chillicott. What did you mean by your last remark?"

Brad said nothing, his eyes going from face to face.

"Well, anyway, it appears we owe you something," Jacob said grudgingly, simultaneously shoving Jeff back toward the door. Hand on the knob, he paused and nodded stiffly in Brad's general direction. "Much obliged. We'll be taking her home now."

Ramsey cast Brad a last helpless look as Jacob took her firmly by the arm and propelled her toward the door, an errant child being chastised.

"I'll see you later, Chillicott." Jeff turned at the door and gave Brad a slow smile. "That's a promise."

Karl moved after the other three, a powerhouse of a man, ignoring Brad as completely as though he didn't exist.

Brad waited until he heard the group mount up and the last murmur of voices had faded away down the trail. It was very nearly dark; he should be getting out of here, too. It was a long way back to where he had parked his horse trailer. He'd wait, though, until they were well ahead of him; the Carmichaels didn't want his company and he damn sure didn't want theirs.

He sat down in the chair by the table, absently picked up

the half-empty bottle of wine, then put it back on the pine-wood surface. He rarely drank much and never when he was alone; perhaps the thought of his father inhibited him, or perhaps he just wasn't that fond of the stuff. More likely it was because he never wanted to be out of control, and alcohol had a way of blurring concentration and judgment. He sure didn't need that right now. Right now he needed to think.

He tipped the chair back, propped his boots on the table, which shivered under the weight, and clasped his hands behind his head. In spite of the interruption, he still felt as though he were on a roller coaster. Every nerve end was alive and tingling, every cell retained the memory of Ramsey's fervent response to his love. What had happened tonight was almost too much to grasp. The girl he had loved since high school, the girl who had filled his dreams during so many long lonely nights, first when he was a vulnerable boy and later as a mature man, had actually been his. He had loved her, felt her fiery passion as he had always imagined it would be. Only it had been so much more devastating, so much more powerful, than he could ever have conceived. Just remembering the feel of her in his arms caused his pulse to start pounding in his temples as loud as the mating call of a ruffled grouse!

There wasn't any doubt about one thing: he loved her. But there was plenty of doubt about everything else.

In retrospect, he was glad for the interruption; her family barging in like firemen at a four-alarm blaze put things back in perspective. For a moment, looking at her lying beside him, her hair fanned out over the flowered pillow like corn silk on a verdant meadow, he'd nearly lost control. He had nearly told her he loved her, opened his heart to her and begged for some hope that they could be together. He knew now, as he had always known, how ridiculous that would have been.

Ramsey wasn't just anybody; the things that separated them were too strong and too painful. Long ago he had dedicated himself to seeing that the Carmichaels were stopped from riding roughshod over the rest of the community, as they had done for so long. He was going to stop their poaching, their cavalier use of public land as their own. It was this driving ambition that had sustained him through many a bitter night.

And now the stakes had escalated. Although the sheriff was stymied, almost ready to consider Arnie's death as unsoluable, Brad was convinced that one of that Carmichael gang had murdered his partner, and he would bring him to justice if it was the last thing he ever did. He would wait and watch. Someday they would slip up. If it cost him Ramsey's love...

He swore and stood abruptly, nearly knocking over the table. What made him think he might have Ramsey's love? She was evasive and tricky, as the matter of her hiding the conch shell proved. Perhaps she even had a motive for the way she acted tonight. He hated himself for the thought, but had she known he was following her all the time, slashed the cinch, released Amber? If not, why hadn't she told her family that the cinch had been cut?

That was ridiculous, he thought, shaking his head angrily, but he had to remember her Uncle Bud was up to his ears in subterfuge, Karl might hide anything behind that glowering exterior and Jeff—well, Jeff reminded him of a half-wild panther: smooth and controlled, but ready to spring at any minute. Why should he think Ramsey was different?

His mouth twisted in bitter awareness. Even if none of that were true, there was still no future for him and Ramsey. She was here for the summer, and then she would return to her existence in Berkeley. She might have an occasional memory of him, a shiver or two of remembered passion to add spice to her life in the city, but that would be it.

Still, the memory of her in his arms burned through every cell of his body, and he was a little ashamed of himself. He had always prided himself on his control, yet he had acted like a wild man, taking her as savagely as the man the Carmichaels thought he was. She deserved better than that. Even though they would have only an interlude of passion, he promised himself that he would give her something beautiful to remember. As he would remember always, after she was gone.

That was another promise he would keep, he thought, clenching his jaw in an involuntary gesture of resolve. He was good at promises to himself. He knew how to wait, and he didn't forget. He put the promise about Ramsey right alongside the other. Ever since he had been old enough to figure out what had happened, and had finally understood what the Carmichaels had done to his family, he had protected that promise as carefully as delicate china wrapped in cotton. One day they would pay...

"Grandfather, I'm a grown woman," Ramsey said, standing stiffly in front of the desk and looking the old tyrant squarely in the eyes. Peripherally she caught Jeff's grin and Karl's scowl, and her resentment grew. Why did Jacob always have to involve the entire family in everything? Wasn't this something he and she could have talked over privately?

All four were in Jacob's office, and she wondered briefly why Uncle Bud wasn't there, too. Then, if she hadn't been so angry, she would have grinned. Uncle Bud was undoubtedly involved in his own escapade, one which wouldn't please his father any more than hers had.

"Ramsey, I'm not saying anything happened," Jacob replied, settling himself more firmly in his armchair behind his battered desk. "I agree that's not my business. But it seems funny to me that Chillicott just happened to be there. And took you to the line cabin—he could have brought you home. He's up to something. You don't know that boy, Ramsey. He's not on our side!"

"Why does there have to be a side!"

"'Cause this murder is just tailor-made for old Brad's

lifelong ambition,'' Jeff said smoothly. ''He'll use any-thing—including you—to bring us down.''

''You're always saying that!'' Ramsey said hotly. ''But has he ever done anything outside the law? No! It seems to me it's the Carmichaels that skirt around it!''

Karl, who had been silent up to now, leaned forward men-acingly. Ramsey took a good look at him; he had been so much a part of the furnishings of the ranch that she realized she hadn't actually directed her attention to him since she came back to the Floating Eagle. He was an imposing man, now in full cowboy regalia: jeans, elaborately tooled leather boots, black western-cut shirt, even a black hat, which he, as most of the western men, apparently took off only at bedtime. A hat with a vibrant, obviously new band of pheas-ant feathers.

Suddenly her heart jumped. Why the new band? Had he somehow lost the old one? At least part of it?

Her reverie was broken by his brusque words. ''None of this would have happened in the first place if you hadn't been snooping, Ramsey. Stay out of the forest. I'm warning you—it's dangerous.''

''I wasn't snooping!''

''What do you call riding out alone all day?''

''That's enough!'' Jacob raised his hand to cut off the discussion, and his voice softened. ''We're forgetting Ram-sey could have been seriously hurt. But I'm surprised at your attitude, girl. Agreed, we may not always abide by all the newfangled rules. The way things are changing, maybe we're going to have to change with them...''

The old shoulders slumped and Ramsey felt the familiar tenderness as an expression of defeat crossed Jacob's craggy face. Was her grandfather thinking of the troubles that were besetting the Floating Eagle? Then the old man straightened, looking again like an imperious hawk. ''But murder! Never! That's where the boy's going too far.''

He sighed and reached across the desk to touch Ramsey's hair. ''That's why I wanted all of us together to talk about

it. Maybe between us we can convince you of the serious-
ness of the problem. Jeff's right, you don't know Brad,
Ramsey. He will use you—he will use anything to get at
us. I think that's what he is doing. I know he's a handsome
boy, but—''

Ramsey looked at Karl and Jeff, then back to her grandfather. "If I'm going to get a lecture, I'd rather it were just
the two of us," she said firmly.

"Reasonable, I'd say," Jeff gave her a conspiratorial
wink, and left the room. Karl, obviously wanting to say
more but finding no permission in the old man's face, followed him, and Ramsey and her grandfather were left alone.
He gave her a weak smile.

"Didn't mean to come on too strong. You mean everything to me, sweetheart."

He was upset and obviously worried; maybe he was vulnerable enough to tell her what was really bothering him.
Anyway, she wanted a change of subject. "Grandpa, you
said the other day that you wanted to talk to me about the
ranch. This seems like a good time."

He sighed. "I was a little premature. There's some things
I got to get in line before I talk to you. But it won't be
long." He suddenly looked very tired. "I'm so very glad
you're here, Ramsey. You and Stevie. I hope—I hope you
don't go away again."

She looked at him in surprise. "My classes start in a few
weeks."

"You belong here."

"I never considered staying…you know that."

He sighed. "Let's leave it for now. I want to go up and
see your grandmother."

As Ramsey started out the door, he called softly, "Remember what I said about Chillicott. You can't trust him."

"And you remember that I'll make my own decisions,"
she replied, but she said it softly and sadly.

Closing the door, she leaned briefly against it, then
walked on out into the yard, the events of yesterday still

blazingly vivid in her mind. Every tissue in her body still ached with the imprint of Brad's caresses. She had been in a daze when Jacob dragged her away, and they had all been too tired and too upset to discuss anything when they returned home. Jacob had called his summit meeting early this morning, and she'd been lectured exactly as though she were a child.

Maybe she was acting like one, she thought uneasily. Was her blind loyalty to her family shutting out everything else? Or were they right about Brad? She knew something was terribly wrong, but she took every opportunity not to see it. Still, it could no longer be ignored. She had to face the unthinkable. Someone might actually be trying to kill her. There had been the fall, where she had luckily escaped serious injury. And the person who cut the cinch had no way of knowing how badly she would be hurt. She could have been knocked out by the fall and left alone in the forest. The person arranging those things had to be one of the family. No one else had access to Amber.

Yet who among the men was actually capable of such cold premeditation? She had thought it might be Uncle Bud, but when she thought of his guileless smile and his ineffectual manner, it just didn't seem possible. As for his having access to the conch, it seemed very little to go on now, after seeing Karl's new hatband. And Jeff was much more likely to choose as a weapon a bon mot at forty paces! He had always been her special friend and confidant. It was impossible to think of his urbane, sophisticated manner as a veneer for violence.

And Karl... She froze suddenly, her hand going to her chest. Karl might very well be capable of violence. Of all the men, he was the only one she could come even close to envisioning as a murderer. He was a brusque, sullen man, more so since she had returned home than she remembered. Even when she was a child and he was teaching her to ride, his tenderness had always been covered by a sharp, no-nonsense manner, and since her return he seemed actually to dislike her. There was nothing familiar about the way he warned her to stay off the forest, accused her of snooping.

He loved guns, she knew, recalling his determination to teach Stevie to shoot. And although all the men were comfortable with weapons, Karl was the only one to use his frequently. She remembered his admission that he had shot over the head of some poachers. What about his unexplained absences? He was always riding off the ranch at daylight, often not returning until well after dark. It was he, also, who usually had Amber waiting for her in her stall.

The more she thought of it, the more certain she became. It was impossible to think of anyone as a murderer, but if there *was* one among her family, Karl was the only possible choice.

But she couldn't do anything on the basis of mere suspicion. She would like to go to Brad and talk it over with him, but that was impossible, too. She had no proof, and Brad was so anxious to find one of the Carmichaels guilty, he would probably have Karl arrested immediately.

How sure could she be of Brad, anyway? Although she tried to resist, the suspicions of Jacob had an effect. She didn't think he could have been faking that molten outpouring of passion, but that might not mean anything. Passion was one thing; it didn't necessarily go along with love, at least in men's minds, or so she'd heard. And Brad had been very careful not to say he loved her.

She had to talk this over with someone, sort out her thoughts and suspicions. Without making a conscious decision, she started down the path that led to Jeff's studio, oblivious to the fragrance of the blooming apple trees, the buzz of honeybees industriously gathering the dusty pollen, the trill of orioles staking out nesting territory. Even in childhood, he had been the one who understood her best, the one she could turn to when she felt lonely and confused. She would tell him her suspicions about Karl, and he would either dissuade her from them or help her decide on a plan of action.

The door was ajar and she knocked softly, then pushed it open.

"Hi, Ramsey." Jeff turned from the canvas and waved his brush at her. "School's out, I see." His wide grin was as familiar and mocking as ever.

She half sat against a stool and pushed back her hair from her face, returning his grin. "He makes me feel about twelve years old."

"I have to admit, he does the same thing to me," Jeff replied. "Always has."

"Do you remember when you first came to the Floating Eagle, Jeff?" she said, her wistful expression revealing her own nostalgia. "You must have been very small."

"I was about six," he said. "The same age you were when you came."

"Were you scared?"

"Of the ranch? Nope. I was petrified they'd send me back to the foster home, though."

"They never would have done that."

"I realize that now. And I soon got to feeling confident. Cocky, even. Jacob was the father I'd never known. Then when I was around ten you came," he said, giving her a teasing grin, "and I even had a little sister."

Not wanting to bring up the painful subject she had come to discuss, she looked around for some means of stalling. "You've done a few more paintings since I was here last."

Jeff stepped farther back from the canvas and she saw the beginning outlines of an almost lifesize figure. It was one of the Indians he loved to paint, she saw, although so far he had merely sketched in the powerful outlines of the commanding male figure.

"I think you're really very good at it," she said slowly.

He gave her a deprecating smile. "It's a good hobby."

"Surely it's more than that. Your paintings are powerful."

He grinned, and shoved his brush into some thinner. "It's

something to do. Riding the range and paperwork for the Floating Eagle doesn't take up all my time.''

He gave her a keen glance. ''Did you come here to discuss my paintings?''

Her smile was a little sheepish. That was the wonderful thing about Jeff. He had always known what she was thinking, sometimes before she even knew herself. ''No. I wanted to talk to you about the things that are going on at the ranch.''

His blue eyes became even more alert. ''Like what?''

''Jeff, you heard what Jacob said about Brad. That he's just trying to pin something on us. But is it possible he may be right?''

Jeff's eyebrows shot up. ''Depends. Right about poaching, sure. Right about our running more cows on the forest land than we have a permit for. But right about murder? Never.''

He came toward her and took her hand in his slender fingers, delicate fingers. ''Ramsey, you know I've always thought of you as a sister. I wouldn't hurt you for the world. But maybe you should hear the truth, even if it does hurt. I agree with Jacob about Brad. He's using you.''

Her heart rebelled at his words, but she bit back a quick denial, insisting stubbornly, ''Maybe Brad's right about some things.''

Jeff's eyebrows shot up. ''You aren't falling for his honest Abe Lincoln act, are you?''

''No, I think he is obsessed about us. But you'll admit there are some strange things going on around here.''

He shrugged. ''Like what?''

''For one thing, what is Jacob so worried about? You do the paperwork—why is the ranch losing money?''

He strode briefly around the only uncluttered space, a frown on his aristrocratic features. ''It's not that much of a mystery. The price of beef is down. As usual, Jacob wants to acquire more land all the time. When you keep cattle

without fences, like we do on the national forest, some of
them are bound to stray away, or get rustled.''

"Some of the rustled ones apparently showed up at an
out-of-state sales yard. Can't anyone catch the rustlers?''

"It's tough. They can drive up in a truck to almost anyplace in the forest and have the cattle loaded and out before
any of us can stop them. Even if we saw them. Karl spends
a lot of his time riding over there, trying to catch them…''

"I wanted to talk to you about Karl," she said slowly.

At his expectant look, she raised her chin and looked
squarely into his face. "I—I think Karl may be involved
with a lot of things.'' She shuddered, but forced herself to
say the words. "Maybe even murder.''

He gave a low whistle. "That's quite an accusation, Ramsey.''

"You know yourself he poaches. And he's very quick to
shoot. Maybe Arnie caught him with a deer. Besides, I
haven't told you everything," she said stubbornly. "I told
you all that Amber threw me. I didn't tell you that the cinch
had been cut, leaving just a couple of strands. Any sharp
jolt would have broken it.''

"And Karl always brings in Amber for you," Jeff said
slowly. "You think he cut it.''

"Maybe. It fits. There was my fall on the stairs, too. Jeff,
I know I tripped over a wire, and it was too much of a
coincidence for the lights to burn out all at once.''

"Is that all?" He rubbed his slender hand across his chin,
his expression thoughtful. "It isn't proof, you know. Those
things *could* have been accidents.''

"The cinch?''

"You can't be positive it was cut. Even a new cinch
might have been defective… Besides, even if he cut it, he
might only have been trying to scare you. I heard him warn
you away from the forest, tell you to stop snooping.''

"So why doesn't he want me there?" she demanded.
"You said Karl spends a lot of time riding in the forest
looking for rustlers. Have you ever considered the possibil-

ity that he might not be looking for them because he knows where they are!''

''That's still not a lot to go on.''

At Jeff's interrogating look, she continued slowly. ''I went to the murder site, Jeff, right after Arnie was shot. I found something the sheriff overlooked.''

Jeff stiffened slightly, but said nothing and she continued. ''It was a silver conch, the kind that's on a Navajo hatband, and dropped very recently. I think it was lost by the killer. And Karl has a very new hatband. Why, unless he lost part of his old one?''

''That's stretching it a bit, I think.''

''Maybe—but I have a very strong feeling about it.''

''Who else knows about the conch?''

''Brad—I showed it to him.''

Jeff scrutinized his paint-stained hands, and she waited for his reply. Finally he sighed.

''You have made some pretty good points, Ramsey. It never occurred to me before, but I'll have to admit Karl is acting strangely.''

''What should we do? Talk to Granddad? Maybe even the sheriff?''

''With no more than we've got? It would break the old man's heart to even suspect such a thing, and if we were wrong he'd never forgive us. As for the sheriff, the Carmichaels have never run to the law with their problems.''

He was silent for several seconds, then turned to Ramsey, clasping both her hands in his. ''Let me look into it, little sister. I'll keep an eye on Karl, scout him out. If it looks like you're correct, then we'll have to think of something. But let's be sure first.''

She gave him a tremulous smile. ''Thanks, Jeff.''

He patted her briefly on the shoulder. ''And Ramsey— maybe you should remember his warning about snooping. If you're right about him, you could be in danger if you go off riding by yourself. Stay clear. Let me handle things.''

''I will,'' she replied, smiling in relief. ''After what happened with Amber, I'm not too anxious to go off by myself."

He gave her a broad wink. "At least check your cinch before you mount!"

"I will, you can depend on it!" She rose, and kissed him quickly on the cheek. "I'd better get back and see if I can round up Stevie. Although he's probably with Karl someplace," she said glumly.

"He'll be all right," Jeff said. "Karl seems crazy about him. What are you going to do for the rest of the day?"

"I'm not going anyplace, if that's what you mean."

He gave her a wicked grin. "Not even if the lawman comes calling?"

"Today I'm going to just hang around the place, and then get to bed early," she said firmly.

Jeff lifted his brush to his temple in a mock salute, then turned back to his canvas.

The figure stood well back in the barn, safe from the moonlight that flooded across the straw-covered floor. In the darkness, he was merely a deeper shadow in the surrounding gloom. Only the convulsive clenching and unclenching of his hands betrayed his agitation. His face, if one could have seen it, was expressionless, but his thoughts were seething as he looked up at the lighted window of Ramsey's room. Did she live a charmed life?

When he'd shot at her and Brad it had been meant as a warning to both of them, meant only to frighten, keep her out of the forest. When he had unscrewed the light globes and tightened the wire across the stairs, he hadn't hoped that he would be fortunate enough to kill her, but he'd thought she'd be immobilized for a while, maybe until the time for her to return to Berkeley. But there was barely a scratch! Cutting the cinch had seemed a masterstroke. Again, a fall was unlikely to result in death, but it conceivably could have. At the very least, it would shake her up, maybe make her think about shortening her stay.

None of that had happened, he thought, cursing softly. Instead, she'd just gotten in deeper with the game warden. Much too deep. He didn't think Chillicott had found out anything yet, but the man wouldn't give up.

Grinding his heel viciously in the straw, he turned back into the darkness. He couldn't wait much longer. Everything was coming to a head. He was absent from the ranch too often, and the old man was getting suspicious. He couldn't let everything he'd worked for crumble into nothing.

No. He would try again. And the next time, he wouldn't care too much whether it seemed accidental or not.

Chapter 11

Ramsey stood at the rail fence looking into the pasture where Amber grazed serenely on the lush summer grasses. By unspoken agreement, the horse had not been waiting for her in the barn, and Ramsey was ambivalent. She resented Karl's apparent assumption that she would not be riding; on the other hand, the thought of saddling up and riding alone around the ranch sent a shiver of fear along her spine.

She pressed her forehead against the cool, peeled railing, and her shoulders slumped. For the first time, she allowed herself to really feel the horror of the situation. The place she had fled to for refuge and security had actually become a quagmire of unknown danger and unseen malevolence. Something sinister and evil lurked under the open, sunny facade of the Floating Eagle—something made more frightening by the fact that it covered itself with the familiar face of someone she loved.

Although she couldn't accept anyone else in the role, the thought that the killer might be Karl was almost equally unacceptable. He was as much her uncle as though they had been related by blood. She remembered her first horse; Karl had lifted her into the saddle, his rough hands surprisingly gentle for so huge a man. They'd never had the long conversations she enjoyed with Jeff, nor the affectionate teasing she'd received from Uncle Bud. Nevertheless, he had always been there, solid and stoic as the land itself.

Where was he now, she wondered. She hadn't seen him since the summit meeting this morning. Wherever he was, Stevie was with him, she thought, a band of uneasiness tightening around her heart. Martha had informed her that the two of them had ridden off together, after Stevie had left a request for chocolate-chip cookies for his supper.

So what was she to do with herself? Her grandfather was closeted in his office, Delia was having a bad day and didn't feel like talking, even to her beloved granddaughter, and Martha had shooed her from the kitchen. If the ranch had been the benign place she had thought it, she would have had no problem whiling away a sunny afternoon. As it was, she found herself jumping at unexpected noises and shying away from shadows.

At that moment, she deeply regretted her decision to come home to the ranch. Nothing was turning out as she had expected. She had been cherishing an illusion. Were her values—home, family, loyalty—also illusion? Were all those things only confined to the illusions of childhood, alien to the real world? As soon as she helped Delia find out what was going on at the Floating Eagle, she would take Stevie and go back to Berkeley.

To make it worse, Brad's image intruded on her consciousness. She winced as she thought of the wild abandon of their lovemaking. She'd never dreamed she could respond like that—completely out of control, swept along by incredible ecstasy. If she didn't love him now, she was very close, she thought, her forehead creasing in a frown. If he weren't so obsessive about her family, if he weren't so rigid, so inflexible, so harsh in his judgments... If he loved her...

She heard the faint ring of a phone, and her pulse quickened, her intuition telling her it was Brad. At some subconscious level of her mind she knew she had been expecting him to call, and she was walking toward the house before Martha called her from the kitchen door.

"Hello." Was that tremulous voice her own?

"Ramsey?" His voice was warm and deep and, she thought, slightly hesitant. "I wanted to be sure you got home okay. Are you all right?"

"Just a few bruises," she answered, unconsciously running her hand along her hip where the soreness was still noticeable. "I'm sorry for the way everyone behaved."

"Understandable, I suppose." His tone was harsh and clipped. There was a long pause, then, "Ramsey, I'd like to see you..."

Emotions coursed through her in rampant confusion. She wanted to see him, too, wanted to see him so desperately that her throat was suddenly dry and her hand trembling on the phone. But was her grandfather right? Did Brad have ulterior motives? Besides, he was doubly dangerous now that she was nearly sure someone in her family had something to hide. Brad would ferret out her suspicions, and Jeff was right: the Carmichaels should handle their own problems.

"Ramsey?"

Perhaps it was the tentative note in his voice, so uncharacteristic of his usual confidence, that persuaded her, or it could have been the memory of the passion that had surged between them last night. Perhaps she had already made the decision on an unconscious level. In a flash, she knew she would make her own decisions about Brad. The thought of being with him, seeing the dark intensity of his face, feeling the strength and masculine energy that emanated from him in a compelling current, washed away any lingering concern about her grandfather's disapproval.

"I'd love to see you."

"Good. I thought I'd make dinner for us."

She remembered when she and Brad ate steak and salad in his apartment after following Ella and Bud to their secret tryst, and the memory of the potent attraction that had flared between them even then made her skin feel hot. It seemed ages ago, so much had happened since that afternoon.

"That sounds good. What time shall I drive in?"

"Don't be silly. When I make a date, I pick the woman up. I'll be at the ranch at five."

"Are you sure—"

"You mean someone may be waiting for me with a shotgun?" His laugh was harsh and faintly bitter. "I'll take my chances."

"I'll see you then..." Putting down the phone, Ramsey glanced at her watch. The hours between now and the time Brad would pick her up seemed to stretch to infinity.

He had never seen her in anything but jeans. Why didn't she forget all the problems between them, the inexplicable happenings at the ranch, and have a happy, carefree evening? Just a man and a woman who were attracted to each other. Who found pleasure in each other's arms. It had been years since she'd had such an evening. Even when she first knew Paul, she didn't remember having the giddy lighthearted feeling that she had now.

Humming tunelessly, she ran lightly up the stairs, mentally going over the wardrobe she had brought with her. Almost every item was casual, but she'd brought one dressy outfit just in case. Her eyes danced and she felt like singing as she pictured Brad's face when he saw her in it.

She spent a long, leisurely afternoon getting ready, amused by her ability to immerse herself in the ritual. She soaked in a bubble bath, inhaling the fragrance of lavender that rose from the steamy water, shampooed her hair, then blew it dry until it framed her face in silken gold and flowed down to her shoulders with a featherlike touch. She put on a little more makeup than usual, accentuating her eyes with shadow and a soft mascara. Her nails could use a little work, she noticed, and spent several minutes gilding them with a

clear pink polish. Holding her hand out, she surveyed it
critically, and felt pleased with the finished look of her slender fingers.

The golden tan on her legs made it possible to omit stock-
ings, she thought as she slipped into her teddy, a shimmering silk accentuated by a froth of delicate lace, colored with
just a wisp of champagne. It slid over her smooth skin like
flowing water. Then she put on the sundress that the clerk
in the exclusive shop where she'd exchanged nearly a
month's salary for it had assured her it could go equally
well to a patio party or cocktails at the Mark Hopkins.

Well, she thought, smiling to herself, it was actually going to dinner at a bleak, sparsely furnished apartment, where
it would probably look completely out of place!

Looking in the mirror, she smiled at her reflection. Of
soft royal-blue silk, the dress had delicate straps above a
fitted bodice that curved lovingly around her high breasts,
narrowed to her waist, skimmed her hips, then flared in a
wide circle to just below her knees. She stepped into a pair
of high-heeled sandals and she was ready, as inappropriately
dressed, she suspected, as anyone had ever been.

She heard the sound of the motor a few minutes before
she saw Brad's pickup come up the long driveway and she
hurried down the stairs, hoping she could meet him before
he got out of the truck. She knew his arrival wouldn't go
unnoticed by anyone who happened to be at the ranch
house, and she wanted to avoid a confrontation if she could.
She wasn't sneaking; she had a right to see Brad, but she
didn't want anyone spoiling the ebullient mood she had
been nurturing all afternoon.

The look in his eyes when he saw her walking to meet
him—surprised, shocked, admiring—made the entire afternoon worthwhile.

He took a deep breath, then gave her a wide grin. "And
I thought you were beautiful before. You're incredibly
lovely, Ramsey. That dress could get you locked up—you're
a menace!"

"I got a little tired of jeans." She smiled as he moved quickly to open the door of the pickup and boosted her inside, acutely aware of the warmth of his hand on her arm.

As he slid behind the wheel and eased the pickup back onto the road, she looked him over carefully. His dark hair was slicked back, damp as though from a recent shower; he was wearing a white short-sleeved knit shirt that accentuated his bronzed skin, and well-tailored chino trousers. He looked fresh and handsome and so sexy she could hardly get her breath.

He grinned at her scrutiny. "Do I pass? Sometimes, when we were kids, I wondered what I should wear if we ever had a date."

"I didn't think men worried about things like that—at least Idaho men."

"Men may not. A kid does, if he's insecure and grasping for the moon."

"If this is a date, aren't we getting things a little bit backward?"

He reached for her hand and stroked her fingers gently, sending little jolts of electricity along her arm and down her spine. "You mean because we jumped directly to the main course, and bypassed the preliminaries? I see no reason to be a slave to convention!" His eyes, usually dark and somber, were dancing with merriment and she felt a sense of relief. The man could laugh after all.

They were quiet, letting the miles flash by, and Ramsey felt no need to break the comfortable silence. It was as though they shared a rapport, which, for the moment, made words unnecessary. She contented herself with looking first at his sharply defined profile, then glancing out at the curtain of evergreens that lined the graveled road.

Suddenly she sat up straighter, her desultory glance sharpening. She didn't think she'd been over this road before, at least not recently. She shot Brad a quick look.

"This isn't the way to Tyler."

"No, it isn't," he agreed.

"I thought you said we were having dinner at your place."

"We are."

"But—" She broke off her protest, watching the half smile on Brad's face. He was up to something, but he wasn't going to tell her what it was until he was good and ready.

Suddenly he braked and brought the pickup to a stop on the shoulder of the road. Startled, Ramsey looked all around, but saw nothing.

"What is it?"

He didn't reply, but slipped quickly out of the seat and walked a few feet up the road. She watched in disbelief as he herded several baby grouse who had been filing down the middle of the gravel track back into the bushes, then jumped back in the truck.

"What was that all about?" She lifted a quizzical eyebrow.

He looked slightly embarrassed. "Just didn't want those little ones to get run over. They don't always have enough sense to get out of the way, and this road is used by logging trucks. Those truckers don't brake for much of anything."

As they drove back onto the road, she studied his face, thinking of the complexity of the man. Harsh, intense, a man who could nurse a grudge for years. And a man who would stop to be sure some helpless little birds weren't run over.

She was still musing when he turned off the road onto a narrow lane and drove through a gate framed with mammoth peeled cedar poles, then down a little lane, finally stopping in front of a weathered frame building.

"Here we are."

"I can see that. But where are we?" Ramsey gave him a questioning glance, then looked back at the house. It was obviously old, but it had been freshly painted, and the roof was new. Much smaller than the ranch house at the Floating Eagle, it was nevertheless a good-size place, with tall windows, an impressive entrance and a veranda running along the front of the two-storied structure.

He didn't answer as he jumped down and walked around the pickup to open the door. "Come on. I'd like you to see a little of the place before it gets dark."

Deciding he would talk when he wanted to, Ramsey followed him on a tour. It was obviously a working ranch. The barn was snug and full of hay; the brown gelding that Brad rode raised liquid eyes, then lowered his head to the grass in the enclosed pasture; they passed a spot that might once have been a garden but now was overrun with weeds. She was getting the picture.

"This is your place?"

"Yep." Even the brusqueness of his reply didn't hide the pride in his eyes.

"I thought you lived in town."

"Just during the days when I'm working. I spend every spare minute I can here."

She thought of her surprise at the bleakness of his apartment; obviously Brad spent all his effort and energy here.

"Now let's go inside."

He opened the front door and ushered her into the house, his shoulders tense as he awaited her reaction. They walked down a narrow hall, then into a large living room. Ramsey caught her breath. If she had wondered about Brad's taste, she no longer did.

The room was obviously old; the walls were of white-washed planks, rising to high ceilings that are seldom seen in newer houses. The floor was of planking also, worn to a high sheen by frequent washings, and was covered by a scattering of bear rugs so luxurious she wanted to slip off her shoes and wriggle her toes in their softness. A fieldstone fireplace along one wall was topped by a heavy stone mantel, and a huge copper kettle glowed on the wide stone hearth.

Although the room itself might have been from another century, the furnishings were not. An eclectic mix, the antiques shared space with clean-lined modern, a large comfortable sofa, an arrangement of soft chairs. An oil painting, a brilliant representation of a sunset over a mountain lake, dominated one wall. Everything combined to give an impression of warmth and solidity and strength.

Ramsey sank down on the sofa. "I don't know what to say."

He was watching her closely, his eyes more vulnerable than she had ever seen them. "Do you like it? I spend a good deal of my spare time here, fixing it up."

"Love it. It has such a warm, lived-in feeling. But I had no idea—"

"I don't talk about the place much," he said, moving to pour her a drink from a bottle of white wine that had been waiting on ice. "It's a small ranch, as ranches go around here. But a small ranch is all I could afford on my salary. I'm hoping to expand, get a few more horses. I'm sticking to horses," he continued, pouring himself a glass and then coming over to sit beside her. "I think there's a good market for them—and I have to admit I like horses better than cows."

"You're full of surprises," she murmured. "What about your job as game warden?"

"Oh, I'll keep it," he said. "I enjoy it; it's what I want to do, and it brings in cash. I'll just go at the ranch little by little." He rose abruptly, as though he regretted saying so much. "Are you ready for dinner?"

She followed him into the kitchen, wondering what other surprises he might have up his sleeve. The kitchen, she saw, hadn't received the attention of the living room, and was quite dated, but still functional. If she lived here, she would certainly get rid of that stove and— Quickly, she squelched the thought. Whatever brought anything like that to mind?

"I fixed everything this afternoon; hope you like it." Brad opened the oven and took out several covered dishes, which he carried a few steps to the tiny formal dining room and placed on the table.

Ramsey glanced at the table setting, then quickly took another look. The linen cloth was obviously old, the china delicate and ornate; the silverware, heavy and old-fashioned, matched the silver candlesticks.

Brad grinned at her expression. "You didn't think a bachelor would have that kind of stuff? It's my grandmother's. What you're looking at represents about all Mom was able to save. She probably wouldn't have saved that, if she hadn't hid it. Near the end, Dad managed to pawn just about everything that wasn't nailed down." His matter-of-fact tone couldn't quite hide the pain she saw flash for a moment in his eyes. She realized that for Brad, accustomed as he was to hiding emotion, even this much of an explanation was uncharacteristic.

Afterward, Ramsey never was quite sure what she ate, although she had a vague remembrance that the dinner was delicious. She was much too aware of Brad sitting across from her, the candles throwing light across the high planes of his face, deepening the shadows so that he looked remote and mysterious. What kind of man was he? Her memory of him as a boy told her nothing. Which was real—the hard, inflexible side he presented to the world, or the open, vulnerable man she occasionally glimpsed?

They talked for a while of impersonal matters, but it seemed to Ramsey that two conversations were going on. Body was talking to body, sexual currents were flowing between them with compelling intensity and the atmosphere had a brooding, waiting quality that made it difficult to concentrate on anything but the man across from her. It was as though both of them knew what the evening would bring, had known all along, and were prolonging the interval, both anticipating the inevitable encounter.

"You love this place, don't you?" she said softly.

"Always have."

"Always? I got the impression you'd only had it a year or two."

He looked at her as though weighing his words, and when he spoke the bitterness was back in his voice. "*I've* only had it a few years; my grandfather homesteaded it. Then it was my father's.''

"But I thought you said your family lived in town."

"We did—after Dad lost everything."

Getting information was like pulling teeth, but she wasn't giving up now. She had a feeling that she was nearing the crux of Brad's bitterness and anger. "How did he lose it?"

He shrugged. "A combination of things. Low beef prices. Poor judgment on a loan from the bank. Other people's cattle breaking the fences and eating the forage."

Her breath caught in her throat. "Carmichael cows?"

He shrugged. "Finally Dad couldn't pay his taxes. The bank wouldn't extend the loan. He could have used a little help, but instead old Jacob enlarged the Floating Eagle; he bought the place for taxes."

His words, spoken without apparent emotion, dropped like stones in her heart. This was the answer. This was the reason Brad hated them. This was what he had brooded over for years, until the need for revenge took precedence over everything else. Her heart grieved for the young boy, torn from the place he loved, seeing his father kill himself before his eyes. He had to blame someone—

"But surely you can't blame Jacob entirely," she said slowly. "It was business..."

"And anything is justified in the name of business, right? Of course, I'm not sure how much Jacob had to do with the bank refusing an extension on Dad's loan—he does have a good friend at the bank."

"Jacob's always been honest!"

"Maybe." His lips twisted in a sardonic smile. "Anyway, we moved out and got a place in town. Dad tried working at the mill, but he didn't seem to have much heart for it. His drinking got worse..." His voice trailed away, and Ramsey was silent, not wanting to break in on the haunting look of pain in Brad's eyes. Then he straightened briskly. "That's about it, I guess. He died soon after that."

"I'm so sorry." Ramsey felt such tenderness that she wanted to rush to him, hold him against her breast until his anguish was gone, but she didn't dare. He would reject it as pity. "Anyway, you got the place back," she said.

His dark eyes glinted. "Yes, I did. Old Jacob ran onto a few hard times himself, and I managed to buy it back for only about double what he paid for it," he said dryly.

She couldn't sit still any longer. Pushing back her chair, she rose from the table and crossed over behind him, placing her hands on his shoulders and laying her head gently against his dark hair. She had to chase away those shadows that haunted him. "Brad, let's forget about them. My family. Arnie Parkins. Let's forget everything for now."

He half turned and covered her hand with his. Still holding her, he rose from his chair and faced her, slowly pulling her against his body until they were pressed tightly together, chest against chest, thigh against thigh. His breath was hot on her cheek, she felt the pounding of his heart, the hardness and rigidity of his muscles, as his eyes probed hers with silent intensity. A question passed between them, an answer was given.

"You look so right in this house, Ramsey," he whispered. "I've wanted for so long to see you in my home, make love to you in my bed."

"I want that, too." She met his gaze fearlessly.

"Do you know what it means? We aren't being swept away this time; it has to be something we both want. Will you have regrets?"

She gave him a tremulous smile. "I won't know that until later, will I?" She wouldn't, she thought. If they never had anything else, she would always see this time as one pure crystal moment in eternity.

"Oh, my sweet darling. If you regret anything, doubt anything, it won't be the strength of my desire for you. I feel like I'm dying of thirst and you're cool spring water." He nuzzled her neck, filling his lungs with her fragrance, then caught her lips in a long, lingering kiss. Finally, with a shudder that seemed to run through his entire body, he moved slightly away. Immediately she felt his loss and instinctively pressed closer.

"If your knees are as weak as mine are, I don't think we should be standing here," he murmured.

"What do you suggest?" She knew her voice was as choked as his had been.

In reply, he bent swiftly and lifted her in his arms. She let her head drift against his chest, all her senses taking him in; the hard muscles of his chest against her cheek, the warm, musky scent of his moist skin, the throb of his pulse in the hollow of his throat, which echoed through her own body. Eyes closed, she smiled dreamily as he carried her down a narrow hall, kicked open a door with his booted foot, then deposited her gently on a bed.

He lay alongside her, his hand gently pushing back the hair from her flushed face, and he smiled softly. "We shouldn't be mussing up that pretty dress."

"Then I guess we'll have to take it off." She stared boldly up into his eyes. This was no seduction; she was an equal partner. Her skin was heated, desirous of his touch, but there was no hurry. She wanted everything, every nuance of sensation and pleasure that could be tasted on the way to fulfillment.

As though tasting her through his fingertips, Brad slowly trailed his fingers over her cheek, lingering on her full, slightly parted lips, then down to where her pulse beat strongly in the hollow of her throat. Gently he hooked one finger under the strap of her dress and slipped it off one creamy shoulder, kissing the spot where it had been, then removed the other, his hand brushing lightly against the tops of her partially exposed breasts.

"I feel like I'm unwrapping a Christmas present," he said huskily as he traced a line down the warm, moist valley between her tender breasts. "A wonderful, incredible Christmas present."

"You obviously aren't the kind who tears off the wrappings," she said, her voice as husky as his.

"True." He lifted his head to smile at her, and she nearly gasped at the raw passion in his eyes. "I did that before. This time I want to savor you, sweetheart, kiss you, caress you, every inch, every beautiful part of you. I want you to want me so much you'll forget everything else."

He drew her dress down over her breasts, unzipped the closure with maddening slowness, and Ramsey raised herself to help him slip it over her hips, leaving only the silk teddy to make a teasing pretense of covering her form.

"I've been wondering all evening what was under the dress," he said, running his hands over the shimmering silk, then slipping the lacy garment down over her legs and tossing it lightly away. "I'd have guessed nothing."

She raised herself and ran her hand under his shirt, feeling the contraction of his muscles along his back. With a moan, he pulled her up against his chest, and she was achingly aware of the texture of his shirt rubbing against her sensitive nipples. His kiss was long and deep and sent such spasms of desire through her that she could only cling to him helplessly.

He lay her back gently on the pillow and straightened up to strip off his clothes, then stood for a moment poised beside the bed, looking down into her face. Her eyes widened as she took him in, every inch of him, from his proud dark head to his long, hard-muscled legs, and heat expanded from her innermost center, fanning out to color her skin a flushed pink, moisten her thighs with desire. My God, he was beautiful.

He knelt beside her, stroking her body in long, slow movements, learning every inch of her with his hands, his lips, as she surged mindlessly and urgently against him.

"I want to be sure I can recognize you in the dark," he whispered teasingly. "No woman but you could possibly have such a long, sweet curve to your hip—there—or such a delicious mound—there."

She ran her hand down his ridged abdomen to tangle her fingers in the secret darkness of his springy hair, searching blindly for the rigid core of his masculinity, feeling a wild, triumphant thrill as she found it. "I never knew— Oh, Brad, Brad…"

But he was in no hurry. He was a gentle, confident lover, leading her along paths of sensuality she hadn't known existed. He inflamed her with his touch until every cell of her body reached for him in fierce and desperate need, every nerve ending cried out for him. She knew from his labored breathing, his husky endearments, his rigid and straining body, that he was as aroused as she, but he was taking them both to the very brink before they plunged into the maelstrom.

Finally, when she was just a seething mass of desire, he apparently could control himself no longer. With the sure confidence of a prince entering his own kingdom, he joined them together and they began the long, slow, age-old dance, culminating finally in simultaneous cries of ecstasy and fulfillment.

As he fell against her, she barely heard his incoherent words gasped into the moist valley between her heaving breasts. "Oh, Ramsey. Beautiful Ramsey. No one can take this away. I will remember this forever."

Drained and panting, they lay in a tangle of arms and legs as the tide ebbed and exhaustion followed. Ramsey was left with an excruciating feeling of love and tenderness. She heard his low words, felt his lips gentle on her cooling skin and snuggled closer. How could her body contain the enormity of her feelings?

Finally, with his dark head resting on her shoulder, his body relaxed and she knew he was half-asleep. She turned to nestle against his body, ready to drift off, too, but something nagged at her, intruded into the perfection of the moment. She loved him, of course. He had insinuated himself deep into her heart. She knew that now, although she had no idea what could ever come of it.

It was no longer just his obsession with bringing her family to justice that bothered her. From what she was beginning to suspect, Brad was right about them. It was something else, something more intrinsic to his character. Even in love, he had held something back, she thought. Not sexually. Oh, no, he had withheld nothing sexually. Her body still sang with the memory of his touch. But she had sensed something dark, some integral part of himself withheld. Even in their most abandoned moment, he had never mentioned love. She had a sinking feeling that he never would.

She remembered the words he gasped as ecstasy gripped him, words that seemed torn from him, wrenching away his protective cover. "I'll remember this forever," he had said.

She felt as though a cold wind had blown across her heated body, and she pulled the sheet up over the two of them. There was something in the tone of his voice, some sorrow in the way he moaned the words. "I'll always remember you."

That sounded suspiciously like goodbye.

Chapter 12

"So you were out with the Chillicott boy." Old Jacob's expression radiated disapproval as he stood ramrod straight in the doorway of Ramsey's room, his eagle eyes missing nothing as she straightened out her bed, then picked up the blue silk dress that she had flung casually over a chair last night and hung it in the closet. "It's time we had our talk, Ramsey."

Ramsey almost made a sharp retort, then shrugged, keeping her head averted so he wouldn't see the tears that constantly threatened. If only her grandfather knew how little he had to worry about. After Brad had brought her home last night she had tossed and turned in bed until the eastern sky was streaked with light, alternately thrilling to the memory of Brad's caresses that had seared deep into her soul, and chilled by the recollection of how little of his inner self he had revealed. Surely his taking her to the ranch at all, a place obviously dear to him, meant he had strong feelings for her. But he had also told her how his dad lost the ranch, revealing for the first time the basis for his unrelenting vendetta. Had he done that to warn her that anything they shared was only temporary?

Certainly the intimacy she and Brad had achieved last night when they found ecstasy in each other's arms hadn't lasted long. He had brought her home just before daylight, as remote and reserved as ever, although she thought she detected a deep sadness in his expression. Confused and heartsick, she had accepted his taciturnity; certain now that she loved him, she suspected it was best for both if they pretended that what was between them was mere sexual attraction. Lust. Whatever Brad might feel for her, he was apparently determined that although she might be in his arms, she would never be in his life. God, how it hurt.

"Let's go to the office," Jacob said, turning and starting down the hallway without waiting for her reply. Ramsey nodded at his back and followed the old man down the stairs. He was being unusually terse, even for him. Was this the serious discussion Jacob had promised, or was she going to get a lecture about the dangers of seeing Brad?

To her surprise, the old man shut the door firmly behind them; this obviously wasn't an open meeting, she thought, suddenly uneasy. It wasn't like Jacob to exclude Jeff and Karl, and the omission made her apprehensive.

"Grandpa—about Brad, I—"

He raised a hand to silence her and sat down heavily behind his desk, waving her to the side chair. "Never mind Chillicott for now, Ramsey. I don't think you should be seeing the boy, but I know you. You're loyal to your family. You won't do anything to hurt us."

His rebuke was almost gentle, and Ramsey gave him a quick glance. He was frowning thoughtfully, as though searching for just the right words.

"Ramsey," he finally said, "I wanted to wait to talk to you about this until I cleared up a few things. But I decided it had better be now, before you start thinking about going back to California."

Her pulse quickened. Was Jacob going to open up at last and tell her what was worrying him so?

"What things did you want to clear up?"

He sighed. "You've suspected things weren't right around here ever since you came. Maybe Delia put you on to it; I know she's upset. Or maybe it's obvious to anybody. You've tried to talk to me, but I put you off, thinking I could work it out myself. But things are getting worse, sweetheart, and I don't know—I'm beginning to think—"

He broke off and Ramsey waited, letting him tell it in his own way.

"The Floating Eagle has been losing money for years. At first, just a little, but more and more lately. I can't figure out how—the money just isn't there. Cattle rustling has increased, too, no matter how hard Karl and Jeff try to catch the thieves. I just got a call that some more of my missing cattle have turned up in Nevada."

"But how can they sell them there? Don't they check brands?"

"The honest ones. There are ways around anything, if you look hard enough."

He twisted a pencil absently in one hand. "Then my banker called. He wants me to come to town today. Says it's urgent." He swung his pale blue eyes back to Ramsey. "I wanted to solve these problems, get everything squared away, so when I talked to you I could offer you a ranch without encumbrances."

He half smiled at Ramsey's startled look, and held up his hand to silence her protest. "The Floating Eagle means everything to me, Ramsey. I want it to continue on in the family, and I've been worrying about what will happen to it when I'm gone."

Ramsey's mouth hung open in complete surprise; this was the last thing she had expected—the last thing she wanted.

"I always supposed you'd split it," she floundered. "Uncle Bud, Jeff, Karl, me—"

"I don't want to break it up. And can you imagine Bud

running a ranch?'' he said dryly. ''The boy hasn't got the backbone of a snake. The ranch will always be his home, but it will take someone else to run it.''

''Jeff? Karl?''

''Karl's a good hand, but he's no manager. Jeff—'' A puzzled look came over the old man's face. ''Jeff's got a good brain, but I feel, sometimes, he's thinking about something else.'' He shrugged, and gave her a direct look. ''Anyway, you're my granddaughter. Stevie loves it here, he's a born rancher. If you'll stay, make this your home, I'll deed the ranch to you and Stevie.''

''But what about the others!''

''I love them all, but you're my granddaughter. Stevie's my great-grandson.''

''I never heard you make that distinction before,'' she said slowly. ''I always thought Jeff and Karl were as much family as Bud and I.''

The old man shrugged. ''Blood's blood. Anyway, there's no need for any change. They can live here, get room and board and a salary, like they always have.''

She jumped up and paced agitatedly about the small room. ''It's impossible, Grandpa. You know it. I can't live here. I have my own life, a job I love—''

His keen old eyes fixed hers with dry humor. ''Do you love California all that much? I had a feeling you were getting to like ranch life.''

She took a deep breath and sat back down. She hadn't thought about Berkeley or her job there for days, and her entire past life suddenly seemed slightly unreal, as though it had happened to another person in another lifetime. Had it been as perfect as she'd thought, or had she been living out Paul's ideal for her—a professional woman in the rarified atmosphere of academia? She thought of the politics, the intrigue, the soul-killing pace...

Oh, she enjoyed part of it, certainly. The teaching, the contact with students, but there had been stress also, the constant pressure to publish...

"I kinda thought you came home to search for your roots," the old man said slyly. "Isn't that the jargon?"

"This was never meant to be more than a vacation," she said firmly.

"Everybody's got a place where he belongs," the old man said just as firmly. "Sometimes you have to look a while to find it, go someplace else till you recognize it. I knew this was my place the minute I saw this little valley. It wasn't much then. I put my heart and soul into it, building it into the biggest spread in the county. Only part of me can die, as long my family has the Floating Eagle. I didn't build it up to have my heirs sell it, either." His old eyes were predator sharp. "It's your place, too, Ramsey."

"Grandpa…"

"What about Stevie? He takes to ranching like a duck to water. You brought us a scared, angry little kid. He's blossomed into a happy, independent boy. This is his home, he's found the place where he belongs." He gave her a shrewd look. "Do you have the right to deprive him of his inheritance?"

"No fair! You could leave it to Stevie no matter what I do."

"Nope. He's got to live here, grow up here. Nothing else is any good. Then there's Delia and me," the old man continued slowly. "We're getting old. We need you, Ramsey. You left us once before, was it so much better? Aren't you ready to acknowledge this is where *you* belong?"

"Don't try to work on my sympathy," she said dryly. "You're made of rock, Grandpa."

"Maybe. But even rock crumbles." For a moment, the old man did look mortal, and Ramsey forced herself to hold back an automatic sympathetic gesture. He was used to having his own way, but this time he was asking too much. It was true she had come home to find her roots, to rebuild her shattered life and to find safety and security for Stevie. Perhaps, as Jacob said, the thought of staying had even been in the back of her mind. That was before she realized you can't go home again.

She looked at Jacob's time-battered face, and felt a catch in her heart. She'd accepted love from him and Delia all her life, taking it as her due. Did she owe a debt? And what about Stevie? For the first time, she wondered how he would react when it was time to leave the ranch. Would he resent her?

Sensing her ambivalence, her grandfather reached over and patted her shoulder. "Think about it, Ramsey."

In the silence that followed his words, Ramsey thought she heard a soft shuffling at the door, then the sound of footsteps. She wondered who had paused there, but dismissed the thought. Probably one of the men had come to see Jacob and, finding the door closed, had gone away.

Jacob rose from his desk, terminating the discussion. "I've got to go now, sweetheart. I'm driving to Nevada again, and I'll stop by the bank on my way back. We'll talk more later."

She started to leave, her hand on the doorknob, but at his next words she turned slowly to face him, stiffening her spine and raising her chin.

"Ramsey," he said softly, "about Chillicott..."

She might have known she wouldn't get off so easily!

"What about him?"

"Watch out for him, girl. He's not just an old school friend, he's dangerous. That boy's got a one-track mind. He's tough and he's smart, and not many people will ever get the best of him. And he's out to bring us down."

Incredibly, she thought she detected a trace of admiration in the old man's words, but she responded quietly.

"The way he sees it, he's just doing his job. A man was killed. Besides, maybe he has reason not to trust us. You did buy the Chillicott ranch away from his dad."

Jacob snorted. "A weakling. And a drunk. The boy's got more guts than his dad ever had. Besides, he's got the ranch back now."

"At quite a profit for you."

"I didn't get this ranch by being a namby-pamby!" Jacob turned and looked out the window, and when he spoke he seemed to be thinking out loud. "He's going to cause us trouble. Things are changing around here, Ramsey. I'm getting old—I'm not sure of anything anymore. The rustling, Arnie Parkins killed—I just don't want you hurt—stay away from him."

Ramsey slipped out the door and closed it softly behind her, not sure he even noticed she was gone.

Head down, lips pursed in concentration as she thought over the recent conversation, she nearly ran into Uncle Bud walking down the hall from the kitchen. A thought flashed through her mind. Had he been listening at the door? She as quickly dismissed the idea and gave him a warm smile.

"Hello, Bud. Just had breakfast? I've missed you the past few days; I hardly ever see you around. What are you up to?"

He gave her a sweet smile. "Yes to your first question, I just had a pot of Martha's good coffee. And what have I been doing? You may have noticed that the ranch gets along very well without me, Ramsey." He gave her a deprecating smile. "I have things to do in town."

"Why do you stay here, Bud?" she said impulsively, remembering her grandfather's gruff dismissal of his younger son. "Just a room of your own, and they all ignore you. You can't be happy."

"Happy? I suppose not. Although I really do love the ranch." His tone was momentarily wistful, then he gave her a fond look. "You're right, I should go. But there are reasons why I can't right now."

"What reasons?" she demanded. She'd had more than enough evasion from everyone. Someone was going to have to level with her. She thought she knew all about Uncle Bud's reasons, but maybe he could explain away her doubts. Karl fit her perception of a villain much better than her uncle, but Uncle Bud certainly had plenty of things to hide!

He moved closer and ran his hand gently over her hair. "I always loved your hair, Ramsey. You were such a happy, sunny little girl, after you got over being scared of your shadow. Don't let them change you. Don't let them take over your life."

"What do you mean?"

"I saw Brad bring you home last night—or was it this morning?" His smile was fond and teasing; then his mouth tightened, and he gave her a quick squeeze. "I also saw you come out of the old man's torture chamber. I suppose he was telling you to stay away from Chillicott."

How had the conversation switched from Bud's concerns to hers? As she opened her mouth to reply, his embrace became almost painful. "Don't let him do it, Ramsey. Don't let him ruin your life. He's good at that."

Before she could think of a reply, he released her and moved off quickly down the hall.

Brad twisted in his chair, propped his feet up on the desk and stared morosely at the phone. All he had to do was pick it up and he would hear her voice: breathless, husky, with the little tremor that turned him to jelly. Not that he had far to go before turning into jelly. He'd never know how he managed to allow her to go home last night, even though he'd realized that if he had kept her at the ranch the whole bunch of Carmichaels would have been swarming over him like killer bees.

All he had to do was pick up the phone. And he couldn't do it.

He had been right in his fantasies about how perfectly she would fit into his ranch. Even in that incredible dress that accentuated her elegance and serenity, even as it reminded him of the gulf between them, she'd been right at home. And without the dress! At the thought of her naked and glowing in his arms, he caught his breath and his fingernails bit into his palms.

He knew at his gut level that things were coming to a

head. Tension was building, and he fully expected some Carmichael to slip up and make a mistake that would allow him to bring him to justice. When that happened, things would be over for him and Ramsey. He had wanted to make everything perfect for what he was afraid might be the last time between them; he had tried to orchestrate a slow, sensual evening, lingering at every stop, culminating in love-making that he could remember through the cold, gray days that were sure to come.

Had he merely succeeded in binding himself to her with bands of steel? He wasn't so sure anymore that her response was just momentary sexual passion, either. How could she respond as fervently as she had, unless she felt something much, much deeper? For a moment last night, when she had cried out his name in an ecstasy of fulfillment, he had been nearly sure she loved him.

As he loved her, he admitted. As he always had. He had wanted to tell her so the first time they made love, and last night it was all he could do to keep from pouring out his heart. Only a lifelong habit of guarding his emotions had saved him. He wasn't so sure that her response to his confession would have been negative, either. He could feel her turmoil. Already she seemed to have a few questions about her family. She had defied them to come with him. She hadn't told them about the cut cinch. At times he had caught an uneasy, evasive look when she talked about her relatives. Maybe, in spite of everything he'd ever believed, dreams did come true. Maybe things would work out…

At the click of the door he lifted his head and saw Sheriff Thorenson walk into the room. The man strolled in and plunked himself solidly in the chair in front of the desk.

"Hi, Brad. Busy?" The sheriff's eyes took in Brad's posture, scanned the pile of papers in the in-basket, then went significantly to the bare out-tray, and he lifted a sardonic eyebrow. "Interrupting your paperwork?"

Brad gave him a wry smile. "As you've obviously noticed, I'm not doing much of anything."

"Been out riding lately?"

"Some."

"Anything I should know about?"

Brad frowned. In spite of the fact that his thoughts had focused most often on Ramsey, he'd kept his eyes open, and he'd had reports. A discreet inquiry to an old—and nosy—friend had revealed that Bud Carmichael was seeing Ella Parkins almost every day. Several people had seen Jeff driving through Tyler on numerous occasions, and word had come from a ranger that Karl had been seen several times riding on forest service land. They were all on the move, much more so than usual. None of it was necessarily damaging, though, and he was no further along in his inquiry into Arnie's death than ever.

He swung his feet to the floor, rose and came around to lean against the corner of the desk, looking down into the sheriff's florid face. "You still think Arnie was killed by a poacher? Just a random hunter?"

Thorenson leaned back in his chair and stuck his thumbs under his belt as he took a long breath. "No. No, I don't. I'm beginning to see it your way, Brad," he said softly.

Brad jerked himself erect, his eyes never leaving the sheriff. "Why? I thought you believed I was just following a grudge."

"Oh, I never thought that," Thorenson said smoothly. "I just didn't see a bit of evidence against them. I still don't have anything real hard, but a few things don't add up."

He rose and paced a few steps, lips pursed, a frown on his heavy face. "I've had a report from Jim Clark, the sheriff over in Camp County. Seems like there have been a lot of trucks coming out of the forest on some old logging roads that are hardly ever traveled. Unmarked trucks. Could carry cattle, though. And Karl Powers seems to be awfully fascinated by public land—he's riding there nearly every day, I hear. I don't see how he could help running into them. But you probably know that."

When Brad didn't answer, he continued. "I put out a few

more feelers—Carmichael cows have been showing up in sales yards in at least two other states.''

Brad gave a low whistle. ''Good explanation of why the ranch is losing money.''

''But not the only reason,'' Sheriff Thorenson said grimly. ''The banker, Old Man Tanner, got back from vacation yesterday. Seems he spent several hours going over some records at the bank. Then he called Jacob, pretty upset. Wanted to see the old man right away.''

Brad raised an eyebrow. ''Do you have the place bugged?''

Thorenson grinned. ''No need to. Not with my niece, Betty, working there.''

''Did she tell you why he wanted Jacob to come in to the bank?'' Brad asked sardonically.

''She couldn't hear everything,'' Thorenson said cheerfully. ''Just that something was haywire with the balance. Some missing money.''

Brad's look was respectful. ''I hope I'm never in a position where I have to try to put something over on you.''

''Don't try it, boy.'' Thorenson's grin broadened. ''I just stopped in to tell you I'm driving over to Nevada to check on those cows. See if I can get a lead on the rustlers. You keep your eyes open around here.''

''How do you figure it?''

''Don't, yet. Lot of possibilities, but to me they point to an inside-job at Floating Eagle. Maybe Arnie wasn't jumped by a poacher. Maybe he caught somebody rustling, and the deer was a smoke screen.''

''But which one—''

''Maybe we'll know more when I get back. I shouldn't be over a couple of days.''

Brad stood silently until the door clicked behind the sheriff. Then he picked up the phone, hesitated and put it back in its cradle.

His feeling that Ramsey was in danger was stronger than ever, but his hands were tied. If he told her his latest suspicions, he might just put her in more danger; she wasn't the kind who could dissemble, and if, as he suspected, someone there was poised on the verge of further violence, that might just push them over. He couldn't just burst in on her and demand that she leave the Floating Eagle, either. Even if she, too, had her suspicions, she would undoubtedly insist on handling things herself.

A muscle twitched in his jaw. That seemed to be an attitude all Carmichaels shared; they would handle their own problems, without recourse to the law. He doubted that Ramsey would deviate from that tradition unless he had some hard proof.

Well, it was up to him to get it. He had let Ramsey divert him from that necessity, but perhaps it wasn't all bad. There had been too many "accidents," and things were piling up. Someone must be getting spooked by now, and if he just kept cool, they would smoke themselves out. He just had to be constantly alert, run down every lead no matter how minor, and before long, Arnie's murderer would be where he deserved to be.

In jail.

And, he thought, his head sinking down into his hands and his stomach churning, that someone would be Ramsey's relative. Someone she loved. He doubted that she would shield a murderer, but the fact that he, Brad, was instrumental in harming someone she cared for so deeply and trusted would always be there between them. She might even understand that he had to do it—but it would be forever between them.

Damn, how he loved that woman! It was a constant, aching pain in his gut. Since he'd first seen her, when he was just a boy, she'd spoiled him for anyone else. She had been his fixed star as he tried to better himself, reach the goals he had set so early in life. He wondered if everything he'd ever done, ever accomplished, hadn't been for her.

Then she'd come back, a lovely, desirable woman, and

he had even allowed himself to hope a little, to dream that she wasn't as unattainable as he'd thought.

He'd been kidding himself; he could never have her. She might understand that he had to do his duty, but she would always believe there might be something more behind it. She might, intellectually, even agree that justice should be served. But neither of them would ever be able to overcome the fact that he would be the instrument of that justice. He could never be her husband.

Could he drop it, then? Turn everything over to the sheriff? Thorenson seemed to be going in the right direction. Then he thought of Arnie, gunned down just for doing his job, and he gritted his teeth in anger. He had to do what he could.

Damn the old bastard! The man pacing back and forth in the shadows of the barn pounded his clenched fist again and again into his open palm, his face a mottled mask of anger and hate. His head felt as though it would explode. All these years of slaving and kowtowing, and now Jacob would give the Floating Eagle to the woman and her brat!

It was a good thing he'd seen them go in the office and shut the door and had listened in. It jolted him to action, speeded up the timetable. He'd been fooling around, waiting for just the right time and place to eliminate her, maybe even hesitating a little, hoping she'd get scared and go back to where she belonged. Now he had no choice. It had to be done before the bastard wrote his new will.

The old man's assurance that nothing would change when Ramsey inherited the ranch seared into his brain like a hot branding iron. Believing that things would change had been the only thing that had kept him going for years. He'd made his plans, and everything he'd ever wanted was close to culmination. Nothing was going to interfere.

The hot flush of rage ebbed, leaving a cold, purposeful

anger. Killing her wasn't going to be enough, wasn't going to make him safe. The kid would still be around. He'd have to take care of him, too.

Chapter 13

Ramsey waited until her grandfather's car disappeared into the distance, then walked back into the ranch house, faced with the prospect of another long day. Ordinarily she would have loved to be out riding, or working in the rose garden, or talking with Delia, but every activity she could think of palled. So many things had to be settled before she could immerse herself in happy routine.

Perhaps she should discuss her suspicions with Delia. Immediately she rejected the notion. Delia was too frail to bear the burden of additional worry. In fact, after alerting Ramsey to her fears, she had settled back contentedly, seeming to feel that she had done everything necessary by placing the problem in Ramsey's hands.

She thought of taking Stevie fishing, and the impulse triggered recollections of Brad. He had been so good with the boy, and after his initial hostility, Stevie had liked him, too. The promised fishing trip had not yet materialized, although she had to admit both Stevie and Brad had been fully engaged in other things. Then she rejected the idea of fishing, too; right now, Stevie was out in the corral patiently teaching a yearling colt to lead with a halter, and he would probably consider a visit from his mother an interruption. Brad—who knew what Brad was doing?

She walked to a window and drew aside the curtain, remembering the day she had returned to the Floating Eagle and Brad had driven up into the front yard. Recalling the instantaneous shock of sexual awareness, she sighed. At the time she had explained the immediate attraction by loneliness, vulnerability, but now she knew it had been much more than that. What might have happened between them if Arnie Parker had not been murdered? Could Brad have managed to overcome his aversion to the Carmichaels?

Her grandfather's disclosures had added to her anxieties. The cattle rustling apparently wasn't a random, sometime thing as she had supposed. It was well organized and effective, and the Floating Eagle was suffering from it. She wondered, too, about the problem at the bank. Until these mysteries were solved, she couldn't think clearly about her grandfather's offer to will the Floating Eagle to her and Stevie.

She started to let the curtain fall, then hesitated as a horse and rider left the barn and cantered out into the open field and along the trail that led into the mountains. Karl, as usual riding toward national forest land. She watched him, an ironic smile on her face. Who was doing the chores around the place? She'd heard a car leave earlier this morning, and suspected that Uncle Bud was keeping his daily rendezvous, and she hadn't seen Jeff for hours, although she'd made a quick check of the office and his studio. Whatever the men were doing, they apparently weren't interested in day-to-day ranching.

Suddenly she stiffened as the impulse hit her; there was one thing she could do. She had been passive too long, and although she had planned to investigate Arnie's murder, that had been before she had begun to suspect someone in her family was involved, before the series of accidents that she was certain were meant to frighten, if not seriously harm, her. But now she was alone and it was a perfect opportunity to search the house for anything that might give her a clue.

What did she have to go on? Everything that had happened pointed to the involvement of someone at the Floating Eagle ranch, but aside from vague speculations concerning cattle rustling, money problems, which she didn't see tying into the murder, did she have anything concrete?

There was the silver conch, the link that had evidently been lost from a hatband. It was a slim piece of evidence, but it did exist; she had held it in her hand. If she found the person who had lost it at the murder site, she would at least have a start. Brusquely she swept aside her qualms at spying on her family. If she could find a silver hatband with one link missing, she might also find the man who had killed Arnie and was causing all her accidents. Although the knowledge sent a shiver down her spine, she knew the two had to be linked.

She had been in Uncle Bud's room, and she hadn't found the hatband. But the picture of him accepting the rodeo award proved he had owned one, even if it was no longer in his possession. And Karl, with his new hatband of pheasant feathers, was a likely prospect.

She walked quickly from the room and down the long hall, cringing to hear her own footsteps echoing on the hardwood floor. Although most of the bedrooms were on the second floor, Karl's was a room near the kitchen and could be entered both from the hall and from outside the house. Gingerly, holding her breath, she tried the knob. She wasn't cut out to be a burglar, she thought, almost amused by her apprehension.

She wasn't surprised when the knob turned beneath her hand. Doors at the ranch were seldom locked. Quelling a feeling that she was intruding on the man's privacy and that he might appear at any moment, she stepped inside and looked around; it was the first time she had been in Karl's room.

It was a large room, well proportioned, and not as Spartan as she had remembered; the furnishings, although tailored, were comfortable, the colors of the walls and bedspread vibrant and deep. Rugs of cowhide were on the floor and a deep armchair was pulled close to a table that was covered with magazines.

She let her eyes rove over the walls, not surprised to see gun racks and a scattering of leather tack. What did surprise her were a few good prints of western scenes, painted by well-known local artists. Here was a side of Karl she rarely glimpsed.

She stood still, allowing the overall personality of the room to flow through her: masculine, solid, the room of a person who knew who he was. The room looked like a home, but how could it be enough, she wondered. He was a mature man, and all his personal belongings fit into the one room. For the first time, she wondered how Karl really felt about his position on the Floating Eagle. He was a valued foreman, but what did he have to aspire to?

Gingerly she began to explore. His closets revealed no surprises: a suit, which she had never known him to wear, a couple of pairs of casual pants, a few shirts; everything else was ranch work clothing. She touched the neat stack of jeans, the rows of chambray shirts, saw several hats, all black with varying bands, hung on nails. She felt a faint sorrow. This seemed very little for a grown man to have accumulated.

His dresser yielded little more; then she opened a drawer, and caught her breath. A profusion of belts, bolo ties and hatbands. The belts had the familiar silver buckles, the bolo ties were mostly of turquoise and there were several silver hatbands, all of them sporting different designs. She wished she hadn't given the conch to Brad; she would have been able to see if it matched any of those before her. In any event, any of the bands, some in various stages of disrepair, could easily have been the source of the conch she had found at the murder site.

Barely daring to breath, she closed the door and stepped slowly out of the room. She had found nothing definite, just another link in the mounting evidence against Karl. If he were the killer, he was the man who was also threatening her life, and she would have to be extremely careful.

Her thoughts flew to Brad. They had promised to investigate together, before the passion between them swept everything else aside. Should she go to him now, discuss her suspicions? But she really had very little to go on, just a gnawing uneasiness about the man. She would have to find out more before she accused him.

Like where he rode every day, she thought, a sudden resolve straightening her shoulders and quickening her step. She was tired of being the quarry, of looking behind her every step she took. Let Karl feel how it felt for a change!

She walked quickly to the corral and lured Amber from the pasture with a bucket of oats. After carefully inspecting the cinch, she threw on a saddle, then led the mare out into the open and slipped the bridle bit between her teeth. He couldn't have too far a start; if she was lucky, she might be able to find his trail.

Resolutely putting aside any thoughts that she might be running into danger, she set out at a fast clip and soon left the valley behind and began the steep climb into forest service property. She knew she was on the right track; her grandfather had said rustling was increasing and she had heard a motor the day she had been riding and had been thrown from her horse. The two things had to be connected.

Several hours later, Amber was blowing and sweating, Ramsey was tired and she still hadn't seen anything out of the usual. She hadn't picked up Karl's trail, and looking for him in the vastness of the forest was like looking for a needle in a haystack. Still, he had to be out here somewhere, she thought, sighing and digging her heels into Amber's flank.

Where was he likely to be? If he were involved with the rustlers, then he had to go near a road sometimes. The rustlers could hardly drive the cattle across the ridge into another county. It would take too long, leave them vulnerable to discovery. Besides she had heard the sound of the truck engine. But that still left a lot of territory; the forest was crisscrossed with logging roads, unused for years, but probably still passable for a powerful vehicle.

It was getting hot, and she rubbed her hand across her damp forehead, the fears she had managed to inhibit now leaping strongly into her consciousness. She thought she was on Karl's trail—was he really on hers? He knew the forest much better than she did, and he was probably an expert tracker. She swallowed, wondering what he would do if he found her alone. She remembered the scowl on his dark face when he warned her not to snoop, and his remark that she might get hurt if she did so now seemed a sinister threat.

Suddenly she heard the roar of a motor, and she stiffened in her saddle. It sounded close; maybe luck was with her!

She kicked Amber and headed her toward the sound. The engine roared again and she knew she was going in the right direction. She urged Amber forward, reaching for the binoculars she had thrust into her saddlebag.

She burst through a screening of trees, then pulled Amber hastily back into their shelter as a truck sped by on the narrow road in front of her. It was going fast, and she barely had time to see that it was a large, unmarked cattle truck before it vanished around a bend. She saw, too, that it was loaded with cattle.

Peering through the trees, she saw a horse and rider several hundred yards along the road in the direction the truck had come from, and she swung her binoculars to her eyes. Her lips tightened, but she wasn't surprised. Karl, his expression closed and enigmatic, was watching the truck disappear. Then he spurred his horse and vanished back into the forest.

A sour taste rose in her mouth as she watched him disappear. She had hoped, in spite of everything, that Karl was not involved. That no one from the Floating Eagle was involved, even though she knew the hope was in vain. But she couldn't keep her head in the sand any longer. She had seen Karl with the rustlers. He had probably helped load up the cattle, and was now on his way back to the ranch.

So this was why he spent so much time in the forest! He was up to his neck in the rustling, a partner in the theft. Karl liked to brag about his poaching; apparently poaching wasn't his only excursion outside the law.

She was afraid she knew now what had happened to Arnie, the unfortunate game warden. The man had just been in the wrong place at the wrong time, and had stumbled upon Karl and the rustlers. That was the reason he had been killed; he was a danger to Karl's operation. The deer was there only to confuse the motive.

Anger, so fierce she nearly fell from the saddle, shook her slender frame. Karl had received the same love and affection from Jacob that they all had, arriving on the ranch a frightened, confused kid. He had been taken in, trusted, become a part of that extended family, the Carmichaels. And he had repaid that trust with theft and murder!

She turned her horse and headed home. She owed her family a lot, but it didn't include shielding a murderer. Karl must have known that it wouldn't when he arranged her "accidents."

She debated her next move all the way home, but still hadn't reached a decision by the time she arrived back at the ranch. Noting that Karl's horse was back in the stable, she unsaddled Amber and turned her out in the corral, hoping that Karl wasn't watching. If he knew he had been seen, he might be capable of anything, she thought, a shudder running through her as she thought of the things he had already done.

Undoubtedly she should call the sheriff, but she hesitated, stopped by two equally compelling concerns. Although she herself was convinced of Karl's guilt, more might be needed before the sheriff could actually arrest him. Equally pertinent was the ingrained habit of consulting the family before making a decision that concerned one of them. She had to talk to someone about this.

This time there was no one in the family she could talk to, but Brad, as biased as he was, still might help her. If she could just talk to him without being explicit about what she had actually discovered. Just talk about Karl, the situation in general, maybe just a hint. If he knew everything, he would immediately arrest Karl, and that would be premature. But if she could just talk to him, hear his voice, it would shore up her own strength.

She picked up the phone and dialed his office, admitting to herself that if she hadn't had Karl to talk about, she would have thought of another excuse. The impassioned warmth of his arms around her, his fevered kisses lavished over every inch of her sensitive flesh, his hot body moving urgently against hers, everything about that night was emblazoned not only in her brain but on every nerve ending. She relived every ecstatic moment again and again, her skin flushing and her pulse racing with each repetition. When had she realized she loved him? Now it seemed she had always known.

She heard the buzz of the phone and braced herself for his reply, then slumped with disappointment at the light feminine voice.

"Fish and Game, Ginnie speaking. May I help you?"

"Uh—I'd like to speak to Brad Chillicott, please."

There was a slight pause as Ginnie took in the request, and from the curiosity in her voice when she replied, Ramsey knew she had placed the caller.

"He isn't in the office just now. Can I take a message?"

"Do you know when he'll be back?"

"He didn't say, but I doubt he's gone far. Can I have him call you?"

"Yes. Ask him to call Ramsey Delacroix, please. It's—it's important."

She replaced the phone and turned to find herself looking directly into the black hooded eyes of Karl Powers.

Her heart thudded against her chest in a wild tattoo.

"Karl! You startled me!"

His eyes narrowed, and he stepped closer. "Didn't mean to scare you." From his flat tone, she was sure her obvious fright worried him not at all. "Who were you talking to?"

"I—I was calling Brad," she said, wishing immediately she could recall the words. Delia had always said she couldn't lie. Now, when she would have liked to, why did the truth just automatically come out?

He frowned. "I thought you were warned to keep away from him."

"I don't need anyone to tell me who to see!" she flared, then stopped as his frown deepened.

"We don't need outsiders mixing in family business. Where did you go today, Ramsey? I saw you ride in."

"I—I just went for a ride."

"I thought you weren't going to ride around by yourself anymore. Thought we all agreed it was dangerous."

Did she really know this man who was facing her so accusingly? "I can take care of myself."

A derisive grin split his heavy face. "Yeah, sure seems like it. At least we're not packing you home this time. Did you ride on the forest?"

When she merely looked at him, he took her wrist in a fierce grasp and pulled her toward him. "Did you see anything?"

She jerked her arm away and rubbed her wrist. "What was there to see?"

"Ramsey, listen to me," he whispered between clenched teeth. "Stop snooping around. Stop it! Go back to California. If you don't, you may get hurt."

He turned and stalked away as she watched, openmouthed. Karl must have known she had seen him with the rustlers and was warning her again. If she'd had the tiniest doubt about his involvement before, it was gone.

And she was in danger. There had been no mistaking the threat in his voice. For a minute, she thought of the Karl she had known since childhood and wavered. Then she straightened, her chin thrust out. This was now. Karl was dangerous. From the implacable look on his broad face, she didn't doubt that for a minute. He had threatened her. She needed help.

At least she knew now who her enemy was. She had no idea when Brad would call back, and she certainly didn't want to be alone with Karl. Uncle Bud was gone, her grandfather might not be back for a day or so, but maybe she could locate Jeff. Just possibly he might have returned to his studio.

Feeling better at the thought, she took a deep breath and started walking briskly toward his studio, trying not to look back over her shoulder.

"Hey!" As she approached the little room, Jeff glanced up from his newest painting, the Navajo Indian in full regalia, and waved his brush at her, and Ramsey stepped quickly in through the open door. He gave her a warm smile. "I was getting lonesome. You've been neglecting me."

She paused to catch her breath, quivering with relief, and returned his welcoming smile. "I wasn't sure you'd be here."

He glanced down at his jeans and riding boots. "Oh, I spent some time this morning riding over on the north forty. But I've been here for the past hour or so. What brings you to my hideout, pretty Ramsey? Want to buy a painting?"

"Jeff, I've got to talk to someone!"

He gave her a keen look, laid his brush down slowly on the easel and came toward her, putting his hand under her chin and raising her face to look into her eyes. "Sounds serious, princess. What's the trouble?"

"Jeff, I know who killed Arnie Parkins!"

He stiffened, his hand tightening hard on her chin. "What are you talking about?"

Taking a deep breath, she leaned briefly against his chest, then moved away, the words coming in a flood.

"I told you my suspicions about Karl. There's more."

"You didn't have much to go on before," he said slowly, moving to lean against his easel as he watched her face. "What else have you found out?"

"Now I know the reason Arnie was killed! It wasn't a poacher at all, it was to cover up rustling! Grandpa says that cattle rustling has increased a lot! He's gone off to Nevada right now to see if he can get a line on the rustlers."

"Is that where he went?" Jeff said thoughtfully.

"Yes, and then he was going to stop at the bank on the way back. Some problem with the balance." She moved quickly about the cluttered studio as she eagerly presented her conclusions. "Then today I saw Karl with the rustlers."

Jeff jerked around to face her, his mouth a tight line. "You actually saw Karl with the rustlers? Where was that? Where were you?"

"I followed him into the forest, and I saw the unmarked truck go by on a logging road. Karl was just a few yards down the road."

"Hmm." Jeff rubbed his chin thoughtfully. "It does seem you've got a case, all right. Have you talked to Karl?"

"No. But I think he knows I suspect him. He caught me on the phone calling Brad."

"You talked to Brad Chillicott?"

"No, he wasn't in, but he's going to call me back."

"What do you plan on telling Brad?" Jeff said slowly.

"Everything," she replied. "I know I don't have enough to convict Karl, but maybe Brad can find something else."

"It's still not conclusive," Jeff said thoughtfully.

"No, but I searched Karl's room. He could have dropped the conch—he certainly has access to them."

"You put a lot of credence in a person having access to the conch," Jeff mused. "I'm not sure I see it, myself. Maybe we should take things a little slower, handle it ourselves…"

"Jeff, I think it's gone beyond that. The man is dangerous. I know the Carmichaels take care of their own, but we can't shield a murderer!"

"No, of course not." He frowned slightly. "But Karl— I think maybe I should talk to him before we make any decisions that are irrevocable…"

"It's too late for that," she said firmly. "The man is dangerous. He threatened me. I know how you feel, I'm sorry about Karl myself, but we have to let the law handle it."

"I suppose so." Jeff sighed, and rose to look briefly out the wide window he had cut into the frame building to let light into his studio. The first faint stars of evening were flickering in and out of a bank of clouds rising to the west. "But if he's threatened you, I don't want you further involved, Ramsey. I can handle it from here."

She slumped with relief, and gave him a tremulous smile. "What do you plan to do?"

"I had planned to go into Tyler this evening," he said slowly. "There's no reason to involve Chillicott in this; you know his agenda. I'll stop in and see Sheriff Thorenson, and let him take it from there."

She came to him and kissed him lightly on the cheek. "When will you be back? I hate for Stevie and me to be alone in the house."

He gave her a squeeze and glanced outside at the darkening sky. "It's getting late. I'll just go in and see the sheriff, take care of my business and come right back."

Her voice conveyed her gratitude. "I hate to be a baby about this, but I have to admit I'm glad you've taken over. You always did take care of me, Jeff."

He gave her his sweet, familiar smile. "I'll take care of you, Ramsey."

Chapter 14

Picking her way through the darkness along the path that led from Jeff's studio, Ramsey was more at ease than she had been in days. Jeff's taking over the problem of Karl left her with a vast sense of relief. Everything would work out.

She paused under the outstretched branches of an apple tree, lifting her face to take in the suddenly cool breeze. It was out of her hands now. Jeff would talk to Sheriff Thorenson, and he would decide what to do about Karl.

And Brad—as soon as Brad got her message he would come to her. There was something so strong between them, that he would recognize the urgency of her call. She knew it, knew it as surely as she knew she would always love him, whatever happened...

Surrounded by the haunting fragrance of the orchard, she watched the cloud bank scurrying to completely cover the stars, and felt an overwhelming sense of belonging. It was so tempting to accept her grandfather's offer and stay on the ranch. He would never suspect that the main attraction was its nearness to Brad. Even if she could never have him, even if his dark, revengeful nature would always stand between them, she knew that she wanted to be near him. He had made her his, and whatever came of that, there was no retreat. Musing on the way his eyes darkened when he bent his proud head to kiss her, the feel of his hand on her flesh pulling her close to his hard chest, she bent to pick a sprig of blooming clover. Perhaps the idle action saved her life.

Her head exploded in hot fire as the blow fell. Pain burned along every nerve. Waves of nausea churned in her stomach; instinctively she tried to break her fall, but her body refused to respond. She didn't even feel the impact of the hard earth as she toppled heavily into a swirling pool of darkness.

When she finally regained consciousness, she lay for several minutes trying to get her bearings. She had no idea how much time had passed. Her head screamed with throbbing pain, her throat was dry and she felt as though she had been beaten over every inch of her body.

Gradually it all began to come back, and she struggled with the panic that threatened to immobilize her. But she had to get up; someone had tried to kill her. She managed to lift herself to a sitting position, then fell back down in a spasm of dizziness.

She knew she had been hit over the head and dragged back into the darkness of the orchard. Karl must have followed her to Jeff's studio and overheard their conversation, then waited alongside the path for her return. Perhaps she had bent just in time to deflect the full force of his blow. Had he left her for dead, or just wanted her unconscious and out of the way while he made his escape?

With strength she didn't know she had, she hauled herself up the trunk until she was standing erect alongside the tree, and looked back at Jeff's studio several yards away. There was no light, but the outlines of the structure were faintly visible. Jeff had obviously gone on to town as he had promised, and had never seen her lying unconscious off the path. There was no help from him.

Sheer terror lent strength to her weak legs as she stumbled along the path to the ranch house. Her aching head made it difficult to concentrate, but she knew she had to get to a phone. She had to call Brad. It was the thought of him, strong and steady as a pine, a beacon at the end of a dark tunnel, that propelled her through the darkness.

Bursting inside the house, she picked up the phone, then let it drop from her trembling hand as tears of anger and disappointment stung her eyes. The lines were cut. Karl was taking no chances on her getting help.

A shudder went through her body, and she grabbed a chair for support as the thought hit her. She and Stevie were alone. Martha had gone home long ago, and Delia was undoubtedly sleeping under the mild tranquilizer the doctor had prescribed. The knowledge galvanized her into action. Wild with fear, she raced up the stairs to Stevie's room, spurts of adrenaline speeding her heartbeat and strengthening her legs. She threw open the door, and felt as though someone had punched her in the stomach as her eyes went frantically around the empty room. She had known what she would find before she opened the door. Stevie was gone.

For an instant, she leaned against the doorjamb, taking deep, gasping breaths, unable to move. Karl had kidnapped Stevie. But maybe he wouldn't harm him. She was the one he wanted to get rid of. Maybe he would just hold Stevie hostage, use him to bargain with. His escape—for Stevie. Oh, God, she half prayed, half pleaded, don't let Karl harm him. A cold, icy hand squeezed her heart. She had to find her son.

With energy born of desperation, she ran to the garage, and jumped into the only vehicle there. She would drive to Tyler; with luck, she might even meet Brad on the road. Reaching to switch on the ignition her hand froze in midair. The key—the key that was always left in the ignition—was gone.

She forced back the paralyzing fear, willing herself to think logically. There was no help; it was up to her. Jeff's little sports car was gone, her grandfather had the sedan and Uncle Bud had undoubtedly taken the other pickup. Karl had not left the ranch by automobile.

She ran blindly into the barn, lungs heaving, breath coming in short, painful gasps, and saw that Karl's horse was no longer in the stall where it had been earlier this evening. She managed a grim smile; she was right. Wherever he had gone, he had gone on horseback.

She never knew how she got through the next period of time; she didn't even know whether hours or minutes passed. In a daze, she saddled Amber and headed out into the night. If Karl had Stevie, he couldn't go too far in the darkness. He might hole up somewhere for the night, and she thought she knew where that might be. The old line cabin. She knew Karl and Stevie had been there often; she had even seen the empty cartridges where, against her express instructions, he had taught the boy to shoot.

When she got to the cabin and saw the faint light shining under the door, she didn't even pause. Rage clouded her judgment, eliminated her fear, and she burst into the room to confront him.

"Where is he! What have you done with Stevie!"

"What!" Karl sprang from his chair, a dumbfounded look on his face. "Ramsey! What in the devil are you doing here?"

Like a wildcat, she flew across the room and pounded his chest with frantic hands, her fear for her child overriding everything else. "Tell me! What have you done with him?"

He grabbed her wrists and held her away from him, surprised eyes taking in her appearance. "What happened to you? There's blood on your face."

"Don't pretend!" she screamed. "Maybe you thought you killed me, like you killed Arnie Parkins! But you won't get away with it! Where's Stevie?"

Still holding her wrists, he pushed her down into a chair. "What are you talking about?"

Looking into his astonished face, she began to have her

first doubts, but she tilted her chin and spoke decisively, spilling out her suspicions, and accusing him of Parkins's murder and the attempts on her life.

Incredulity gave way to exasperation. "If you think all that," he finally said, "you sure did a dumb thing coming here like you did. You always were too impulsive. I warned you. But what's this about Stevie?"

"He's gone." As she watched the rage color Karl's face a deep red, she had a huge hollow feeling in the pit of her stomach, and she knew she had made a big mistake. She had accused the wrong man.

Things she'd paid no attention to before flashed through her mind. She remembered her last glimpse at Jeff's studio, and the painting of the Navajo in full costume, and the awful realization hit her. The black hat with the silver band. Jeff often painted Indians. Why hadn't she realized he must have a collection of Indian regalia?

She had been misled by his affectionate manner, the memories of their childhood together, and had confided everything. That old Jacob was on the trail of the rustlers. The trouble with the bank—why hadn't she remembered that Jeff kept the books and handled the checks? The last straw must have been when she told him of her decision to tell everything she knew to Brad. He had realized the net was closing.

"Jeff...it must have been Jeff." She raised a tearstained face to Karl. "What can we do?"

"Get back to the ranch as fast as we can," he said grimly. "If that little snake has hurt Stevie, I'll kill him with my bare hands. I never did trust him."

"Never trusted him? But I thought you liked him," she faltered.

"Liked the supercilious little bastard? Hah! I've suspected he was pulling something with the books for years. And I've been trying to catch him at the rustling. Almost caught him today."

"But I saw *you* with the rustlers."

With a disgusted look, he grabbed her arm and pulled her toward the door. "I got there too late, just as they drove off. But I figured you'd been out there, snooping around, when I saw you ride in. You wouldn't take a warning. I told you it was dangerous to ride around on your own. Now let's get out of here."

They mounted quickly and pushed the horses into a hard gallop.

"When you warned me about snooping, I was sure you were the rustler," Ramsey called over her shoulder.

"Hah! Only a fool would have needed a warning after what was happening to you," Karl retorted. "You never could see what was right under your nose. Always had on rose-colored glasses."

Brad was just driving into the yard when he saw the horses pull up. He knew immediately that something was wrong. Even in the partial darkness, he could see the two had been riding hard, and Ramsey was slumped in the saddle as though expending the last of her energy. He jumped from the pickup and ran toward them, lifting up his arms to Ramsey. His anxiety increased at her little sigh as she slid down along his body, and his arms tightened convulsively. With an agonized moan, he buried his face in her disheveled hair, for a moment not able to say a word. She was safe.

"Brad!" she choked. "Oh, Brad—I knew you'd come."

He'd had to come. When Ginnie had reported that Ramsey had sounded frightened, nothing on this earth, or any other, could have kept him away. His response was as elemental as life itself, as primitive as man's age-old necessity to protect the one he loved. His woman needed him. He might never have her in the conventional sense, but in every way that mattered, she was his.

"Ginnie told me you called," he said, pressing her against his body and stroking her until her trembling finally lessened and her heartbeat slowed. "I tried to call back, but your phone was out of order."

"The lines were cut," she managed to whisper.

His arms tightened around her until she nearly gasped with pain. "What's going on?"

Karl had come up by then, and he and Ramsey told Brad everything that had happened. There was an instant of silence. When he replied, his voice was as cold and deadly as a timber rattler coiled to strike.

"So it was Jeff. I rather suspected it, but I had nothing concrete to go on. And now he has Stevie."

"His car is gone," Ramsey said, lifting her head from the security of Brad's chest. "He must have a big head start. I don't know how long I was unconscious, and then I went to find Karl…"

"He's pretty limited in where he can drive in that little toy," Karl said. "The little coupe would never make it over most of the logging roads. He must have gone toward Tyler."

"Maybe he thought that was where he was going, but I don't think he got there," Brad said grimly.

"What do you mean?"

"It was dark when I left Tyler, but I think I saw his car pulled off the side of the road. I didn't stop to investigate, but it sure looked like it from a distance."

"Why would he leave his car along the road?" Karl demanded.

"Couple of reasons," Brad said thoughtfully. "Maybe he had engine trouble, and couldn't get any farther. That machine's made for smooth pavements. Or maybe he never planned to escape by automobile, and just pulled off the road thinking no one would see it until he was long gone."

"Then let's see which it was," Karl said. "I'll follow you down the road in the pickup."

"The keys are gone," Ramsey said weakly. "I found that out when I tried to go to Brad for help."

Karl flashed a mirthless smile. "I keep an extra set of all keys."

Ramsey jumped into Brad's pickup, and the two vehicles

sped back down the road. They didn't speak as Brad cast an occasional glance at Ramsey, wide-eyed and frightened beside him. He winced as he got a good look at her face, and his hands tightened on the wheel as though they were around Jeff's throat. Blood was matted in her hair and smeared across one white cheek. He wished he had time to check for the extent of the damage, but when he'd tried she had angrily brushed aside his suggestion. All her thoughts now were for Stevie. She must not be seriously hurt, he thought, anger darkening his face. If she were, nothing could save Jeff. He would hunt him to the ends of the earth.

She was doing very well considering what she had just been through. She sat erect, but very close, her thigh pressed against his, as though she was soaking up his strength. He took one hand from the wheel and squeezed her hand hard. "Okay?"

"Okay," she said tremulously. "We'll find them, won't we?"

"We'll find them," he promised.

When Brad braked and pulled onto a small side road, they were only a couple of miles from the Floating Eagle.

He swung his spotlight on the tiny car that was off the road and almost covered by the high underbrush. "Good thing my lights picked it up," he said, stepping down and moving quickly toward the abandoned coupe, followed closely by Ramsey, and by Karl who had pulled in behind him. "It's pretty well hidden."

He and Karl inspected the vehicle quickly, then Karl straightened and spoke in a low voice. "He must have hit that pothole and broke an axle. Looks like he was going like a bat out of hell."

"And this accident meant a change of plans," Brad said just as grimly as he peered into the darkness of the forest. "He's on foot."

"Unless he got a ride," Karl offered.

"Possible, but doubtful. Hardly any traffic, and he

wouldn't chance it anyway with Stevie. Still, he could be walking toward Tyler.''

He frowned, assessing the possibilities. He didn't like any of them. The clouds that had been threatening a storm all evening were blacker than ever, and he suspected a thunderstorm would hit before long. Even as well as Jeff knew the forest, he wouldn't want to be out in the darkness in a thunderstorm. Too many chances for a misstep, a fall. Where would he have gone? The odds against finding him were astronomical, but he looked at Ramsey's strained face and didn't voice the thought.

He felt the rage building inside him. Jeff had a good head start, but he was tricky. Right now he could be peering at them from the darkness of the forest, or he could be miles away. The question was, where?

He felt Ramsey shiver and drew her closer against his side. "We'll find him—don't worry."

"He could be anywhere," she choked. Brad knew she was thinking of Stevie, as he was, scared and bewildered, not knowing what to make of a friend turned enemy, and a muscle twitched in his clenched jaw.

"I can't think he's gone far," he said firmly. "He might make a run for the other side of the mountain into Camp County where he's got friends. But it's miles over rugged terrain. He's on foot, a storm's coming up and I think he's likely to hole up someplace. If we just knew where to start looking…''

Ramsey's eyes widened and her grip on his arm dug into his flesh. "I just remembered something—''

"What is it?"

"It's a long shot—but it's possible. There's an old mine shaft near here where Jeff and I used to play when we were kids. It's sheltered. Close. He might take Stevie there."

Brad gave her a quick look. "Can you find it?"

"I'm sure I can."

"Then it's worth a shot. But let's not put all our eggs in one basket. I'll radio the office. The sheriff's out of town, but there will be someone around. Karl, you start up the road toward Tyler, and keep your eye open for Jeff and Stevie along the way. Bring back all the help you can.''

Karl nodded curtly and started for the pickup. Brad put his hands on Ramsey's shoulders and turned her to face him, feeling her trembling, assessing her capacity to continue the search. He nodded briefly as he met her gaze. She looked pale and shaky, but quietly determined, and he knew that her initial panic had subsided.

He kissed her gently, putting his entire heart into the caress. He hoped she could read it all: his love, his absolute determination to find her child and to keep them both safe. He would give his life for that. But they had better get started.

"You and Jeff played in a mine shaft when you were little? That sounds dangerous. Didn't your grandfather object?"

"He never knew. I did get lost a couple of times, and I was pretty scared until Jeff finally found me. He made me promise not to tell."

"I'll bet he did." Brad's mouth set in an implacable line. So even in childhood Jeff's feeling about Ramsey had been at least ambivalent. You didn't scare a little kid if you really liked her.

He snapped a thin coil of rope to his belt, patted the pistol in his holster to reassure himself that it was there, then took Ramsey's hand and led her toward the ominous darkness of the forest, just as a crack of lightning flashed across the sky.

"Lead on, sweetheart."

Chapter 15

The storm, which had threatened for hours, now burst on them with all its fury. Lightning slashed with jagged red streaks against the somber sky, followed almost immediately by rolling thunder. Ramsey knew that one could tell how close a lightning bolt was by the elapsed time between the flash and the thunder, and she bit her lip nervously. There was no space at all.

She staggered under the force of driving rain against her face, and knew they were in for a deluge. Summer storms in the high country were brief and infrequent, but they were savage when they came.

"Can you find the way in all this?" Brad raised his voice in order to be heard above the pounding wind and rain.

"I think so." She paused in the partial shelter of a pine and looked around, unsure of her next move. They seemed to have stumbled on a trail of sorts, the one she had been hoping to find. Still, she had been only a child when she came here before, and many of the markings she remembered had vanished. One thing couldn't have changed; she remembered the abandoned mine shaft jutted out of the side of a mountain just above a stream... She would recognize the rock formation of the mountain if she could just see it.

If she could just see anything. Even with the storm, the darkness wasn't total; there was a faint and eerie glow from the cloud-covered moon; still, it was close enough to complete darkness to make her wonder if the next step would send her plunging into a ravine. They managed by waiting for each lightning flash, taking a quick look around and then moving forward with the aid of Brad's flashlight.

She wasn't entirely happy about the flashlight, either, knowing that it would point out their whereabouts to Jeff if he were anywhere near. Still, it couldn't be helped. They had to take that risk, since without it they had no hope at all of finding the old mine shaft.

She trudged forward, trying to ignore the thoughts that would lead to despair. What if Stevie wasn't there, even if they did find the mine? What if she had been wrong, and Jeff knew of other, better hideouts? She couldn't face that possibility now. She clutched Brad's hand and took another step forward.

She lost track of time, concentrating only on going forward along what appeared to be a faintly marked trail. Brad was right beside her, holding her hand firmly in his, reaching to steady her as he tried to keep his body between her and the main brunt of the storm. Her terror diminished as she sensed the outline of his broad shoulders beside her. She felt an implicit trust that somehow, someway, they would find their way through this nightmare together.

Suddenly she stopped, and her heart plummeted like a shotgunned pheasant. Just ahead of them a sheer drop into a churning canyon effectively barred their way.

She took a choked breath. She hadn't remembered this cliff; she was lost.

Brad cuddled her close, holding her head against his chest as he looked down into the rushing water below. His shirt was soaked through, and she could feel his wet skin against her cheek. She pressed closer, seeking comfort. The search couldn't end like this; they had to find Stevie.

"It's all right," he murmured, his lips brushing her sodden hair. "We'll go back; perhaps we lost the trail…"

There was nothing to do but retrace their steps. She thought the rain might be letting up and wondered if the storm were fading, then jumped as a particularly loud clap of thunder rolled above them. They were going to get no help from the weather.

They backtracked a few hundred yards, and Brad gave a low whistle, his hand tightening on hers. "Look, Ramsey. Isn't that a trail going off in the other direction?"

Without waiting for her reply, he struck out ahead of her, and with renewed hope she scrambled along behind him. The landscape did indeed look more familiar; she was almost certain she was on the right track. If there were just a little more light, she could see whether the mountain looming ahead of them had the unique rock formation that she remembered.

Suddenly Brad stopped and pulled her up beside him, and she saw that their way was blocked again. A creekbed that had been dry all summer was now swelled by the rain into a flash flood, and the turbulent water ran in a swift torrent in front of them.

"Can we wade it?" Ramsey whispered.

As she spoke, a large log came swirling by in the current, and Brad shook his head. "Too deep, and it's running too fast. But there's got to be a way across."

They walked a few yards downstream, holding on to willows to keep from slipping off the bank, but the creek narrowed, finally plunging into a canyon that was obviously impassable.

"Maybe it's better upstream," Brad said, already moving up the side of the mountain.

Ramsey followed, nearer to exhaustion than she had ever been. Although the sharp pain in her head had subsided to a dull ache, her lungs felt as though they were bursting, and her knees threatened to crumble with every step. Worse, she wasn't even sure they were going in the right direction. Jeff and Stevie might be miles away by now, while she and Brad stumbled around helplessly in the darkness.

She took a deep, quivering breath, and set her chin stubbornly. Whether it was the right direction or not, it was the only direction they had. She wouldn't give up.

Brad put out a restraining hand and motioned ahead of them. "That may be what we're looking for," he said softly.

Ramsey's eyes followed his gaze, and she felt a tiny spurt of hope. The wind and rain had increased the stream flow, but it might also have provided the means to cross it. A fir tree, roots upended by the storm, lay across the creek like a natural bridge.

"It's pretty narrow," Brad said. "Only room for one at a time. It will be slippery. Can you make it?"

She looked down at the water raging underneath and shuddered, then squared her shoulders. "I can make it."

Working quickly, Brad took the coil of thin line from his belt and looped it around Ramsey's waist. "Just in case." He gave her a grin that didn't hide his anxiety. If she hadn't been so scared she would have grinned back. An Idaho man never felt completely dressed without a gun and a rope.

She stepped gingerly out on the fallen tree trunk, inching her way forward, while Brad stood on the bank and played out the rope. She tried not to look down at the white churning water, and kept her eyes fixed on the opposite bank. It was comforting to know that if she fell he would manage to tow her back to the bank, but she didn't relish the prospect. Moving slowly, she peered into the darkness ahead of where the natural bridge disappeared in a clump of brush and thickly growing evergreens.

She took a quivering breath of relief mixed with excitement as she reached the other side, and she half turned to call to Brad. She never completed the movement. Even if the thunder hadn't crashed at that exact moment, he would never have heard her cry. She tried to scream, but a hand tightened cruelly over her mouth, stifling all sound; a knife slashed the thin rope around her waist, and she was dragged backward into the dense foliage.

She heard Brad shout, and the hand increased the pressure on her mouth, cutting off most of her breath. She tried to struggle, but in her exhaustion she was no match for the hard, lean man that half carried, half pushed her over the steep terrain.

She had a moment of black despair. Brad couldn't hear them over the whining and howling of the storm; even if he crossed the bridge without slipping, he couldn't track them in the darkness. And the man who had captured her seemed to know exactly where he was going as he covered the rough terrain with the speed and stealth of a mountain lion.

He pushed her inside a narrow opening in the face of the mountain with such force that she sprawled face forward on the dry dirt of the mine shaft.

"Mom!"

Dazed, she raised her head as Stevie came hurtling toward her. Even lying there in the dirt, she felt a flash of sheer joy, her pain momentarily forgotten in her relief at seeing him alive.

"Get back over there, kid." The voice was cold and remote as a glacier, but she had no trouble recognizing it. Jeff, as she had known it would be.

She saw the frightened look in Stevie's eyes as he scurried back to the rock ledge along the far side of the shaft, and anger lent her enough strength to struggle to a sitting position. She had been correct in her assumption that Jeff would bring Stevie to the old mine shaft. Hastily she surveyed the place, hoping to see something that would help them escape, but there was nothing. The small enclosure was cold and dank as she had remembered, but Jeff had built a small fire, and for a moment she felt a flash of hope. Perhaps Brad would see the glow. The hope died as she watched Jeff cover the shaft entrance with brush; from outside, the entrance would be completely invisible. Brad might even be close behind them, but he would never find them; he had no idea where the old mine was located, and would stumble right by it in the darkness.

She thought of screaming and rejected the thought. That would do nothing but lead Brad into a trap.

She started to struggle when Jeff tied her hands and feet securely with rope, but stopped when he hit her almost casually across the face. At the blow, Stevie started forward, but stopped, uncertain, when Jeff waved his pistol in his direction.

"It's all right, Stevie." She gasped. "Don't worry, we'll be all right."

The low laugh from Jeff sounded so little like her familiar cousin that she swung her head around to give him her full attention. He looked the same, she thought, yet completely different. The old, lazy, affectionate man, the one she'd always called brother, was gone, replaced by a stranger whose expression sent cold chills down her back.

"Why, Jeff?" she whispered.

He shrugged impatiently. "You're a smart woman in some ways—surely you've figured it out. When you came home, and the old man trotted out the fatted calf, I knew I'd have to do something about you sooner or later, but when I heard him say he was willing the ranch to you and your brat, I knew it had to be sooner."

"And Arnie Parkins," she whispered, her wide eyes on his face. "You killed him, didn't you? When he caught you rustling."

He shrugged. "The fool kept meddling where he had no business to be. He planned to tell Jacob. Then you and Chillicott came nosing around. I knew I had to get rid of you."

"It was you who dropped the conch shell."

He gave her a hard grin. "Anybody in the county could have done that. But I saw your face tonight when you looked at my painting. I knew it would come to you pretty soon. And then you said the old man had found some problem with the bank balance." He shook his head in near amusement. "The old fool. I've been forging checks for years, transferring money to my own account, and he never caught on to it."

"So you ran out behind me and hit me over the head," she said slowly. "Then you grabbed Stevie, cut the phone wires and took the keys so I couldn't get help."

"It was just a precaution. I never thought you'd make it to the house. You're a hard one to kill," he said, his voice as matter-of-fact as though he were discussing the weather. "The wire across the stairs, the cut cinch—you have a lot of luck, Ramsey." He gave her a wide, teasing smile, the more chilling because it was so familiar. "I think your luck just ran out, princess."

Her eyes went miserably to Stevie, who was sitting so unbelievably still against the hard rock wall, his little face white as paste, his eyes wide with fright. "Let him go," she said. "I'm the only hostage you need."

He shook his head slowly, the smile still on his face. "No hostages, princess. I planned on using Stevie as a hostage, to get you and Chillicott off my trail. But things have changed. I can travel faster alone. I've friends waiting for me in Camp County, and I can't leave you two alive to point out my trail. We'll just stay here until ole Brad comes by—he's bound to be running up and down this mountain like a hound dog after a coon—and then I'll have to shoot all three of you."

She tried not to look at Stevie's face, but he drew her like a magnet. She was surprised that some of his fright seemed gone, and his face was screwed up in concentration as he listened carefully to Jeff's words.

"I've been planning on this for years," Jeff continued. "I can't leave witnesses. I've got money in another bank account, another name—I'll be out of the country before you're found."

She had to think of something. Everything he said was true; Brad would be looking for them, and even though he would be alert, Jeff could easily shoot him from his vantage point at the mouth of the shaft. Her mouth felt so dry she could hardly swallow. Brad and Stevie—the two people she loved most in the world. She had to stop him, but how? If she could get him talking, that might at least buy some time.

"Why did you do it, Jeff?" She raised her eyes to his face. "We all loved you—trusted you. You had everything."

"Everything!" His voice was a snarl, and she watched the civilized mask crumble to reveal a deranged man. A man corroded with hate. "I've slaved for that old pirate for years! For what! Room and board, and a salary you couldn't buy chicken feed on. I told him I wanted to leave, wanted to study painting, but would he let me! No! He said art was for sissies. He wouldn't help me at all."

His face twisted in rage as Ramsey murmured softly, "You could have gone, anyway. He couldn't have stopped you."

"And starved? I've worked for my freedom, Ramsey, and I don't plan to enjoy it as a pauper. I figured when he died, the Floating Eagle would be sold. I'd take my share, and that, plus what I've managed to accumulate by other methods—" he gave her an evil grin "—would set me up just fine. Let me live as I should have lived. I guess I'll miss the income from the sale of the ranch now, but I'll get by."

"But what about me, Jeff? I've never done anything to you—we were always close—"

"Close!" He cut in with an explosive oath. "God, if there's anything worse than a miser, it's a Pollyanna! So sure the sun rises and sets with her, that everybody loves her!" The enmity in his eyes was so raw that Ramsey shrank back involuntarily against the mine-shaft wall. "Everything was fine until you came, Ramsey. They loved me, Delia and Jacob. Nothing too good for me. Bud never counted, Karl was just hired help. I was the only one who counted."

His eyes changed, became paler, and Ramsey knew he

had lost all semblance of sanity. "After you arrived, every-thing was for you. It was princess this, princess that. They didn't even know I existed." He parted his teeth in a feral grin. "Well, they'll know it now."

Ramsey felt as though she had been walking along a smooth meadow and a pit full of vipers had suddenly opened beneath her. How could she have been so wrong? Even as a child, Jeff had hated her, envied her. All the time she had thought he loved her, he had been plotting against her. It was chilling to finally realize that his affectionate teasing, his big-brother manner, had always masked an im-placable hatred.

She froze at the sound of rustling branches outside the mine opening, and Jeff stepped quickly to the entrance, pushing aside the brushy cover. "He's here," he whispered exultantly. "A few more steps and he'll be right where I want him."

Without turning his head, he motioned to Stevie. "Bring me the flashlight, boy, and be quick about it. Or you'll be the first to go." He gave an obscene chuckle. "You've heard of flashing coyotes, haven't you, blinding them so you can shoot them... With the light shining in ole Brad's eyes, I'll have him down before he knows what's happening."

"Stevie, no!"

Stevie shot her a furtive look as he started toward Jeff with the flashlight in his little fist, and she dropped her head in her hands. There was nothing she could do; she couldn't stop him. Stevie was just a little boy, cowed by Jeff's bru-tality, trained to obey adults.

As Jeff reached for the flashlight, Stevie dropped it at his feet, then moved like a darting fish to slip the pistol from Jeff's holster. Before Ramsey could close her mouth, or Jeff turn, the boy was back at the far side of the tunnel, the gun pointed squarely at Jeff's chest.

Jeff gave a startled oath, then grinned as he started walk-ing toward the small boy, his hand outstretched.

''Don't be silly, Stevie. You're not going to use that. You don't know how.''

Stevie didn't reply. He clenched his small jaw, stiffened and, with the pistol held firmly in both hands, fired.

The sound of the shot bounced wildly around the confines of the tunnel. Ramsey screamed. Jeff spun around, then fell heavily against the dirt floor. Clutching his shoulder with one hand, he struggled to his feet and staggered toward the small boy.

''No closer,'' Stevie said, his voice a mere squeak as he raised the gun again.

Then the brush at the opening flew aside and Brad burst in. Taking in the situation at a glance, he lunged at Jeff. He held him upright while he savagely smashed his fist into the man's face, then let him fall in the dirt in a crumpled heap. Moving swiftly, he bent to tie him securely, then raised his eyes to Ramsey.

In that moment there was just the two of them, a man and a woman linked by a force as powerful as life itself.

Then her eyes went to Stevie, who still stood against the wall. He had dropped the gun, and his wide eyes moved from her to Brad like an anxious chick. He and Brad both started toward her at once. Moving swiftly, Brad knelt beside her, his knife making swift work of her bonds, as Stevie flew toward her, little arms outstretched. With one arm, Brad crushed her against his chest, so tightly she wasn't sure where her heartbeat ended and his began, while his other arm gathered Stevie close. Wordlessly, all three rocked together in a paroxysm of joy and relief.

When she could finally speak, her voice was only a soft croak. ''Thank God. He was going to kill us all. If it hadn't been for Stevie—and you—''

He ran his hand softly over her hair, his eyes so full of emotion she found it hard to believe she was looking at the reserved man she thought she knew. ''You didn't do so badly, sweetheart. You got us here. And thank Stevie. If I hadn't heard the shot, I would never have found you. We were all lucky.''

Lucky? Yes, luck was part of it. But they'd had both good and bad. What had really helped was Jeff's overconfidence. So sure of his ability, his innate superiority, he had never dreamed he should be wary of a small boy. He had never spent time with him, never seen Karl give Stevie his painstaking lessons with a gun.

Ramsey managed to move enough to shift her grip on Stevie so she could look into his beaming face.

"You were wonderful, Stevie. And so brave. How did you ever think of doing that?"

He moved out of her arms and stuck out his chest. "Karl taught me. He says a man's got to outshoot 'em and outthink 'em if he wants to survive in these parts."

In a spasm of laughter, Ramsey collapsed in Brad's arms.

Chapter 16

The faint light of dawn was staining the eastern sky a soft rose, and the call of a rooster echoed faintly from somewhere near the barn, but the lights in the Floating Eagle ranch house blazed as though it were midnight. Ramsey slumped in her chair; as tired as she was, she was still acutely aware of Brad standing behind her and leaning down to tenderly adjust the bandage around her head. His face was so close to hers that she felt his warm breath on her cheek. Although she had protested that she was all right, he had paid no attention, carefully cleansing the wound and covering it with clean gauze. She knew he would insist that she see a doctor tomorrow. She leaned back, reeling with exhaustion, and surveyed the other occupants of the room through half-closed eyes.

The scene was not as frenzied as it had been an hour earlier, when Karl, Ramsey and Brad had returned to the ranch house after handing Jeff over to the authorities, but it was chaotic enough. Jacob had returned from his trip, and been informed of what had happened. After a fiery display of temper and incredulity, he now sat mutely in front of the fireplace. Uncle Bud had just arrived and been filled in on events by Karl; even Delia was downstairs, perched like a bird on a chair near her husband, her anxious eyes on his face, her hand in his. Only Stevie and Jeff were missing from the family gathering, Ramsey thought, leaning her head back against Brad and placing her hand over his. Stevie was in bed; Jeff, hopefully, was in jail.

"I still can't believe it," Jacob said, staring into the empty fireplace. "Jeff was like a son to me."

"Oh, much more than a son," Uncle Bud murmured ironically.

Jacob's head jerked up, and Ramsey waited for the explosion, but the old man merely sighed, a bewildered look on his face. His broad old shoulders, usually so erect, looked almost frail, and he slumped in dejection. He looked, Ramsey thought sorrowfully, like a beaten man.

And why shouldn't he? His world was collapsing around him; he was drowning in a sea of betrayal, she thought bitterly.

"All this was going on," he repeated, "and I never knew. Maybe I could have done something. Maybe I did something wrong…"

What he had done was run things his way, Ramsey thought. For all that he had loved them, he had treated Jeff, Karl and his own son like children, weakening them, finally depriving them of hope. Oh, it wasn't all his fault. Perhaps something had been wrong with Jeff from the beginning; maybe he had been warped by unknowable circumstances before he came to the ranch, but the old man's dictatorial manner and lack of understanding hadn't helped.

Delia leaned over to kiss his weathered cheek, and suddenly both her grandparents looked very vulnerable and very old.

The old man made a valiant effort to straighten up and assume command. "What's done is done. We've all got work to do. Bud, I'll want you to take over some of the book work—''

"I don't think I'll be able to," Bud said quietly. "I'm going to marry Ella Parkins, and we won't be living here."

"Marry Ella Parkins!" A flash of the old Jacob returned. "You know how I feel about that!"

"I don't really care how you feel about it," Bud said calmly. "You know we've loved each other for years. We planned to leave together, and then Arnie was killed. Naturally we couldn't go then. We would have been accused of killing him for sure. But we're leaving now."

He straightened his shoulders, and Ramsey saw an uncle she had never seen before—confident, assured and determined. So that was the reason for his clandestine meetings with Ella, and the fear she had seen in the woman's eyes. But at last they were free to be together.

"You've a duty to the ranch—''

"I've always loved the ranch, but I never seemed to be necessary here," Uncle Bud said softly. "You'll get by without me—you always have."

Jacob's suddenly keen eyes searched his younger son's face, almost as though he had never seen him before. It was as though a pigeon had suddenly turned into a fighting hawk. Then the old man sighed and rose heavily from his chair. "We're all too tired to decide anything now. We'll talk in the morning."

He looked at Ramsey, frowning as he noted her hand nestling in Brad's. He started to speak, then shrugged, and reached for Delia's hand. "Let's go to bed, sweetheart."

There was silence as those left in the living room watched the old man and woman slowly ascend the stairs. Jacob seemed to be leaning on the frail woman beside him, and Ramsey swallowed to keep back tears. He was a broken man, his posture signaling resignation and defeat like that of a captured eagle.

Karl, with a curt nod, left the room, and Uncle Bud soon followed, leaving Ramsey and Brad alone, and suddenly very ill at ease. So much had happened in such a short time, and Ramsey didn't know which was the most traumatic: the wild abandon of their lovemaking, which she would never forget or get over, or the danger they had so recently faced together.

He moved from behind her and knelt beside her chair until his eyes were level with her own. Even exhaustion couldn't completely dull the swift passion that surged through her when she looked into his darkening eyes and read the desire and tenderness in their depths. He raised his hand and ran his finger softly over her cheek, leaving a tingling trail of warmth. Her response to his nearness was more than physical sexuality, she knew; it was a spiritual awareness, a consuming need of her entire being, that leaped up to meet him eagerly, although her tired body couldn't have made it off the chair!

The moment of incredible rapport accentuated an infinite sadness. "Brad, we have to talk," she murmured, unconsciously catching his finger between her lips and nibbling softly.

"I know." He leaned forward to brush her lips with his, a light, featherlike kiss, which nevertheless burned all along her spine. "But not now. You've been through enough for one night."

"But—"

"Everything can wait, Ramsey," he said firmly. "I'm going to see you safely to bed and leave. I'll be back tomorrow after you're rested."

There were so many things that needed saying between them, things she dreaded saying, but Brad was right. The thought of bed—alone—had never been so seductive. He took her hand, steadying her as she rose from her chair on trembling legs.

"I can at least get to bed on my own," she said, giving him a wistful smile.

"I'll watch from here to be sure you make it," he said firmly.

She walked slowly up the stairs, conscious of his eyes on her back, then turned and waved from the landing. He nodded, and turned from the room. Ramsey waited until she heard the click of the front door closing behind him, then continued on to her bedroom. She would have liked to collapse on the bed, fully clothed, but managed a quick warm shower. It took some of the aching from her bones. Naked and flushed from the hot water, she crawled in between the scented sheets and collapsed.

Her last thought, before dropping into a dreamless sleep, was how much things had changed in the past few weeks: the family unity that she had always considered a mainstay was broken; a once-loved relative was in jail; a son who had always been treated with contempt had fought back; and the game warden, a man who was barely allowed in the house a few weeks ago had made himself right at home tonight, seeing the last of the Carmichaels to bed. The enemy, she thought wryly, was within the house. And her heart.

She stretched luxuriously, then opened her eyes to see the sun streaming across the bed in a wide band. Confused by sleep, it took her a while to remember why she would be in bed when it was obviously late afternoon.

When she finally remembered the events of the previous day, it took all her determination not to huddle back down under the covers. She touched her head gingerly; she had removed the bandage last night when she showered. There was still a dull, persistent ache, but she thought it was nothing serious. No, not nearly as serious as everything else that had happened.

She supposed it would take a while to get everything in perspective, but she was sure of some things. Her world had crumbled, along with her illusion of her family. She had come home for unconditional love, believing in a family where everyone loved and supported one another, no matter what happened. She had found betrayal, with every hand turned against the other, found currents of hatred and envy that had run undercover for years. Everything she had ever believed in had been a lie.

She supposed she had been unbelievably naive; certainly everyone seemed to think so. Brad had been right about all of the Carmichaels.

At the thought of Brad, her heart seemed to twist inside her chest. She must lose Brad, too. Nothing was what it seemed; her judgments had all proven to be based on illusion. She'd thought she loved Brad, and that only his vendetta against the Carmichaels stood between them. She had thought it was his harsh, uncompromising nature that doomed their love. Now she knew the problem was with her; she could never trust her own judgment again. Her love for Brad was probably based on the same need that had brought her running to her family, a need for security, for safety. A child's reasoning.

Sighing, she pushed aside the covers and dug her toes into the slippers beside her bed. There was no use prolonging the agony. She would pack and leave the ranch immediately, and go back to Berkeley where she belonged. It was time she became an adult. There was no deep, undying love. There was no Santa Claus.

She started at the knock on the door and slipped back under the covers. "Come in."

"Hi." Brad stood framed in the doorway, a smile on his face, a huge bunch of roses in his hand. "Feeling better?"

"Hi." She couldn't help the way her heart pounded and her pulse raced when she saw him, but she wouldn't let him see. Only a fool failed to learn from experience. "I didn't know it was so late; I'll get right up."

"No hurry." He crossed to the bed and handed her the roses, seeming almost diffident as she took them, inhaled the aroma and then put them on the bedside table.

"Thanks, Brad. They're lovely."

"I'm glad you're finally awake; I've been here since morning, even looked in twice. You were sleeping like a baby.'' He sat down on the bed and took her hand between his own hard palms. It felt so much like coming home that she immediately jerked her hand away. Not that trap again.

So she had been sleeping "like a baby." Well, she'd certainly acted like one long enough. Her face flushed as she thought of her unreasoning trust.

"Where is everyone else?"

"Your granddad and Bud are in the office. Delia told me Jacob has asked both him and Ella to stay on after they're married. Seems he's quite excited by the fact that Bud finally showed a little backbone."

He frowned slightly at her lack of response. "Are you sure you're all right?"

"I'm sure." She lifted her head to look into his concerned eyes and her painfully acquired resolve nearly failed her. Surely she could trust him, trust the feeling she had for him. Then the thought of Jeff's face livid with anger floated between them, and his words rang in her ears. *Pollyanna. Thinks everyone loves her.*

If Karl had been the murderer, she might have been able to accept it, but her feelings for Jeff had gone much deeper. His betrayal throbbed like an open wound. And Paul. Paul had said he loved her, too, until he had decided he loved someone else better. No, you had to grow up sometime. You couldn't depend on anyone else. You were responsible for your own life.

"You were right about them, Brad. I was wrong."

"Hush. We can talk about that later. How's your head?"

"Much better than it ought to be, I suppose."

"Do you feel like getting up? I thought maybe we could drive out to my ranch house, just you and Stevie and me. I did promise him some fishing. There's a little stream there where he can fish, and you and I—''

She took a deep, unsteady breath. "I don't think I'll have time, Brad. I want to start packing right away. I'm going back to California."

He went very still, hardly breathing. His expression didn't change. Only in his eyes did she see the force of the blow.

"When did you decide that?" His lips thinned, and he gave her a long, level look. "No, I guess I mean, *why* did you decide that?"

"I've always planned on it…"

"I rather believed you might have second thoughts."

"Just because you and I made love?" She forced herself to meet his eyes, to ignore the hurt in them. "That's no basis for anything lasting, Brad. You know that."

"No, I don't know it. I want you, Ramsey. Always."

Want, not love. She faced him defiantly. "I thought you had what you wanted. A Carmichael in jail, Jacob a broken man."

"You blame me for that?" He rose and paced the room. "It's true I wanted Arnie's murderer in jail, but I didn't make Jeff what he is."

She had to be honest. "I don't exactly blame you, but it worked out well for you, didn't it? You've always hated us…"

"Not you, Ramsey," he said softly, "never you. But the others? I've been doing a little thinking myself, and I'll have to admit, seeing old Jacob brought down doesn't bring the satisfaction I expected."

At her surprised expression, he sank down on a chair and stared moodily into space. "I've come to believe I owe the Carmichaels a lot."

"You owe us!"

"Maybe what I felt all these years wasn't just hatred." He spoke slowly, as though thinking out loud. "Oh, there was plenty of that. I had to blame someone for Dad's losing the ranch, his drinking, his death, but I've always known, when I was honest with myself, that he was drinking long before he lost the ranch. That's one of the reasons he lost it. His death, our poverty, the way people looked down on us, wasn't entirely Jacob's fault."

He sighed. "But when my dad died, I made up my mind

that I'd show the Carmichaels they couldn't lord it over me. They couldn't beat me down. I'd show them all that I was their equal. I'd get everything back that I blamed them for taking away.'' He gave her a bitter smile. ''So you see, Ramsey, I'd say my hatred was equal part envy.''

When she started to speak, he held up his hand. ''Ramsey, I think the reason it hurt so much to see old Jacob lowered to the level of common mortals last night was because, in a twisted kind of way, he's been my inspiration. A challenge. Without him—without all of you—I might never have gone on to college, never saved enough to buy back my ranch.''

His eyes searched her face anxiously. ''Do you understand?''

Ramsey watched him in absolute astonishment as the hard facade fell away, and she saw the warm, vulnerable man underneath, opening the anguish of his heart to her. It was all there: the years of loneliness, of striving, of desperate need. There was agony in his face as he crossed to the bed and snatched her up in his arms, crushing her violently against his chest.

''And you, Ramsey,'' he whispered, his voice hoarse with emotion as he buried his face in her tousled hair. ''I've always loved you. Always lived for you. You were my guiding star, and you still are, only you're a warmer, more accessible star than I'd ever dreamed of. I can't think of letting you go.''

His voice was muffled, but she heard every electric word. ''Oh, Brad, I don't know what to say.'' She drew back a little and raised her eyes to his face, feeling more miserable than she'd ever imagined she could. She had thought his hard, revengeful nature stood between them, she had thought him incapable of love. That obviously wasn't so, but the tragedy was that it didn't matter. It was her own emotions she didn't trust. Never could trust.

''You could say you loved me,'' he said, his burning gaze drinking her in like cool water.

"That's just it," she said, desperately twisting away from his touch. She couldn't think straight, couldn't say what had to be said if he insisted on being this close. "I thought I loved you. I thought I loved Jeff. I thought my family was one big, happy group. How can I trust what I think I feel?"

"You have to trust yourself, Ramsey."

"How can I, after all that's happened? I'm so confused. I've been running around in a dreamworld. Everyone has told me it's time I grew up, and they are right. I'm going to take Stevie and go back to San Francisco and try to think things out."

"It seems to me you let everyone else define what you are, Ramsey," he said slowly. "They say you're a child, you think you're a child. What's running away going to prove?"

"Don't you see?" She clutched his arm, desperate to make him understand. "Everything I ever believed is a lie! All my values have proven false. Family, love, trust, none of it's real!"

Slowly, deliberately, like an irresistible force, his eyes never leaving hers, he put his arms around her naked back, and pulled her up until her face was only an inch or two away from his. She shivered convulsively as his hands on her bare flesh sent showers of warmth all along her body. He drew her even closer, until the rigid tips of her breasts pushed against the fabric of his shirt. Through the thin material, she felt the ripple of his muscles, the rhythmic pounding of his heart. The heady scent of him, crisp after-shave and all his own special aroma, enveloped her in a warm cocoon of sensuality, and she could only stare at him, like a bird in a snare, breathlessly waiting.

He bent his head, and his warm mouth claimed her lips with a fierce intensity. She made a weak attempt to pull away, but he ignored her struggle, deepening the kiss, until she opened her lips in tremulous welcome. With his honeyed tongue probing and searching the velvet dark recesses of her mouth, he stroked her back, caressed her slender shoulders, ran his hand down her quivering skin, finding and lingering at last on the soft, tender flesh of her hips.

She couldn't have stopped them if she'd wanted to, and she didn't want to. Not now. Her flesh was singing, her pulse pounding all through her body. Seemingly of their own volition, her arms went around his neck, pulling his dark head down even tighter against her searching mouth. Desire burst inside her like an exploding star, sending sparks of fire through every nerve and cell. She was weak with longing, desperate with need.

As she trembled against him, he continued his caresses, running his hand over the sweet curve of her hips, tightening and pulling her inexorably against the hard rigidity of his body. She felt the intensity of his desire singing like flame along her every nerve, and in spite of her resolve, she gave herself over to the frenzy, tangled her fingers in his hair and, with a strangled gasp, molded her seeking body to his.

He drew back slightly, his breath hot on her cheek. "This isn't real?" His voice was choked, husky with yearning.

At the moment, nothing else *was* real. She was a more than willing participant as he lay her back against the pillow, one hand reverently stroking her breast. As he buried his hot face in her neck, searched the moist hollow of her throat with insistent lips, she noticed with horror that the door to her bedroom was still open.

She stiffened, struggled to sit up. "We can't, Brad! Not here!"

Reluctantly he released her, but he didn't seem half as concerned about the open door as she was. "They'll get used to it," he said, kissing her lightly on the forehead.

"Brad, I told you how I feel—"

"Your family is human, darling. Maybe you saw them through a romantic haze, maybe I saw them as devils—but they're both good and bad. Like everybody else."

"No, you don't understand. The warmth, the closeness, the loyalty—it was all a myth!"

"Not a myth! You had the right idea, sweetheart; that

hasn't changed. In fact, it's just the kind of family I want to build with you.''

She stared up into his face, still unable to leave his encircling arms, but not entirely convinced. ''Brad, how can I ever be sure?'' she whispered. ''I was so wrong, so gullible...''

Propped on one elbow, he traced the bridge of her nose with a tender finger, and one dark eyebrow quirked upward. ''It's cowardly to withdraw from love, Ramsey. Maybe it's the one unforgivable sin. Sure you're wrong sometimes, and it hurts. But that's nothing to the hurt that comes from not accepting love when you finally find it.''

Warmth, sweet and golden, seemed to spread through her entire body as she read Brad's devotion in his eyes. It was all there: the desire, the hunger, the steadfast loyalty. How could she ever have thought him remote and withdrawn? Was he right? In spite of everything that had happened, could she take a chance?

''I love you, Ramsey, I need you desperately. It's a little hard for me to say these things; I've kept things bottled up so long. But we'll be the family you always wanted. That I've always wanted. We'll give our kids the security that you and I have spent a long time looking for. The best security there is—parents who love each other desperately.''

Suddenly he tensed, and his fingers dug into her arm. ''You do love me, don't you?''

''Yes. Yes, I love you.'' As soon as she said the words, a fierce certainty swept through her. She loved this man, she really did! Everytime she needed someone, he had always been there, and she knew in her heart he always would be. Not to mention the way he made her body sing with ecstasy, her spirit flow and merge into his. Maybe growing up was taking a chance on love.

And loving was feeling the security to tease. ''We don't have a very big family.'' She laughed. ''Just you and me and Stevie.''

''Not much at all! But I certainly intend to change that

as soon as we're married.'' A faint uncertainty softened his features. ''You do want more children, don't you?''

''I want your children,'' she whispered, suddenly, exultantly, sure of both herself and him.

He started to reach for her again, but she leaped nimbly out the other side of the bed. ''If you'll get out of here, I'll get dressed and we can go over to our ranch house.'' Her eyes glowed with radiant promise.

His eyes danced. How different he looked without the tense, reserved expression he'd worn when she'd first known him.

''Hurry. I don't want to shock your grandparents, but I warn you I'm only human. And you don't have a thing on.''

She gave him a mock frown, but she didn't flinch from his ardent gaze. ''You're not suggesting we start on our family before we're married?''

He grinned as he ducked out the door. ''Well, we shouldn't wait too long. Stevie's not getting any younger, and he'll need a playmate soon.''

She heard his soft chuckle as he closed the door just before the pillow she threw slammed against it.

* * * * *

SILHOUETTE Romance™

Escape to a place where a kiss is still a kiss...
Feel the breathless connection...
Fall in love as though it were
the very first time...
Experience the power of love!

Come to where favorite authors—such as
Diana Palmer, Stella Bagwell,
Marie Ferrarella *and many more—*
deliver heart-warming romance and genuine
emotion, time after time after time....

Silhouette Romance—
stories straight from the heart!

Silhouette®
Where love comes alive™

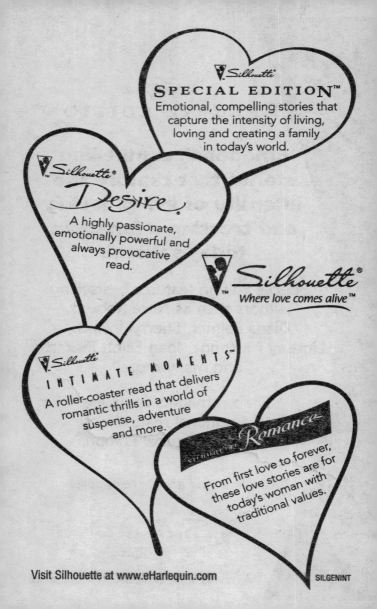